RANDOM SHOTS.

Random Shots

By

CHARLES HEBER CLARK

(Max Adeler, pseud.)

American Fiction Reprint Series

BOOKS FOR LIBRARIES PRESS
FREEPORT, NEW YORK
1971

First published in 1879
(Item #1052; Wright's AMERICAN FICTION 1876-1900)

Reprinted 1971 in *American Fiction Reprint Series*
from the Ward, Lock, & Co. edition

INTERNATIONAL STANDARD BOOK NUMBER:
0-8369-7033-0

LIBRARY OF CONGRESS CATALOG CARD NUMBER:
70-164557

PRINTED IN THE UNITED STATES OF AMERICA

RANDOM SHOTS.

BY

MAX ADELER,

AUTHOR OF "OUT OF THE HURLY BURLY," "ELBOW ROOM,"
ETC., ETC.

WITH NUMEROUS HUMOROUS ILLUSTRATIONS

BY

ARTHUR B. FROST.

COPYRIGHT.

London:

WARD, LOCK, & CO., WARWICK HOUSE,

DORSET BUILDINGS, SALISBURY SQUARE, E.C.

PREFACE.

THIS volume of stories and sketches is offered to the public with a confidence born of the fact that the two books which preceded it from my pen, "Out of the Hurly-Burly" and "Elbow-Room," have been sold in numbers so large as to leave no room for doubt that they have been received with favour. That this unpretentious work will prove equally popular is a reasonable expectation, for some portions of its contents are at least equal in merit, and in attractiveness to lovers of honest fun, to the best that may be found between the covers of its predecessors. Doubtless, also, it has its full share of faults; but if these are forgiven by generous readers as readily as others have been in the past, I shall have no reason to complain that I have been treated with unkindness.

It is only fair to say to the reader of the Mormon story in this volume that if he is reminded of Artemus Ward by a phrase which alludes to a number of hearts "beating as one," he cannot excuse me upon the theory of unconscious plagiarism. I took the idea deliberately, because it exactly suited the place into which it was put.

MAX ADELER.

CONTENTS.

❖ RANDOM ✦ SHOTS. ❖

Professor Quackenboss.

WHERE the Professor came from originally, or how he even obtained the title of "Professor," nobody knew. He appeared suddenly in the village one day, and renting a small shop, he hung out a sign bearing the inscription, "Professor S. Quackenboss, Phrenologist and Indian Herb Doctor," and sat down to wait for business that never came.

A week or two after his arrival, he determined to give a free lecture upon phrenology, for the purpose of introducing himself to the people of the community. He rented a hall, and obtained quite a large audience. When the hour for beginning the lecture arrived, the Professor advanced and explained the science, and then invited persons in the audience to come forward and permit him to examine their skulls, and tell what were their characteristics. Several men offered themselves for this ordeal, and the Professor contrived to come so near to the truth in describing them, that he more than once excited a good deal of applause.

Finally, old Mr. Duncan stepped up for examination. He is an absent-minded man, and he wears a wig. While dressing himself before coming to the lecture, he had placed his wig on the bureau and accidentally tossed his spectacle case into it. When he put the wig on it was just like him not to notice the case, and so, when he mounted the platform, he had a huge lump just over his bump of combativeness. The Professor fingered about a while over Mr. Duncan's head, and then said—

"We have here a somewhat remarkable skull. The perceptive faculties strongly developed ; reflective faculties quite good ; ideality large ; reverence so great as to be unusual ; and benevolence very prominent. Secretiveness is small, and the subject, therefore, is a man of candour and frankness ; he communicates what he knows freely. We have also," said the Professor, still ploughing his fingers through D.'s hair, " acquisitiveness not large ; the subject is not a grasping, avaricious man, he gives liberally, he—he—he——. Why, it can't be ! Yes. Why, what in the—! Munificent Moses ! that's the most awful development of combativeness I ever heard of ! Are you a prize-fighter, eh ?'

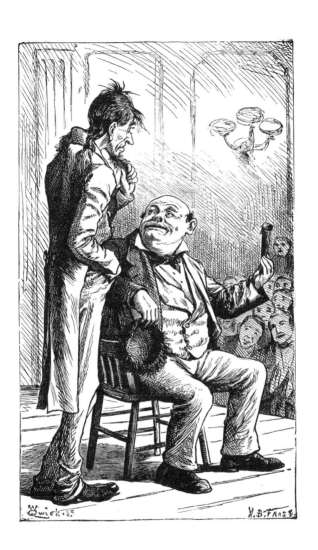

"Prize-fighter!" exclaimed Mr. D. "Why, what do you mean?"

"Never been a soldier, or a pirate, or anything like that?"

"You certainly must be crazy."

"Ain't you fond of going into scrimmages and rows and hammering people?"

"Certainly not."

"Well, sir, then you're untrue to your nature. The way your head's built qualifies you, I should say, in a special manner as a pugilist or a soldier. If you want to fulfil your mission, you will devote the remainder of your life to battering up your fellow-man and keeping yourself in one interminable war. You've got the most fearful fighting bump that ever decorated a human skull. It's phenomenal. What'll you take for your head when you die? Gentlemen, this man is liable at any moment to commence raging around the community like a wild cat, banging you with a club or anything that comes handy. It isn't safe for him to be at large."

Then Mr. Duncan put up his hand for the purpose of feeling the bump, and he found the spectacle case. He removed his wig, and there was the case resting upon his left ear. Then the Professor, looking at it for a moment in confusion, said—

"Ladies and gentlemen, we will now—the lecture is— that is, I have no more—boy, put out those lights."

And Mr. Duncan replaced his wig, the Professor disappeared, and the audience laughingly dispersed.

After that the Professor did not dabble a great deal in phrenology. He remained idly in his office during part of each day, but as he was fond of conversation, and rather unduly partial to stimulating beverages when they could be obtained at the expense of other people, he used to spend most of his time either at the tavern or at the corner grocery, where he could give his ingenious views of things generous expression to a crowd of amused listeners.

One evening the Indian question came on for discussion at the grocery, where some of the leading men of the village had dropped in, for it was the post-office also ; and when two or three persons had expressed their opinions, the Professor removed his pipe from his mouth, and placing his feet upon the stove, while he tilted back his chair, said :

" I don't take the same view of the North American Indians that most people do.

" Now some think that the red man displays a want of good taste in declining to bathe himself; but I don't. What is dirt? It is simply—matter ;—the same kind of matter that exists everywhere. The earth is made of dirt ; the things we eat are dirt, and they grow in the dirt ; and when we die and are buried we return again to the dirt from which we were made. Science says that all dirt is clean. The savage Indian knows this ; his original mind grasps this idea ; he has his eagle eye on science, and he has no soap. Dirt is warm. A layer one-sixteenth of an inch thick on a man is said by Professor Huxley to be s comfortable as a fifty-dollar suit of clothes. Why, then, should the child of the forest undress himself once a week by scraping this off, and expose himself to the rude blasts of winter? He has too much sense. His head is too level to let him take a square wash more than once in every twenty years, and even then he don't rub hard.

"And then, in regard to his practice of eating dogs ; why shouldn't a man eat a dog ? A dog sometimes eats a man, and turn about is fair play. A well-digested dog stowed away inside of a Choctaw squaw, does more to advance civilization and the Christian religion than a dog that barks all night in a back yard, don't it ? And nothing is more nutritious than dog. Professor Huxley says that one pound of a dog's hind leg nourishes the vital forces more than a waggon-load of bread and corned beef. It contains more phosphorus and carbon. When dogs are alive they agree with men, and there is no reason why they shouldn't when they are dead. This nation will enter upon a glorious destiny when it stops raising corn and potatoes, and devotes itself more to growing crops of puppies.

"Now, many ignorant people consider scalping inhuman. I don't. I look upon it as one of the most beneficent processes ever introduced for the amelioration of the sufferings of the race. What is hair ? It is an excrescence. If it grows, it costs a man a great deal of money and trouble to keep it cut. If it falls out, the man becomes bald and the flies bother him. What does the Indian do in this emergency ? With characteristic sagacity he lifts out the whole scalp and ends the annoyance and expense. And then look at the saving from other sources. Professor Huxley estimates that 2,000 pounds of the food that a man eats in a year go to nourish his hair. Remove that hair and you save that much food. If I had my way I would have every baby scalped when it is vaccinated, as a measure of political economy. That would be statesmanship. I have a notion to organize a political party on the basis of baby-scalping, and to go on the stump to advocate it. If people had any sense, I might run into the Presidency as a baby-scalper.

"And as for the matter of the Indians wearing rings through their noses, I don't see why people complain of that. Look at the advantage it gives a man when he wants to hold on to anything. If a hurricane strikes an Indian, all he does is to hook his nose to a tree, and there he is, fast and sound. And it gives him something to rest his pipe on while he smokes, while, in the case of a man  with a pug, the ring helps to pull his proboscis down, and to make it a Roman nose. But I look at him from a sanitary point of view. The Indian suffers from catarrh. Now, what will cure that disease? Metal in the nose in which electricity can be collected. Professor Huxley says that the electricity in a metal ring two inches in diameter will cure more catarrh than all the medicines between here and Kansas. The child of nature, with wonderful instinct, has perceived this, and he teaches us a lesson. When we, with our higher civilization, begin to throw away finger-rings and ear-rings, and to wear rings in our noses, we shall be a hardier race. I am going to direct the attention of Congress to the matter.

" Then take the objections that are urged to the Indian practice of driving a stake through a man, and building a bonfire on his stomach. What is their idea? They want to hold that man down. If they sit on him they will obstruct the view of him. They put a stake through him, and there he is secured by simple means, and if it is driven in carefully, it may do him good. Professor Huxley says that he once knew a man who was cured of yellow jaundice by falling on a pale-fence, and having a sharp-pointed paling run into him. And the bonfire may be equally healthy. When a man's stomach is out of order, you put a mustard-plaster on it. Why? To warm it. The red man has the same idea. He takes a few faggots, lights them, and applies them to the abdomen. It is a certain cure. Professor Huxley—"

" That's enough about Professor Huxley," said Miles, the shopkeeper, interrupting the speaker. " We don't care to hear any more about him."

" Don't care to hear any more about Huxley," exclaimed the Professor, with a look of feigned surprise upon his face. " Don't want to hear any more about that great and good man! I can hardly believe it."

" Well, we don't, anyhow," said Miles.

The Professor rose, reflected a moment, and then said : " Strange! Strange! that men prefer darkness to light! That they would rather have blind ignorance than the glorious truth!" Then he reached over the counter, fumbled for a moment in the barrel, came up with a water cracker in his hand, and slowly sauntered through the front door.

His feelings were hurt, but he was a forgiving man, and so, after staying away for a day or two, he came back again one night, and resumed his old place by the stove.

After awhile there was a lull in the conversation, and the Professor, who had hitherto remained silent, cleared his throat, and said, quietly—

" I see that they talk of putting up a monument to Christopher Columbus. It's too bad the way people 've been fooled about him. He never discovered America, and I've made up my mind to let the people see what kind of an old humbug he is."

" You say that Columbus didn't discover America?" said Mr. Partridge.

" Certainly he didn't. He was a mean, lubberly rascal, who went paddling around in a scow, letting on he was doing big things, when he hadn't courage enough to get out of sight of land."

" Who did discover it then?"

" Well, I'll tell you fellows in advance of publication, but mind you keep quiet about it. It was Potiphar!"

" What was his first name?"

" First name? Why, he hadn't any. It was only Potiphar—old Pharaoh's Potiphar, you know."

" How did you find out about it?"

"Why, you know old Gridley, up in the city? Well, last year he was in Egypt, and he brought home a mummy, all wrapped up in bedclothes, and soldered around with sealing-wax. Gridley asked me to come

over and help to undress him, and so we went at that
mummy, and after rolling off a couple of hundred yards of
calico, we reached him.   Looked exactly like dried beef.
Black as your hat, and just about tender enough to chip
down for tea.   Gridley said he'd like to know who the old
chap was, and I looked him over to find out.   You know

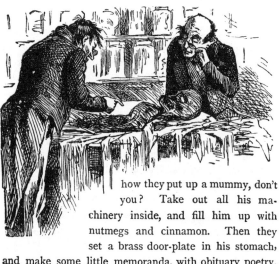

how they put up a mummy, don't
you?   Take out all his machinery inside, and fill him up with
nutmegs and cinnamon.   Then they
set a brass door-plate in his stomach,
and make some little memoranda, with obituary poetry,
and all that kind of thing.   Anyhow, after polishing him
up with a flesh-brush for a minute or two, I found the
door-plate, and with some care I managed to read the
inscription on it.   It was this : ' I am Potiphar, servant of
Pharaoh.   I was buried three thousand years before the
Christian era.   I discovered America.   C. Columbus was
an impostor.'   That's what the inscription said, and, in

my opinion, that settles it. Now, I'll tell you what I'm going to do. I've had a cast made of that dried beef, and I intend to have it swelled all out and made into a statue, and I'm going to set it up at my own expense, alongside the statue of Columbus, and have a sign put on it to the effect that Columbus is a fraud. Then I intend to get up a memorial to Congress, asking it to change the name of the country to Potipharia, and to make Potiphar's sacred animal, the cat, the emblematical bird of the nation, instead of the eagle."

" You say you read the inscription on the plate," said Partridge. " I didn't know you understood the language."

"Can read it as easy as A B C."

" ' Buried three thousand years before the Christian era,' I think you said it read. How did old Pot know anything about the Christian era, if he died that long before ? "

" Blamed if I know. Cast his prophetic eyes over the future, I s'pose."

" Well, how could he tell that Columbus was going to claim to discover America ? "

" That's so. I dunno. Is kind of queer."

" Do you know what I think of you ? " asked Part-ridge.

" What ? "

" I think that if there was a statue of a humbug to be erected, the nation would choose you for the honour, instead of Columbus, or any other man, ancient or modern."

" Maybe it would ! maybe it would ! " said the Professor ; and then he refilled his pipe from Partridge's tobacco-pouch, which was lying in a box by his side, and relapsed into silence.

It was never known why the Professor designed his great Nebuchadnezzar enterprise, but some people had a dark suspicion that he proposed to absorb for his own use any money that he secured. He entered the office of the *Argus* one day, and producing a huge roll of manuscript he said :

" I've got something here that I want you to publish. It's a ' Vindication of Nebuchadnezzar.' "

" A what ? "

" I say I've got here a ' Vindication of Nebuchadnezzar.' The object of it is to set Nebuchadnezzar right with the public, to clear up his record and give him some kind of a chance."

" My dear sir, the public don't care anything about Nebuchadnezzar. Our space is too limited for anything so unimportant."

" I think you are wrong. For about three thousand years people's minds have been prejudiced against that great and good man. I've found some new records about him on some Babylonian bricks in the Patent Office at Washington, which present the matter in a new light. My intention now is that the *Argus* shall create a sensation by publishing these facts, together with fac-similes of a cart-load or two of the bricks, and then I shall ask you to head a subscription list for a Nebuchadnezzar Monument Fund. How much'll I put you down for ? "

" Professor, you must excuse me. The subject is too unimportant for my attention."

"You make a mistake. I tell you the public mind is excited about the matter. Look at the frightful consequences of permitting these erroneous impressions about Nebuchadnezzar to continue ! Your young men are learning them in the divinity schools. They carry them out into the world, into heathen lands. The ignorant African upon the banks of the Niger is taught to stay awake at nights in order to denounce Nebuchadnezzar. The deluded Esquimaux amid the frozen seas paddles about in his canoe harpooning seals, with the conviction that Nebuchadnezzar was a tyrannical old rascal. The red Indian, bounding over his native plains or removing the hair from the summit of his enemy, is instructed to howl as he reflects upon the misconduct of Nebuchadnezzar. The almond-eyed children of China mingle execrations of Nebuchadnezzar with their most ordinary conversation. The whole race is down on him. He is the victim of universal disapprobation, now isn't he ? "

" I don't think he is."

" Now, how would you like it if for the next three thousand years everybody was to believe that you were an old reprobate who ate grass ? "

" I wouldn't care."

" Oh, well, maybe you ain't a sensitive man. Nebuchadnezzar was. His feelings were easily hurt. Old Babylonian bricks all mention that. Now this vindication of him will run through your paper about two months, and it's bound to create such enthusiasm for the old man that people 'll go without food to contribute money to run up some kind of a tombstone for him. And when I get through with him I've got another serial vindicating Belshazzar, that 'll run for a couple of months more, and then people 'll be hungry to get out a monument for *him.* Now you mark me: this nation'll not be ten years older before all those old chaps 'll have monuments strung all along every where to them. There's going to be an awakening on the subject in the popular mind. I'm going to set it up so's when anybody says anything against Nebuchadnezzar the folks 'll turn out and hang him to the nearest tree. A popular idea, you understand. Just wild about him."

" I'm going to try to remain calm."

" Now, what'll you pay me a line for this vindication?"

" Pay you ! Why I wouldn't print it if you'd pay me a dollar a line ! "

"What! Wouldn't give a lift to an old man that's been imposed on for three or four thousand years ? Wouldn't do him a good turn, now he's in his grave and can't help himself ? "

" Certainly not."

" Well, well! I've heard a good deal about the liberality of a free press, and about journalistic enterprise, but I can't see it. I thought, of course, that any newspaper'd come to the rescue of an unfortunate fellow-creature when he's in trouble."

"Well, I won't."

" Oh, all right; all right; but mark me! I'm going to scratch on a brick somewheres that you are a reprobate, with the instincts of a hyena and the intellect of a shrimp; and I'm going to bury that brick where it 'll be turned up in three or four thousand years, so the people of those times 'll know what to think of *you.*   I'll fix you, old boy, you see if I don't."

Then Professor Quackenboss rolled up the vindication, rubbed his nose on his sleeve, and   went down-stairs warm with indignation.

Jerome Pinnickson's Mother-in-Law,

WITH

AN APOLOGY FOR MOTHERS-IN-LAW GENERALLY.

HE mother-in-law has not had fair play. She suffers with the widow and the old maid, but she has been more cruelly abused, more mercilessly ridiculed than either. Like them, she is not responsible for her condition, but, unlike them, the man who complains the most about her is he who elevated her to the position she holds—namely, the man who married her daughter.

She has been the subject of countless brutal stories,

myriads of offensive jests, and quantities of sarcastic rhymes. Into all of these has entered an element of bitterness which does not appear in the jibes that are hurled at the widow and the spinster.

Malice is the inspiration of the assaults upon the mother-in-law. Perhaps it is savagery born of a sense of detected guilt—guilt which has been hidden from the too confiding wife, but detected promptly by the penetrating eye of the mother-in-law. She is not blinded by love for the man; she is made vigilant by love for the wife, and to perfect clearness of vision she adds that large and generous experience of the methods of devious and deceitful husbands, which enables her at once to laugh to scorn the hypocrisy which attempts to excuse late hours upon the plea of business, or to offer the claims of the lodge in explanation of absent evenings that are spent in conviviality.

For men who are guilty of such crimes, the mother-in-law operates as a kind of second conscience. She is an agent of the moral law to convey reproof; perhaps to execute vengeance. In such a character she deserves respect. The sinner who quails beneath her majestic glance of course does not like her. Neither does the thief like the halter. But for the part she plays in the economy of the universe she is entitled to the reverence of the good.

There are diversities of mothers-in-law, as of all other things ; and it does happen sometimes that a worthy and well-conducted man finds himself subjected to a mother-in-law who is a real affliction. But all things are wisely ordered in this world. All the saints have been made perfect through suffering. The thorn in the flesh sometimes points the way to celestial joys. A terrific mother-in-law may be good for discipline. She should be regarded very much as an ascetic regards a hair-cloth shirt: as something which subdues the body with the intent to purify the spirit. She is hard to bear, of course, but so are all the trials of life; and yet if life had no trials nobody would ever want to get to heaven.

There may be men who, when they join the church triumphant, will be largely indebted for their felicity to a fearful mother-in-law. Let them submit themselves to her now, with cheerful resignation, looking upon her as a possible conducer to a blissful hereafter.

It is worthy of notice that the mother-in-law is never spoken of with disrespect in the Bible. Ruth, the most charming woman in the Old Testament history, obtained a husband and an immortality of admiration because she loved her mother-in-law and treated her kindly. One of the signs of the troublous times that are to come upon the earth will be that the daughter-in-law will be against her mother-in-law. Possibly we may attribute the fall of man to the fact that Adam had no mother-in-law to look after him and his wife and to warn them, as the efficient mother-in-law always will, against doing wrong. Solomon was the wisest man that ever lived, and he had seven hundred mothers-in-law, unless some of his wives were orphans, and there is not a reproachful word concerning them in any of his writings. The modern man who has but one, and who growls about her, ought to consider this and refrain.

The chances are that most of the men who make complaint are in fact under serious obligations to the women whom they dislike. A good mother-in-law in a house is really a well-spring of pleasure to a properly constituted husband. She is assiduous in taking care of the baby, and the serviceableness of her knowledge concerning the most effective methods of carrying the infant through criticial periods, the efficiency with which she dispenses

paregoric, measures out ipe-cac, and compounds spice-plaisters, fills the minds of just men with sentiments of admiration and thankfulness.

The average mother-in-law is an over-match for the wiliest hired girl of the period. She knows all about the proportion of soap to the week's washing, and she has some occult power which enables her to detect an un-naturally low tide in the sugar bucket. In a sick room she is a ministering angel, and when the agonies of house-cleaning attack the dwelling she is worth as much as two servant girls and a coloured man.

It is the fate of her sex to be misrepresented. It is a part of the cruel law which maintains the subjection of woman that the mother-in law should be vilified con-tinually. But she suffers and is strong. Who ever heard of a mother-in-law rushing into print with abuse of her son-in-law?   And if mothers-in-law should retaliate how mightily could they prevail!   If every mother-in-law should relieve her mind by telling what she knows of her persecutor, probably many men of fair reputation would have to take much lower seats in the social synagogue than those that they occupy at present.

Jerome Pinnickson had a mother-in-law who was filled with deep anxiety to escape the reproach that attaches to the women of her class as a rule.

As soon as her daughter was married to Pinnickson, and it was arranged that Mrs. Carboy—Mrs. Pinnickson's mother—was to come to live with her child, Mrs. Carboy said :

"Helen, dear! I am very desirous that Jerome shall not regard me as most men regard their wives' mothers, and I am determined to try very hard to make myself agreeable and to do what I can to make Jerome love me."

"I know he will, mother."

"I hope so, Helen.   Most mothers-in-law are so solicitous for their daughters' welfare that they forget the rights of the husbands, and the result too often is that they come between husband and wife and cause trouble and dissension."

"But you won't do that, I am certain."

"No, Helen, I trust not.   I have made up my mind to devote more attention to Jerome than to you ; to show myself eager to make his home happy, to anticipate every want, and to pay him those little attentions for which men are always so grateful.   Ah! my dear, your poor pa used to say that I was the most thoughtful woman he ever saw; and I did try to be very considerate."

"Jerome will say the same thing, mother, I am sure."

And so, upon the first night that Pinnickson went out, as he alleged, "upon business," Mrs. Carboy said to her daughter :

"Helen, darling, suppose you go to bed. I will sit up and wait for Jerome. I am accustomed to it. A man does not like to come home late at night and find the house dark and dreary and every one asleep. We must try to make it cheerful for Jerome. I will sit here and be ready to greet him with a smile when he comes in."

So Mrs. Pinnickson retired, and Mrs. Carboy went on with her sewing.

"Dear Jerome," she said to herself, as she bit off a thread, "how pleased he will be to find that I am so eager to make him happy !"

Mrs. Carboy sat there, hour after hour, until at last she dozed off in her chair. Just as the clock upon the mantel was striking one, the noise of a key in the lock of the front door waked her, and Jerome came in. She sprang to greet him. He seemed a trifle vexed when he saw her, but when she explained her project to him, he thanked her kindly and bade her good night.

If some one could have caught the remark that fell from his lips as he went up-stairs, he would have been understood to say :

"Detestable old idiot ! I believe she sat up because she was afraid I would not come home sober ! She has begun to watch me already."

But Mrs. Carboy went to bed with an approving conscience, and perfectly happy in the thought that she was a kind of guardian angel to that household.

The next time Pinnickson went out alone in the evening he said, as he took his hat:

"By the way, mother, you needn't sit up for me to-night. I shall be detained rather late."

"Dear heart," said Mrs. Carboy to Helen, as the door closed, "he doesn't want to give me trouble. But I will show him that my affection for him makes such a service seem trifling. You can retire as usual, darling, and I will wait for him."

Jerome *was* later than usual. He came in a little before two ; and Mrs. Carboy flew to meet him. He was a shade angry, and he said :

"I thought I asked you not to wait up for me?"

"I know, my son ; but I felt as if I were willing to sacrifice myself for your comfort in spite of your kind protest."

Then Pinnickson slammed his hat down upon the table, tossed his cane on the stand, and went off saying :

"I wonder what game the old girl is up to, anyway? She evidently suspects something."

When Pinnickson had occasion to stay out the next time, he remarked : "I shall be out very, very late. Perhaps I shall not come in at all. I particularly request that you and mother shall both go to bed at the usual time. Remember, now, I do not want either of you to sit up."

"How considerate he is," said Mrs. Carboy, as Jerome shut the door. "He would suffer anything rather than cause me trouble. But little does he know the depths of a woman's love. You retire, Helen, when you wish to, and I will stay up and give him a pleasant surprise."

Late that night Pinnickson opened the front door slowly and softly. He crept in noiselessly, and shut the door. He peeped into the room, and beheld Mrs. Carboy dozing away in the easy-chair. Upon tiptoe he as-

" He beheld Mrs. Carboy dozing in the easy-chair."—*Page* 31.

cended the stairs, and then he went to bed, leaving her undisturbed.

About four o'clock in the morning some one pounded upon his chamber door.

"Who's there?" asked Mrs. Pinnickson.

"I! your mamma. Do you know, Helen, darling, that Jerome has not come home yet? I am afraid something dreadful has happened to him."

Pinnickson was sleepy, but he could not suppress a smile as his wife arose and went to explain to her mother the facts of the situation.

In the morning, Pinnickson tried to smooth matters over by a shuffling excuse, to the effect that he did not look for Mrs. Carboy, after what he had said about not sitting up, and he was not aware that she was waiting for him.

"Never mind," said she, with a serene smile, "it makes no difference. Next time I will stay awake, so that I won't miss you."

Pinnickson looked as if this information did not fill him with joy. In fact, it made him miserable. The thought that he would never, never be able to go out without the certainty that the implacable and indomitable Mrs. Carboy was at home counting the minutes of his absence, was exasperating. The most fiendish of mothers-in-law could not have devised anything that would have been more terrible.

And Mrs. Carboy did not end with this method of torture, in her efforts to make her son-in-law happy.

"Helen," she said, "Jerome loves neatness and order, and I think we ought to have a good house-cleaning every month or two, just to please him. Nothing, my child, makes a man so contented and happy as to find his home a model of cleanliness and comfort."

And so Mrs. Carboy and Helen began the good work.

and when Jerome came home he found the ironing-blanket over the piano, the carpet up from the hall, the chairs on top of the sofas, the hat-rack in the back porch, his coats and boots stuffed away in a strange closet, and the household things generally in a pitiable condition of demoralization. He complained to his wife, and she said :

" Mother wanted to do it. She says we ought to have a good house-cleaning every month or two, so as to make home happy and comfortable for you."

" She said that, did she? Your mother said that ! Helen, tell your mother that the next time I come home and find such happiness as this, either she or I will have to seek for happiness elsewhere."

Then Mrs. Pinnickson began to cry, and when she sought her mother, to cast on her the burden of her woe, Mrs. Carboy said :

" Don't mind it, darling ! Jerome is not well. I have long thought that his liver was disordered. Perhaps he will feel better in the morning. If he does, we will go ahead and tear out the second-floor rooms. I will clean up the library myself, and put his papers away."

And she did. She arranged the papers on Pinnickson s desk, and " straightened up " everything that was crooked or out of place ; and when the shades of evening fell, she said :

" Helen, dear, Jerome will be delighted with the library I wish you would tell him I fixed it. It will make him feel more kindly towards me, perhaps. Don't say anything about it until he sees it. We will give him surprise."

After dinner, Pinnickson went into the library to write a letter, when the women waited to observe the effect of

the surprise. They heard him using some expressions
that seemed to be violent in tone, and presently he opened
the door and called,

"Helen! Helen!"

Mrs. Pinnickson went to see what he wanted.

"Helen," he said, "I want to know WHO ON EARTH
has been in here meddling with my papers?"

"Why, Jerome, I thought—"

"Oh, never mind what you thought. Helen, don't
you know that I cannot endure that any one should dis-
turb these papers? I have said, over and over again
that they were to be let alone."

"I know, my dear; but then, arranging them just a
little would not hurt them; and—"

"Arranging them! Why, they are turned topsy-turvey
—not one is where it ought to be. It will take me hours
to find what I want."

"I am very sorry. I—"

"But why did you do it? What possible reason had
you for disturbing them?"

"Why, you know, Jerome, I didn't do it myself."

"You didn't do it! What other person had the im-
pudence to interfere with my private papers!"

"Well, you see, mother said that you—"

"Your mother! Is this the work of your mother?"

"Yes; mother said—"

But before Mrs. Pinnickson could finish the sentence,
Pinnickson rushed from the room, grasped his hat, crushed
it down on his head, and flew from the house.

"I am afraid," said Mrs. Pinnickson, after telling her
mother of the interview, "that he is very angry."

" Not a great deal, I think, darling," said Mrs. Carboy. " It will pass off. I will sit up for him as usual to-night, and when he comes in I will explain it all to him, so that he will be satisfied."

Mrs. Carboy waited patiently that night, thinking of what she would say, when Jerome came home, to assuage his wrath and make him feel that he had indeed a mother-in-law who loved him.

After a while he entered. Mrs. Carboy met him with a charming smile. She was just about to open a conversation, when he dashed past her, ascended the stairs three steps at a time, entered his chamber, and locked the door.

" Jerome has some business trouble on his mind, dear boy," whispered Mrs. Carboy to herself, as she went to bed.

" I will have that intolerable old hag assassinated, if there is no other way of getting rid of her, ' said Pinnickson to himself, as he prepared to undress.

When the family assembled at breakfast next morning, Pinnickson was gloomy, and sad, and silent. Mrs. Pinnickson said, timidly—

" Are you not well, Jerome, dear ? "

" Perfectly ! perfectly well ! What do you ask that question for ? "

" I thought you seemed somewhat indisposed."

" I thought so, too," said Mrs. Carboy, with a sympathizing smile.

" Well, I'm not," grumbled Pinnickson.

" Doesn't your head ache ? " asked Mrs. Pinnickson.

" Certainly it don't."

" Haven't you a pain in your chest ? " asked Mrs. Carboy. " I thought I heard you coughing during the night."

" No, you didn't."

" Hadn't you better take something for it, dear?" urged Mrs. Pinnickson.

" Something for what?"

" For your cough."

" No, Helen," said Mrs. Carboy ; "what Jerome wants is a mustard plaster. Jerome, may I make one for you ?"

Jerome did not reply. He rose slowly from the table, and with a look of intense disgust upon his face he left the room and then the house.

" Helen," said Mrs. Carboy, when he had gone, " Jerome is suffering, but he has determined to say nothing, for fear of worrying you. Dear soul ! always so thoughtful and considerate ! But we must do something to help him. I always put mustard plasters on your pa when he had a pain in his chest."

" But Jerome will not let me put one on him."

" Then, my child, you have a duty to perform. If he will not admit that he is ill, prove to him that you are more careful of him than he is of himself, compel him to assume the plaster. He will love you more dearly for your solicitude for his welfare."

" How can I compel him to wear it ?"

" Mix a dry mustard plaster, and sew it upon the inside of his underclothing, after he's asleep to-night. He will never know it until it has had a good effect."

" I will try the experiment," said Mrs. Pinnickson.

Upon the following morning, Pinnickson came into the dining-room in a fine humour. He took his seat, and was just in the midst of an explanation of a transaction he had the day before with a business friend, when he suddenly stopped, looked cross-eyed, and a spasm of pain passed over his face. He exclaimed :—

" I wonder what in the— No, it can't be anything wrong."

" What is the matter, dear ? " asked Mrs. Pinnickson.

" I don't know. I felt a kind of pain in my chest ; very queer too. Sort of stings me."

" I knew you were not well," rejoined Mrs. Carboy.

" I am sorry," said Mrs. Pinnickson.

Then Pinnickson began again, and he was just telling how his friend, Jones, had met him at a chop-house, and prevailed upon him to go into a speculation with Gagbury and Pittston Railway Stock, when he suddenly dropped the subject, and, jumping up, said :—

" Goodness ! Halloa ! What's that ? Helen, something dreadful is the matter ! I feel as if I had a shovelful of hot coals upon my chest. "

" Must be the rheumatism getting worse," said Mrs. Pinnickson.

" Oh no ! It's something a great deal worse than rheumatism," said Pinnickson. " Feels like a fire burning into my flesh. Ouch ! Ow-wow-wow ! It is fearful ! I can't stand it another moment ! I believe it is cholera, or something, and that I am going to die."

" Do try to be calm, my son ! " said Mrs. Carboy.

" Calm ! how can a man be calm with a volcano boiling over upon him. Get out of the way, quick ! while I go upstairs and undress ! "

Then he rushed upstairs and removed his clothing. His chest was the colour of a boiled lobster ; but he

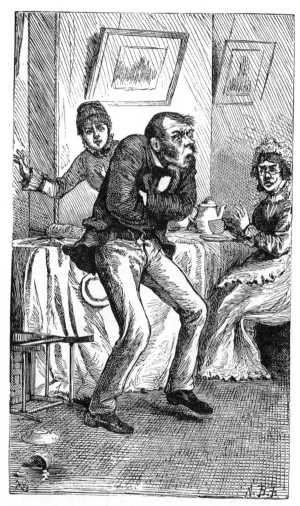

"Calm! How can a man be calm—"—*Page* 37.

could not imagine what the cause of the inflammation could be, when his eyes rested upon something white upon his shirt. He picked up the garment and examined it

Five minutes later he came slowly downstairs with thunder upon his brow and a dry mustard plaster in his hand. His wife met him in the hall. Going up to her, he shook the plaster before her face, and said in a sup-pressed voice :—

" Did you put that thing upon me ? "

" I did it for the best, Jerome. I wanted to make you well, and—"

" Well ! well ! and who said I was sick ? "

" Why, dear, you know mother thought—"

" Your mother ! Did your mother put you up to plastering me with this diabolical contrivance which has nearly eaten me to the bone ! "

" She merely suggested—"

" Suggested it, did she ! Well, now, listen to me. If Mrs. Carboy ever suggests, or thinks, or does, or dreams any more of meddling with me, I register a solemn vow that I will put her out of this house, bag and baggage, finally and for ever, as soon as I can lay my hands on her. You hear me ! "

Then Pinnickson rushed out, and slammed the door fiercely, while Mrs. Pinnickson sat down on the lowest stair, and burst into tears.

" Never mind, Helen," said Mrs. Carboy, who had been listening behind the door of the dining-room ; " he will feel better before evening, and then he will be grateful for what you did."

Pinnickson did not manifest any gratitude, but as the

inflammation upon his chest passed away, his temper improved, and he became comparatively cheerful and agreeable, even to Mrs. Carboy, for whom, however, deep down in his bosom, he cherished a feeling of resentment.

A few weeks later, Pinnickson, while sitting with his wife and Mrs. Carboy, one evening, said :

" My dear, you seem to have given up your piano practice completely. I never hear you playing any now."

" It is true, Jerome ; I hardly ever touch the instrument. I am busy all day with the household affairs, and I seem to have no time for practice."

"Poor Helen is very industrious," observed Mrs. Carboy.

" But I don't want you to keep the piano always closed," said Pinnickson. "You know how fond I am of a little music."

" Well, I really must try to pick up my playing again to please you. But I do not know how I can find the time."

"You must make the effort, dear," said Mrs. Carboy, "in order to oblige your husband. I do wish I could help you in some way. I can't play, but I can sing a little. Perhaps Jerome would like to hear me sing to him in the evening ? "

Pinnickson did not express himself frankly on this point; but he threw out a strong intimation that he would choose almost any other fate than that.

Next morning, when Mrs. Carboy was alone with her daughter, she said :

" My child, a happy thought occurred to me last night after I had retired. Jerome loves music, and you cannot give it to him. Why not buy him a musical-box, which will play without an effort from anybody ?

"That would be splendid, mamma," said Mrs. Pinnickson.

"I will buy one this very day," added Mrs. Carboy. "I would rather spend all I have, than let Jerome think I do not want to make him happy."

When Pinnickson went into his drawing room after dinner that evening, a charming musical-box was upon the table, playing beautifully. Pinnickson was delighted; and when his wife said that it was a present from Mrs. Carboy, he thanked that lady warmly, and really for a moment felt his heart soften toward her.

He listened to the music for some time with pleasure. The box played four tunes. He heard them each five or six times, and then he said:

"I guess that is enough for to-night, mother. How do you stop it?"

Mrs. Carboy said she thought she could show him. But when she had fumbled about the box in a feebly uncertain manner for five or ten minutes, she confessed she did not know how. Pinnickson tried his hand, but with no other result than to accelerate the motion of the cylinder.

"Oh, never mind!" he said, at last. "Let it play. We will have music all the evening."

So he sat down, and began to read. The musical-box produced its four tunes in rapid succession. Pinnickson found his mind following them so that he could not fix his attention upon his book. When an hour or two had elapsed, the performance began to grow monotonous; then it irritated him. Finally, he made another effort to stop the machine, but without success. This failure exasperated him. He felt that he could not endure those four dread-

ful tunes much longer, and he said so, glancing meanwhile
at poor Mrs. Carboy, who sat over by the fire, the picture
of distress.

At last Pinnickson said he should go to bed in preference to going mad over the jangling and twanging of
that fiendish contrivance upon the mantel. So the whole
family retired, and when Pinnickson got fairly settled in
bed, he was indignant to discover that he could still hear,
amid the silence of the house, those four maddening tunes
reeling off in quick succession. He was furious, and as
his anger kept him awake, he got to brooding over his
wrongs, and thinking how beautiful is that social system
in the Cannibal Islands, which compels a man to put his
mother-in-law to death immediately after the marriage
ceremony.

And the musical-box ground out its quartette of melo-
dies with almost malignant persistency.

On towards morning, Pinnickson could endure it no
longer. He leaped from bed, ran down-stairs, seized the
box and flung it from the window into the yard. He heard
it smash, and he gloated over the thought that its musical
performances were ended. But they were not. The
machinery was disarranged, and all night long it gave
queer spurts in which fragments of "Rule Britannia"
were oddly entangled with bits of " Hear me, Norma;"
and odds and ends of "Robin Adair" came booming out
in the most astonishing connection, with suggestions of
"Oft in the Stilly Night." And amid the fits and starts
of the dislocated music, Pinnickson dozed away into an
uneasy slumber, in which he dreamed that Mrs. Carboy
was hovering over him trying to play "Robin Adair" on

the bass drum, while Helen produced the most hideous noises from a trombone twelve hundred feet long.

The memory of the grave wrong that Mrs. Carboy had done him by means of the musical-box lingered long in Pinnickson's mind, and he sometimes felt that he hated her. But for his wife's sake he suppressed his feelings and tried to treat her in a kindly way.

Pinnickson's half-brother, a widower, much older than he, had been taking Mrs. Carboy out a good deal in the evenings, and Pinnickson's heart warmed towards his relative as he realized the blessedness of the relief thus afforded.

One evening, Mrs. Pinnickson said to him :

" Jerome, I have some news for you."

" What is it ? "

" You know mamma ? "

" Well ? "

" Well, she is engaged to be married."

Pinnickson's heart leaped within him.

" Engaged to be married?   To whom ? "

" Your half-brother—John Barnby."

Pinnickson wanted to hurrah, but considerations of propriety restrained him ; so, after a pleasant remark or two upon the subject, he went out upon the porch, and gave expression to his feelings of exultation by various wild and foolish gestures accompanied by quiet laughter.

When he returned to the house his wife thought she had never seen him in such excellent spirits.

A few months later the wedding occurred, and Mrs Carboy (Mrs. Barnby) went to her new home. That evening, as Pinnickson sat in his parlour with his wife, he felt that his real matrimonial existence had just begun. His mother-in-law had ceased troubling him for ever.

"Jerome, dear," said his wife, "I've been trying to think what relation mamma is to you now."

"What do you mean?"

"Why, it's dreadfully mixed up. I can't for the life of me tell exactly how she is related to you."

"I never thought much about it."

"Well, now; let's see. Your father was my father's half-brother, wasn't he?"

"Yes."

"Then my mother is your half-aunt, as well as your mother."

"I s'pose so."

"And now she has married your half-brother, who is the son of your mother's first husband, and not of your father."

"Wait a minute. How was that?"

"Why, I say that mamma's second husband is the son of your mother's first husband; while mamma's first husband was your father's half-brother. Isn't that right?"

"I s'pose it is. It is somehow that way."

"Very well, then; mamma is your mother's daughter now, and consequently your sister; and yet, how can your sister be your aunt?"

"My aunt! My sister be my aunt! Hanged if I know."

"Don't you see, my first papa was really your half-uncle; while my second father is my half-brother; so that —that——Well, don't it seem to you that I am somehow mamma's half-sister as well as her daughter?"

"Well, Helen, to tell the truth, I don't follow you exactly. I have a hazy idea, from what you say, that your mother occupies toward me all the female relationships from grandmother down; but precisely where she stands is the problem that I can't grasp."

"It isn't clear to me either. But let's go over it again. Your father was my father's half-brother, wasn't he?"

"Certainly."

"Well; my father's wife was my mother, wasn't she?"

"How was that? Say that again."

"Why, my father's wife was my mother, and your half-aunt; and now, that my mother is your sister—"

"Yes, my sister."

"Your sister; my mother is your mother's daughter, and consequently, being also my aunt and your mother-in-law—and—and—let me see, where was I?"

"My mother-in-law!"

"Yes, your mother-in-law. What I wan't to know is, how, being my mother and your half-aunt, and having married your half-brother, the son of another half-brother, she could—"

"Helen!" said Pinnickson, with a stern voice, "stop right here! We will pursue this investigation no further. We will drop the subject. You will oblige me by never referring to it again in my presence!"

"Helen, I do not wish to wound your feelings; but ever since our marriage I have been kept in a continual condition of exasperation by your mother. Unintentionally, perhaps, she has irritated me almost beyond endurance. I have suffered and been strong for your sake, because I loved you. You do not know what I have endured. When your mother left this house, a burden was lifted

from my soul; I felt once more that I could be happy. In the midst of my joy, you force upon me this frightful conundrum about half-aunts and grandmothers, and so on. Considerations of that matter, I feel, will finally dethrone my reason. Your mother, fleeing, has left behind her a legacy of woe. I refuse to accept it. I shall have nothing to do with it. I do not care what relation she is to you, or to me, or to anybody. It is enough for me that she has gone. Let her go. Do not stir her up. Do not agitate her. Let us have permanent repose. I have freed my mind. We will now drop the subject for ever! "

And so Jerome Pinnickson's mother-in-law drifted away from that household as a cloud floats from the landscape from which it has kept the sunlight ; and so, in fine, Pinnickson had peace.

The Adventures of Abner Byng;

WITH

SOME REFLECTIONS CONCERNING CERTAIN MORAL IDIOTS.

VERYBODY is acquainted with persons, who in their ordinary conversation, constantly and as a habit violate the truth. It is done obviously in sheer wantonness, when there is nothing to be gained by it, and when no motive is perceptible. One of these persons will begin a conversation with a palpable falsehood which does not even glorify himself, and which, he must be aware, cannot be believed by the person to whom he is talking. That a man should lie for purposes of profit, or even with the intent to exaggerate his personal importance, is perfectly comprehensible; but why a person should, as a rule, set truth at defiance without the smallest provocation, and apparently without any sense of shame at the reflection that his mendacity is perceived by the listener, is a very difficult question.

The habitual liars not only do this, but if their veracity is called in question, or their attention is directed to the nature of the obligations imposed by the Ninth Commandment, they become indignant, and resent the imputation as hotly as if they had sworn fealty to Truth for ever, and were shocked at the impeachment of their honour. The better plan usually is to receive the falsehoods in silence, for an attempt to refute them will probably provoke the invention of a swarm of fortifying fibs. A grey-headed old man, while sailing into a certain harbour with the writer, pointed to a mud-dredge, and calmly said that the machine could excavate twenty-five thousand cubic yards of mud at one revolution. He had no interest in the dredge, neither had his companion. He felt the impulse to lie at that moment, and the dredge happened to cross the range of his vision opportunely. If he had chanced to see a grain elevator or a frigate or a floating barrel, it is likely that he would have organized an equally picturesque falsehood upon another basis. To argue with him would have been more than useless. He would immediately have libelled the multiplication table by trying to prove that four times four are twenty-five thousand.

An officer of the American navy, during the Civil War, wrote home to one of his friends that while his ship was passing the forts below New Orleans, a fifteen-inch shell exploded among a crowd of eleven persons in the engine-

4

room, and didn't scratch a man. Another officer, a captain
in the same navy, used to entertain his shipmates with
stories about two magnificent but wholly imaginary
chargers that he had at home.   One day he said that he
had received a letter conveying the painful intelligence
that the noble steeds were dead.   Pretty soon he forgot
that he had framed that story, and for the remainder
of the cruise he talked about the horses as if they were
living, and he even went so far as to buy a handsome
set of harness for them at the first port of stoppage.
These are but representatives of the great body of liars
who live in every community.   The latter lie about their
achievements, their acquaintances, their houses, their
business, and even their religion.   If anybody makes a
statement in their presence, they cap it instantly with a
stronger statement of the same nature.   Their ingenuity
and readiness are astonishing.   Their complete oblivious-
ness of the fact that they utterly contradict to-day what
they said yesterday, is wonderful ; and it is not less surprising to observe that they will speak in terms of severe
censure of other persons who are suspected of similar
practices.

It is not a little curious to note that this propensity
very often runs in families.   It is, without doubt, sometimes hereditary, and this fact may tend to explain it upon
the theory that it is a peculiar form of moral idiocy.   It
is, perhaps, to the mind what colour-blindness is to the
eye.   In the moral and mental constitution of the habitual
liar there is, as an Irishman would express it, a bump that
is a hole.   The quality which enables ordinary men to
reverence the truth and to feel the shame of falsehood, is

wanting; and, meanwhile, the imagination has undue activity. There is absolute deadness of one faculty, and abnormal development of another. There is the intellectual colour-blindness which is not conscious of the difference between blue truth and red falsehood. A great many good Christian people will scout this suggestion and shake the Ninth Commandment fiercely at the liars. But wise men, who are beginning to appreciate the fact that psychology is a science whose shallowest depths have hardly been sounded, who comprehend that the imperfect constitution of the human mind is the parent of a vast amount of crime, and who realize that a man whose soul has malformation is not more responsible for its faulty action than a man with a misshapen leg is for his awkward gait, will accept this theory readily. The monumental liar always excites derision and scorn. Perhaps he ought to excite pity. The very frequency of his occurrence in ordinary society is a testimony to the fact that he is the victim of a somewhat common malady, rather than a deliberate and malicious sinner.

Whether Abner Byng was a mere wanton enemy of the truth, or only a moral idiot, perhaps cannot be determined; but he has a clear right to rank high as an organizer of magnificent and sweeping falsehoods. He has been a sailor, and when he begins to talk about his voyages he draws the long bow with a vigorous hand.

"You see," said Abner, one day to a little company whom he had met at the hotel in our county town, after the adjournment of the Court—"you see I was once a sailor before the mast, on a vessel which was cruising about in the South Atlantic Ocean.

"She was a very small vessel, and so frail that I was afraid all the time she would go to pieces; but she didn't. It happened one day that I was sent aloft to nail a block of some kind on the top of the mainmast, and as we had no hatchet I took an axe. I hit the mast three or four pretty stiff knocks, when all of a sudden I thought I felt the mast go down with a jerk. But it looked all right, and I thought it couldn't possibly be. So I came down and said nothing about it.

"Three or four days afterwards the mate said to the captain :

"'Cap., it's queer we don't sight land by this time.'

"'Very queer,' said the captain.

"'And what's more funny about it is that for several days past my instruments have made us out to be in precisely the same latitude and longitude.'

"'Maybe something's the matter with the sun.'

"'Or perhaps the parallels of latitude have shifted.'

"'Or you may have made a mistake in your figures.'

"'I didn't think of that,' said the mate.

"So they took another observation, and found that they were in precisely the same place. Everybody was frightened, and it was not until after a close examination that it was at last ascertained that I had actually driven that mainmast through the bottom of the ship into the mud, where it had stuck fast, and the old tub had been spinning round and round, like a weather-cock on a steeple, all this time, without anybody knowing it.

"To say that the captain was mad, don't describe his condition. He roared around so about it, that I got scared and hid myself in an old cask in the hold. There I lay

all day, when it was decided to heave part of the cargo
overboard, to lighten ship, and the cask I was in was headed
up, and the whole concern was tossed into the water.

"I was in that barrel about four days. It was a little
crowded, to be sure, and it would roll some, but on the
whole it was comfortable. One day I felt myself tossed
on shore, and then I was so certain of saving my life, that
I turned over and took a good nap.

"I was waked by something tickling my face. At first
I thought it was a mosquito, but then I remembered that
no mosquito could have got into the barrel. I brushed
at it again, and caught it. It was a straw. I gave it a
jerk. Something knocked against the barrel outside, and
I heard the word :

"'Thunder!'

"Then another straw was inserted, and I pulled it
still harder ; I heard this exclamation :

"'Thun-der-r-r-r !'

"Still another straw came through the bung-hole, and
as I caught it, I saw there was a man outside trying to
suck something through the straw; and whenever I pulled
it it knocked his nose against the barrel. So I gave it
one more pull, and then, kicking the head out of the cask,
I introduced myself to him.

"He was a Dutchman named Schuyler, and he told
me, in his native tongue, which I spoke with difficulty,—
that I had come ashore in Dutch Guiana. He was a good
sort of fellow. I went up home with him, and was introduced to his wife and his three daughters.

"The latter were splendid girls ; but they were so
much alike, that I could never tell one from the other. I

Kicking the head out of the cask, I introduced myself." —*Page* 53.

fell in love with one of them—I never could tell which, and I courted them just as they happened to come along.

"One day they all came into the drawing-room together. They were furious. They said I had promised each of them to marry her, and each repeated the fond words I had whispered to her, and accused me of treachery.

"It looked stormy for me. To conciliate them, I offered to marry them all, and to take them to Salt Lake; or to cut myself in three pieces; or to drown myself with them and perish in four watery graves.

"Respectfully and firmly declined.

"Then they all went out. After a while one came in and said:

"'Abner, dear, let us elope together, and leave these horrid women, and go to some sunny clime, where we can be happy in the fulness of each other's love.'

"'I will think it over, my angel,' said I.

"She passed out. Then one of them came in again.

"'Abner, dear, let us fly together, and leave these horrid women, and go to some sunny clime, where we can be happy in the fulness of each other's love.'

"'I say, I will think it over, my own angel.'

"And she disappeared. But she seemed anxious, so in she came again.

"'Abner, dear, let us fly together, and leave these horrid women, and go to some sunny clime, where we can be happy in the fulness of each other's love.'

"'You've said that three times, and that's enough. My mind fully grasps the idea. I say I'll think it over.'

"'Why, I never said it before,' says she.

"'You didn't?' I exclaimed.

" ' Certainly not ! '

" I saw it all. Each of them had approached me with
the same proposition. It was clear that I must fly. I
made up my mind to take the first boat that left Dutch
Guiana for anywheres.

" That night I walked to town, and shipped on a
barque that had just loaded a cargo of mahogany for
Liverpool, and next morning I was at sea.

" I have been subject all my life to cataleptic fits,
during which I seem to be dead. On the tenth day out,
one of these fits attacked me, and the doctor, after feeling
my pulse, said I was a corpse.

" They determined to bury me. Contrary to custom
at sea, they made me a substantial coffin out of mahogany
boards ; and as they were rather short of nails, they tied
the lid on with pieces of marlin-twine. A hundred-pound
shot was fastened to the foot of the coffin, and the Epis-
copal service was read over the body. Then the word was
given, and the whole concern was launched into the sea.

" All this time there I had been lying, unable to move
hand or foot, or to speak, but I was conscious, and I had
heard all that went on around me, and even followed every
sentence of the Burial Service.

"You can imagine the frightful agony I endured. The
plunge into the cold water, however, revived me, and I
recovered the use of my faculties only in time to find
myself going down to the bottom of the ocean at the rate
of about one mile a minute. The water was just two
miles in depth, and before I could budge, I had struck
bottom. Fortunately they had buried me in my sailor
clothes. and I had a jack-knife with me. I instantly

drew it, slipped the blade in the crack between the lid
and the coffin, cut the marlin-twine, severed the rope that
held the shot, clutched the sides of my narrow apartment,
and began to ascend with frightful velocity.

"When I reached the surface the impetus gained,
threw the coffin three feet into the air, and it came down
right side up, with me lying in it snug and comfortable,
only I was a little wet and hungry. I had been
under water precisely
five minutes, and I
couldn't possibly have
held my breath a se-
cond longer, so it was
lucky the sea was not
deeper just there. I
must have drifted
somewhat for the ves-
sel was just visible
on the horizon. The
velocity of the ocean
currents will account
for this.

"While coming up,
the end of the coffin
struck against a large
fish, stunning it so,
that I secured it with-
out difficulty when I got to the top, and despatched it
with a knife. I tied it to the coffin with a piece of
the marlin-twine, and as I floated along day after
day, I cut steaks off the fish to support my life. It

was fortunate that I was buried in a coffin, as I must inevitably have been drowned otherwise. I was lucky, also, in capturing the fish, or I would have starved to death.

" Well, I sailed along nicely enough for about a week, only I began to get tired of such close quarters, when one day I ran against an iceberg of the most enormous dimensions. I immediately clambered upon it, dragged the coffin up after me, and sat down to consider what I had better do next.

"An idea struck me; I would explore the iceberg, which was about five miles long, and, in some places at least, half a mile high. So I pulled the fish from the water, or rather the remains of the fish, and, taking two of the largest bones,

I made myself an excellent pair of skates, which I tied to my feet with marlin-twine. I found that I could get along very rapidly with these, and at once I started upon a tour.

" I hadn't gone more than a mile and a half, when I stumbled over the dead body of a sailor, with a fishing rod and line in his hand. The man, evidently, had come off of his ship to catch some fish, and had been lost and frozen to death.

"I took the rod and line from him, together with one or two articles of clothing, and proceeded to return to my coffin. After lighting a fire with some splinters of the coffin, and cooking some of the fish I already had, I concluded to go a-fishing. Baiting the hook, I flung it overboard. I got a few nibbles at first, but directly I felt a good bite, and I pulled up. It was an ordinary herring. Before I got it fairly out of the water, a fifty-pound sea-bass leaped up and swallowed it.

"'All right,' thought I, 'I'd rather have you anyway,' and I hauled in on it.

"Strange to say, I hadn't more than got the sea-bass's tail out, than a sturgeon appeared and took it down at a gulp.

"'Still better,' thought I, as I kept on reeling in my line. But I was destined to further annoyance; no sooner had I got the sturgeon pretty well up, than the biggest shark I ever saw, stuck his nose out and took the sturgeon down without chewing him.

"'Very extraordinary, upon my word,' thought I, as I still pulled my line in. But hardly had I comprehended the situation, when a whale swam up, and seeing the shark swallowed it.

"I was pleased; any man would be under such circumstances. I tied the line to a huge icicle, and so held the whale fast. The whale died that night from indigestion, and I, drawing the other fish from him, began to enjoy myself as well as I could.

"The days were very short, and I experienced much annoyance from the continual darkness, until another idea

struck me.   I took the dead sailor's shirt, tore it into
narrow strips, ran the strips through the bamboo fishing
pole, and stuck the pole into the fattest portion of the
whale that floated alongside.   I then lit the end of the strip
that protruded from the bamboo, and produced a most
brilliant light.   The rays were reflected from the whole
iceberg, and the glare was so intense that the sea was
lighted up for miles, and I was compelled to look away
from the ice to avoid going blind ; but my left eye was,
nevertheless, somewhat injured.

" Thus I lived for nearly a month, until one day I happened to observe a piece of wood sticking out of the wall
of ice beside me.   I grasped it and tried to move it, but
without success.   While I was working at it, the iceberg
chanced to run aground, and it split into pieces with a
noise like the firing of a million cannon.   I felt the ice
giving way beneath my feet, and I grasped the piece of
wood and hung on.   As the berg fell to pieces, I found
that I had hold of the bowsprit of a ship which had been
embedded in the ice, but which was now floating, as good
as ever, in the ocean.

" To clamber down and get on the deck was the work
of an instant.   And there I found the captain and crew
all frozen to death.

" It was lucky that I found this ship, or I would certainly have been drowned when the iceberg went to pieces.
There were twenty dead men on the vessel, and after
having twenty funerals, I set to work to load the craft
with the pieces of ice which floated around me.   Having
secured a full cargo, I set sail, and proceeded due south, to
hunt for a market for the ice.

"On the third day, I was chased by a pirate, and having no artillery on board, and with such a small crew, too, I took a barrel of gunpowder, stuck a half-hour fuse in the bunghole, lighted the fuse, and flung the barrel overboard, right in the track of his vessel. The pirate struck the barrel, there was an explosion, and the pursuer was blown to atoms. Only one man was picked up, and I made him one of my crew. But the man mutinied, and I formed myself into a court-martial, brought the man before me, tried him, found him guilty, and then the court took the crew out and hung him at the yard-arm.

"At the end of a month, I ran into the harbour of one of the Fejee Islands, and, just as I dropped anchor, a canoe put off from shore and came alongside. It contained the chief of the tribe which inhabited the island. I gave him a salute of twenty-one guns, with an old blunderbuss which I found on board, and received him, hat in hand, as he came over the gangway.

"'How are you, sir?' said I to the chief; 'I hope you're well. I just dropped around to see if you should be wanting any ice. I've got a fine cargo here, which I'm selling off at reduced rates.'

"There was yellow fever in the island, and ice was the very thing the chief wanted worse than anything else. So I cleared my cargo out at an immense bargain, and went ashore with the chief.

" When the people heard I had brought them a whole ship-load of ice, they went frantic with joy. A public reception was tendered me, and I was voted a national benefactor. The people rehearsed my praises all over the island, and a grand mass-meeting was held, at which I was proclaimed Prime Minister of the country, and second only in authority to the chief who had come off to see me. I left the vessel at anchor in the harbour, accepted the office, and lived there for four years and eight months, enjoying myself hugely, and amassing great wealth.

" The people were cannibals, but I could never entirely overcome my aversion to man-meat, and, one day when they had roast missionary on the table at a public banquet, I refused to touch a morsel, and left the room in disgust. This enraged the fickle mob, and I was arrested, tried, and condemned to be broiled to death on the state gridiron. On the appointed day, a huge fire was built in the square of the city, and, when it had burned to coals,

the immense gridiron was placed upon it, and I was stripped and carefully laid upon the gridiron.

" I bore the inexpressible torture for a time, but after a while, making an excuse that I wanted to turn over, I leaped up, seized the gridiron, and bravely attacking the crowd, killed two hundred of them with the hot gridiron, and put the rest to flight.

"About three hundred of the more timid savages, in an agony of terror, swam out in the harbour, and secreted themselves in the hold of my ship. I also sought refuge there, and, finding my enemies in the vessel, I fastened down the hatches, weighed anchor, and sailed out to sea

before the people on shore could recover from their alarm.

"I hadn't proceeded more than twenty miles before I observed three shipwrecked sailors floating on a hen-coop. I picked them up, and, strange to say, they were my two brothers and my nephew, whom I had not seen for twelve years. Of course, the meeting was affecting beyond expression, all four of us melting into tears, and sobbing as if our hearts would break. Now that I had a crew, I had no trouble in navigating the ship, so I sailed for Cuba, where I sold the three hundred natives in the hold for slaves, at one thousand dollars a-piece, and then I set sail for Philadelphia, and got home just in time to receive the dying embrace of my mother, who very naturally had mourned for me as dead for ten years."

When Abner Byng finished this recital, he cleared his throat, called for a mug of ale, drank it, lighted the stump of a cigar, and said :—

"Some men lie about their adventures, but that always

seemed to me to be wrong.   When I deviate from the truth a half-an-inch, I want somebody to kick me—to kick me hard."

Then slowly uprose Thomas Dundas, a farmer who had been on the petit jury that day.   Coming near to Abner, he gave him a fearful kick, which moved him a dozen feet or more toward the door.

At first Abner seemed indignant ; he appeared to be eager for war.   But when he had eyed Dundas for a moment, a smile stole gently over his face, and he said : –

"Squire, you're the quickest man to take a hint that I ever come across."

And then Abner Byng adjourned.

How Jack Forbes was Avenged.

EVERYBODY agreed that Jack Forbes had not been treated fairly. The squire, the clergyman, the cackling old ladies at the sewing bee, the baker, the milkman, the members of the Cecilian Society—in fact, all the prominent people of Banglebury admitted that the treatment which Jack Forbes had received from Jenny Brown, was the roughest that had ever been inflicted upon a clever young man by a good-looking girl.

The whole story was as follows : In May, Miss Brown had come to Banglebury, fresh from a winter's gaiety in the city, where her parents lived. It was whispered about that she was sent to the village to remain with her uncle, Judge Bates, in order to separate her from a youth who had made a deep impression upon her at home. But this was merely a rumour, which seemed to be denied by the light-heartedness and joyous spirits of the fair maiden.

At any rate, it did not deter Mr. Forbes from falling in love with her, after a very brief acquaintance, and show-

5

ing her that devoted attention which is the usual method
of expressing such a tender passion.

Miss Jenny received these little demonstrations as if
she liked them ; and although Forbes never could get his
courage quite up to the point of declaration, he did not
entertain a single doubt of her devotion to him. Night
after night, he took her to concerts and lectures, and singing-school, and sociables, dancing and singing with her,
and walking home with her in the moonlight and the
starlight, with his heart knocking at his ribs as if it was
bent upon fracturing them, and his soul so full of tender
fear that he could talk of nothing but the most absurdly
commonplace and prosy subjects.

Of course Forbes behaved very foolishly. He could
not reasonably expect Miss Brown to parade around the
country with him for ever without having an understanding, particularly when the whole village talked about the
matter : and Forbes, therefore, had no right to complain
when Mr. Dulcitt, the new singing-master, soon after his
arrival in the town, began to trespass in Forbes's baili-
wick, and to engage an unpleasantly large share of Miss
Brown's time and attention.

Mr. Dulcitt was a mild young man, with light hair and
weak eyes, which were protected by spectacles. He had
a room at Mrs. Megonegal's, where he used to practise
upon the flute, until the other boarders would rage and
tear up and down the entries, and consign Dulcitt and his
flute to a place which Dulcitt, we sincerely hope, will
never reach, and where a flute, under any circumstances
would be entirely useless.

But Dulcitt's strong point was vocalism. He could

sing with such tremendous power that people wondered
how he contrived to get so great a volume out of so small
a body. A rumour spread about that his legs were hollow, and constructed like organ pipes, and that he had
bellows in his boots. However, he was a good singer—
there was no manner of doubt about that ; and when he
stood up in front of his class in the town hall, and led
them through some spirited chorus, he created so much
enthusiasm for himself, that the miserable Mr. Forbes
cowered in the back part of the room so angry that he
could hardly help along the chorus with that dreadful
bass voice of his.

But his anger was mere good-humour at such times,
to the ferocious rage with which he regarded the mild-
eyed Dulcitt when he descended from the platform and
beamed through his spectacles upon Jenny, as he offered
her his arm and swept her past poor old Forbes, without
even a glance at his rival. To make matters worse, everybody in the class understood the situation, and all eyes
were turned upon Jack to see how he would bear it.

Everybody considered Miss Jenny's conduct highly
improper. The young ladies thought so because Mr.
Dulcitt had neglected them. The young gentlemen
entertained the opinion because each man had a private
impression that such behaviour would have been justifiable
only if Jack had been forsaken for him.

One cold night in December, the Cecilian Society met
to practise some music for a concert which was to be
given during the holidays. Dulcitt, and all the members
of his singing-school were present. After the rehearsal,
Dulcitt and Miss Brown went away arm-in-arm, as usual.

Forbes decided to bring matters to a crisis that very
night. He resolved to watch the house of Judge Bates
until Dulcitt and Miss Brown should part at the front
door, and then to plunge in and propose to his fair deluder
at once. He lived next door to the Judge ; and so putting
his hat firmly on his head, he left the hall and darted
quickly around through a back street so that he might
reach home before Dulcitt and Jenny arrived.

As he entered the gate of his front yard and sat down
in the darkness of the porch, he saw them coming slowly
down the street. His dog ran up to him and began to
caper about and bark ; but Jack forced him to lie down
beside him and keep quiet, while his rival approached
with his enslaver.

They came very deliberately and passed by, conversing
in such soft tones that the wretched listener could not
understand a word. She reached the Judge's door. Dulcitt
stood and talked for a while, Forbes meantime shivering
with cold and impatient for his departure. But after a
little parley, Dulcitt actually went into the house. Jack
Forbes groaned aloud ; and then, after giving his dog a
kick that sent him howling away behind the house, Jack
cleared the fence at a bound and was in Judge Bates's
garden.

The Judge had his library room upon the second floor,
and Mr. Forbes had just gotten beneath the window when
the lamp was lighted and Miss Jenny appeared in the act
of removing her bonnet. It was a mean thing to do, a
mean thing even for a desperate lover, but Forbes decided
to clamber into the tree that stood by the window so that
he might look with his own eyes upon the perfidy ot the

woman to whom he had given his love. After a series of difficult gymnastics, during which he tore his coat and knocked the skin off his hands, he reached a place from which he could peer into the room. Yes, there was Jenny, sitting in front of the fire, and Dulcitt by her side, with his arm on the back of her chair, with his glasses turned full upon her, and his faded eyes gazing at her, just as Jack's used to gaze. Forbes felt his heart sink within him at this spectacle, but he determined to sit on that limb all night if it was necessary, in order to see all that happened, and to ascertain precisely how matters stood. Hardly had he formed the resolution, when Jenny came to the window and pulled down the curtain.

"It's of no use," said Jack, in despair; and he began to descend the tree, when the door of the house opened and somebody came out. It was so dark that Jack could only distinguish a figure which he thought resembled that of the Judge.

The Judge walked towards the stable whistling, meanwhile, to a large dog that accompanied him. Jack had heard the Judge express his determination to procure a dog to protect that very stable. Doubtless this was the animal.

"But the best thing for me to do will be to keep quiet until the Judge goes in," said Jack. To his horror, however, he saw dimly the figure of the dog coming towards the tree, and a moment later the animal stood beneath him barking loudly. Jack thought then he should surely be discovered. But no, strange to say, the Judge walked slowly back to the house and closed the door, leaving his dog under the tree. After barking a few moments more,

the brute lay down, and seemed determined to make a
night of it.   Mr. Forbes, from his cool and lofty perch, regarded the indistinct black figure beneath him with anguish.

"Good gracious," he said, "suppose the confounded
brute should stay there all night!"

Then he thought he would wait until the dog got to
sleep, and creep gently down without waking him.

Ten, fifteen, twenty minutes passed, with Jack blowing the fingers of one hand while with the other he balanced himself on the limb. He began to descend. But at the very first motion the dog leaped up and began barking again. He tried the experiment a second time, and, just as the ferocious brute stretched himself upon the ground, after another demonstration, Jack caught sight of two shadows kissing each other upon the curtain. Then the light was turned out, and presently he heard the front door open, and saw Dulcitt dance along beneath the street-lamp, as if he were practising a fandango.

It occurred to the unfortunate Mr. Forbes to call to him. "But, no!" ejaculated Forbes; "I will freeze into solid ice first; hang me if I don't!" and he stamped on the limb so violently that it roused the dog, who barked savagely.

"Let us try what kindness will do," said Mr. Forbes, making that peculiar noise which resembles the sound of kissing—a noise which is supposed to soothe a dog, but which cannot be written.

"Poor fellow! poor old dog! come here, poor fellow!" (Kissing noise again; then a whistle.)

But the dog barked more vociferously than ever, and pranced around the tree as if the only boon he wanted in this life was a chance to bite a chop from Mr. Forbes's leg.

"Here, Pont! here, old fellow! (kissing noise again) —come here, old dog! here, poor fellow! here, Jack!"

More violent demonstrations of blood-thirstiness on the part of the now franctic animal.

"Here, Jack! Here! Rats! rats! rats! ketch 'em, Jack!" exclaimed Mr. Forbes, with the ingenuity of despair. Rats were not the game wanted at that moment, apparently, by " Jack." Meditation upon the succulency of Mr. Forbes's calf seemed to have filled him with frenzy, for he capered and howled, and howled and capered, worse than ever.

" Lie down, sir !" said Jack, trying a new plan ; " lie down, sir ! keep quiet! go home! go home, I tell you ! " and he descended two or three feet upon the tree. This seemed to make the animal more outrageous, for now he leaped up the trunk and tried his very best to get even a nip at Mr. Forbes's boots, barking all the time as if he had been wound up and his vocal apparatus was kept going with a spring.

So Jack climbed back to the most comfortable place he could find, reluctantly convinced that he should have to stay in the tree until morning.

He seated himself astride of a limb, with his back against the trunk, and put his hands in his pockets to keep them warm. Presently the dog became quiet, and Jack sat there looking up at the stars, which seemed to wink at him through the frosty air as if to say, " Got you now, old fellow. Nice fix you're in, isn't it ? "

Then he began to think about trees in general. He thought of Wm. Penn's treaty tree, and of the picture that he had seen of the proscribed royalist hid in a hollow tree, with a pretty girl giving him food. And he wished Jenny would only come downstairs and hand him something warm and comfortable. He remembered that cheerful anecdote which relates how the 'coon, which was treed by Captain Scott, of Kentucky, promised to come down if the Captain would not shoot, and Mr.

Forbes thought what a lucky 'coon it was to be able to come down when it chose. And there was the old story about Charles the Second hiding in an oak, with the soldiers beneath looking for him. Jack thought that he would rather have a whole hostile army encamped under that tree of his, at the present moment, than that infernal dog, which lay there as calm and quiet as if nothing was the matter.

Then the stars began to dance about in the sky, and to multiply, and Jack caught himself nodding and dreaming so that once he nearly lost his balance and fell. He had always heard that sleepiness was a symptom of freezing to death, so he jumped up and began clambering up and down the branches to keep himself warm. This set the dog to barking again, and it made such a fearful racket that at last Judge Bates flung up his window and threw a missile of some kind at the animal, accompanied with an angry word or two. Jack could stand it no longer ; so he cried out :—

"Judge ! Judge Bates ! "

"Holloa ! Who's there ? " said the Judge, nervously.

"I ; Jack Forbes ; I am up this tree, and I can't get down because of this confounded dog of yours."

"Of mine ? I have no dog," said the Judge.

"Well, at anyrate, there's a ferocious dog here, and I can't get down. I am freezing to death ; actually freezing," said Jack, pathetically.

"Wait a moment, until I get dressed," said the Judge, closing the window.

In five minutes or ten, the Judge came to the door with a lantern in his hand, while Mrs. Bates, and Jenny

Brown, and the three servant girls stood at their respective windows, wrapped in shawls, surveying the scene with eager and excited interest.

The Judge came forward, cautiously, and spoke to the dog. It leaped toward him instantly. The Judge laughed. " Why, Jack, this is your own dog," he said.

" No! that can't be," replied Jack.

" But it is, though," said the Judge, convulsed with laughter, and holding the lantern close to the brute.

It was too true. Forbes, in his nervousness and fear, had mistaken the friendly capers and yelps of the dog for manifestations of ferocity on the part of some other animal.

Mr. Forbes slid down from the tree hastily, but sadly ; and while he explained the whole matter frankly to the Judge, begging him to say nothing about it, the Judge laughed so violently that Mrs. Bates and Jenny came running downstairs, thinking he had a hysterical fit. And Mr. Forbes climbed over the fence hurriedly, and went shivering to bed, without even saying good-night to the family.

It was useless to try to keep the matter quiet. It was absurd to suppose the Judge would neglect to tell such a good story. But if he had remained silent, it would have been of no use ; for Mrs. Bates, and Jenny, and the servants, each related it to a different circle next day. And so everybody in Banglebury knew about it before another sun had set, and Jack had fun poked at him everywhere he went. Even in the Singing Society those who had at first given him their sympathies turned against him, and laughed at Dulcitt's jokes upon the subject.

Jack went downstairs and swore an awful oath that he would be revenged. But how? Assassination of Dulcitt, with a butcher-knife, in a dark corner, some night, suggested itself; or the intermixture of bug poison with Mrs. Megonegal's hash, or hurling Mr. Dulcitt into the river; or blowing out his brains with a pistol—all occurred to him, but he gave them up as promising unpleasant consequences to himself. Then he thought he would smash Mr. Dulcitt's spectacles with his fists; he pondered upon horsewhips, and considered their relative severity to clubs and canes. He went home and retired to bed, trying to decide precisely which would be the best method of making Mr. Dulcitt suffer.

He had hardly touched the pillow before an idea struck him. He remembered a curious incident that he had read in one of Jean Paul's stories; and he felt certain that he had found what he wanted. He was so much pleased that he leaped from bed, and executed a fandango upon the floor with so much energy that Mrs. Megonegal sent a servant up to ascertain the cause of the disturbance, and to request " less noise." Then Forbes turned in again with mingled feelings of joy and bliss. He felt a good deal mortified when he thought of that wretched adventure in the tree, and of the publicity that had been given to it. He experienced a kind of ferocious joy as he reflected upon the manner in which he would bring that wretch, Mr. Dulcitt, to grief.

The next evening the grand concert was to come off. The Cecilians assembled early upon the platform, with music-books in their hands, eager to begin. Dulcitt strutted about, busily important, giving whispered directions, arranging the singers, distributing music, and making his spectacled self very conspicuous.

The hall was crammed absolutely full. The people occupied the very window-sills ; while certain small boys, filling the gallery, yelled at each other, and stamped in rhythm upon the floor. In the very front of the audience sat Mr. Forbes, where he could be seen by every singer upon the stage. He looked very grave, and in answer to numerous inquiries, he said that he felt rather unwell, and believed he would not sing this evening. Dulcitt congratulated himself in getting rid of a man who, as he said, " made a noise like a rip-saw, when he tried to sing."

The first piece upon the programme was the Hallelujah Chorus. Mr. Dulcitt seized his baton, and ascended to the leader's stand ; he tapped once or twice, and the very small band played a small overture in a very small sort of way. Then the chorus dashed into the magnificent music, singing it bravely, while Dulcitt, with his back to the audience, beat time with both arms and his head.

When the chorus got fairly under way, Mr. Forbes dived into his overcoat pocket, and produced a huge lemon. Cutting the top off, he made motions to attract the attention of the singers, and having succeeded in getting some of them to look at him, he raised the lemon to his mouth and began to suck it. The effect was instantaneous and marvellous. The mouths of those who saw him instantly filled with saliva, and as they made vain attempts to swallow, and to keep along with the music, a series of the most horrible discords was produced, so that Dulcitt grew frantic, and danced and beat more violently than ever. The strange interruption excited surprise in

the minds of those who had not seen Jack, and they lifted
their eyes from the music to ascertain the cause. When
they saw the lemon, the same result was produced ; and,
in a minute, the whole chorus was upset, knocked out of
tune and time, and at last brought to a stand-still.

The audience was amazed. Dulcitt, red in the face,
turned around, and seeing Jack hard at work at his
lemon, comprehended the situation in a moment. Re-
covering himself, he determined to defy his enemy.
Directing the singers not to look at Forbes, he began
again. But it would not do. Every man and woman
knew Jack's lemon was there, and they all found it impossible to get rid of the thought or to stop the filling of their
mouths. The flute-player found his instrument swamped ;
the clarionet was water-logged ; the trombone dripped ;
the hautbois and the cornet were filled with moisture.
Three or four spurts were made by the orchestra, and a
phrase or two was attempted by the chorus ; but the
result was horrible. The audience hissed ; the young
men on the front bench, seeing Jack's manœuvre, laughed ;
the boys in the gallery whistled like miniature locomo-
tives.

At last, beside himself with rage, Dulcitt leaped from
the platform, and rushing up to Jack, struck him in the
face with his *baton.* Mr. Forbes responded promptly
with his fist, shattering Dulcitt's spectacles to atoms.
Then they grappled, and after rolling around among the
benches on the dusty floor for some minutes, they were
separated. Dulcitt, red and bleeding, shook his fist at
Jack, and, struggling with those who held him, said
breathlessly :

" Dulcitt shook his fist at Jack."—*Pagé* 77.

"This is not the last of the quarrel. Pistols, you know—you've got to fight—to fight—death, you know— *death*—death—DEATH!" yelled Dulcitt, as he was dragged away by his friends.

Jack smiled contemptuously, but said nothing until Dulcitt had departed; then, as the half-angry, half-amused audience slowly dispersed, Jack deigned to give some explanation of the difficulty. He had fairly turned the tables on his enemy : and disappointed though they were at the failure of the concert, the people laughed, and agreed to forgive him for the ingenuity of his revenge.

Jenny Brown sat on the platform, cool, silent, and indifferent, until a strange young man, whom Jack had never seen, climbed up by her side and spoke to her. She coloured a little, seemed pleased, and finally rose up and went out with him.

Jack marched home in triumph, worried about Jenny, and yet exultant over the success of his pleasant little scheme.

His joy was short-lived. Hardly had he reached the house, when a friend of Mr. Dulcitt's called, and after explaining that he came upon a disagreeable errand, handed Forbes a note. It was a challenge from Dulcitt.

" Tell him," said Jack, with an air of defiance, "that I will meet him at seven to-morrow morning, in Duby's Woods. Weapons, pistols ! "

Mr. Dulcitt's second withdrew, and Jack went upstairs to bed. While he was undressing, he began to think about it. Was it worth while after all to fight that idiot for a girl?—for a girl, too, who very likely cared nothing for Mr. Forbes, and who might only be flirting with

Dulcitt, to test Jack's devotion to her? Pistols, too! it was deuced unpleasant: somebody might get hurt. Suppose he should put a ball through old Dulcitt, and be arrested and hung for murder? Worse than that; what if Dulcitt should blow Jack's brains out on the spot! It wasn't nice to consider such a probability. What good would any girl be to him if his brains were blown out? Why, none at all. It was all confounded foolishness. Better remain a bachelor his whole life, than die like a dog at seven o'clock in the morning, by the hand of a weak-eyed singing-teacher.

"I'll be hanged if I'll do it," said Jack, as he got into bed. "I won't go. I'll pack up and leave town by the six o'clock train, and write a note saying that I had to go to the city on important business. I'd be a fool to fight such a fellow as Dulcitt, anyhow. I'm not going to make a target of myself for any man or woman either," ejaculated Forbes, as he turned over and tried to go to sleep.

But in vain. Haunted by thoughts of the duel, of the danger or one hand, and the disgrace on the other, Jack passed the night without a moment of repose. It was not pleasant to picture Dulcitt and his friends upon the ground, waiting for him with sanguinary impatience, until the hour passed, and then coming into town to post him as a coward. But Jack thought he would rather look upon this picture than upon that other, which showed his lifeless remains extended upon the ground, and soaked in gore.

So at five o'clock he got up, dressed himself, crammed a few things in a satchel, and stole softly downstairs. When he flung open the hall-door, the street was so dark,

and cold, and desolate, that Jack felt very forlorn and
miserable, and was half inclined to stay at home and
brave the shame that would be heaped upon him for his
cowardice. After a moment's hesitation, however, he
closed the door gently, and crept down the street, with as
much dread of being observed by the early risers, as if he
were a criminal fleeing from justice.

As he came near to the railroad station, the lights and
the glow of the
warm fire in
the depot looked
so cheerful and
comfortable that
Jack's heart
grew lighter, and
he thought that
upon the whole
it was a good
thing he had
come. He walk-
ed briskly upon
the platform, opened the door of the waiting-room, and
entered.

There was one other passenger going by the early
train ; he was sitting on the other side of the stove, with
a carpet-bag by his side. His head was bowed down and
rested upon his hands. His elbows were upon his knees.
Jack got close to him before he looked up.

It was Dulcitt, bent upon the same errand as Jack's
own.

When Dulcitt saw Jack, he started to his feet, stepped

6

back a pace, and grew very red in the face. Jack also retreated and blushed. Dulcitt was the first to recover his presence of mind. He determined to make what profit he could from the situation.

" So, you scoundrel, you are trying to run away, are you ? " he said to Jack.

" No, I am not," Jack replied—" no, I'm not. I heard that you were scared to death, you coward, and intended to bolt, and I came here to stop you."

" That's a lie ! " exclaimed Dulcitt ; " you never heard anything of the kind. I expected you would try to escape my vengeance, and so I determined to block your game."

" You didn't, you blackguard," replied Jack ; " you were running away, for you've got your valise with you."

" So have you got yours," said Dulcitt.

Jack coloured deeply, and looking at his carpet-bag, said in a hesitating voice :

" I—I—know—I—well, I've got my pistols in it."

" All right, then," said Dulcitt, fiercely, " let's go outside and fight now."

Jack was stunned for a minute, and then he said :

" No, I won't, either ; if I do anything I'll kick you, you miserable cur.'

" Then you're a mean, dastardly scoundrel," yelled Dulcitt, in a frenzy, shaking his fist in Jack's face.

Before Jack had a chance to reply, the door of the room opened, and in walked Jenny Brown, accompanied by the strange young man who leaped upon the platform upon the evening of the concert.

Forbes was bewildered.

Dulcitt was stupefied.

Jenny gave a little scream as she beheld her two victims, and very likely would have fainted but for the promptness of the strange young man, who put his arm around her instantly. When she had recovered, she looked at Forbes and Dulcitt for a few minutes, and then, comprehending the situation, burst into a fit of hearty laughter. The strange young man smiled, but the two duellists looked very glum and surly.

At last Miss Jenny went up to them and said :

" Well, gentlemen, as there is no help for it, I must take you into my confidence and trust to you not to betray it. This is Mr. McFadden, the gentleman to whom I am to be married this morning. I have been engaged to him for several months, and I regret to say I am obliged, after all, to marry him without the consent of my friends. May I hope that you will keep this matter secret for a time ? "

" Miss Brown, deeply as I regret to learn this from you, I can assure you that I shall regard your wish as an obligation," said Dulcitt, bowing sadly.

Jack Forbes gulped down a big sob, and then, with a faltering voice, said :

" I won't tell either, but I don't think this is exactly the right thing, and I don't think you have treated me fairly. What did you lead me to believe that you loved me for, say ? "

Before Jenny could reply, Mr. McFadden stepped up and said :

" See here ! none of that, you know ! If you talk in that manner to this young lady, you know, I'll punch your head, you know ! "

As Mr. McFadden appeared to be equal to the task of fulfilling his threat, Jack turned away in gloomy silence and went home again, and Dulcitt followed him.

As they walked down the street, Jack halted until Dulcitt caught up to him, when he said :

" I say, Dulcitt, let's make it up ? "

" All right," said Dulcitt, extending his hand.

Jack shook it heartily, and looking his late enemy in the eye, remarked :

" And I think, perhaps, it would be better if neither of us said anything about this matter ? "

" I think so, too," observed Dulcitt, " decidedly."

" For to tell you the honest truth," said Jack Forbes, " she isn't much of a girl anyhow, and I wouldn't fight for her."

Babies.

CERTAIN FACTS CONCERNING THEIR DEMORALIZATION.

VERYBODY, we believe, excepting a few misanthropists, admits that the human race, as a whole, has been steadily growing better under the beneficent and extending influences of civilization. The careful observer, especially if he be a parent, will, however, have a strong inclination to protest that the modern baby—regarded merely as a baby— cannot fairly be included in the number of those who are moving onward toward perfection.

Concerning the characteristics of the babies of remote antiquity, we have no accurate information. We know that Moses, lying in the bulrushes, attracted the attention of Pharaoh's daughter; but there is nothing in the Scrip-

tural narrative which warrants the assumption that he did
so by lifting up his voice and weeping. If an average
baby of the present period could be placed in such a
position, the chances are that it would howl so as to
arouse the whole land of Egypt. But we have reliable
accounts of the conduct of babies of the early part of this
century, from elderly people who cared for them, and the
evidence of these persons is that the babies of the period
were stuffy and sleepy, and addicted to indulgence in a
remarkable amount of silence.

The infants of the present day are not thus. They
come into the world apparently with two fixed resolves :
Aot to stay asleep more than an hour or two in each
night, and to give their lungs and vocal chords the largest
opportunities of exercise. The old-fashioned baby
slept serenely though cannons were fired by its ears. The
modern baby considers it necessary to awake and remon-
strate if the nurse steps about with a squeaking boot. The
ancient baby merely warbled a little as a suggestion that
it needed nourishment, or a few drops from the paregoric
bottle. The preposterous baby of to-day cries loudest
when it is fullest, and stays awake most when it has
largest doses of narcotics.

There is an element of ingratitude in this behaviour
which, unless there is a speedy reform, will be likely to
create a permanent prejudice against the modern baby.
Mankind has done a great deal for him. The old-time
baby considered itself lucky if it could obtain an occasional
ride in a rude box fastened to four uncouth wheels. The
later baby goes out sumptuously in a gilded coach with
falling-top and springs. The primeval baby was hushed

to sleep with harsh and melodious rhythm. The present baby has had cradle-songs written expressly for it by Gounod, and Gottschalk, and Schubert, and Abt, and many other great composers — songs which ought to send a baby whirling into the land of dreams.

The pre-revolutionary baby was rocked in a cradle the only motor of which was an intermittent and irregular maternal toe. The baby of our time is vibrated beautifully by clockwork. The baby of the misty past had but one food supply, and it had to use that or go hungry. The baby that howls beneath the brilliant light of our later civilization has the choice of many viands, from oatmeal gruel to toasted buns ; and for it were reserved the blessings of the patent bottle with the india-rubber nozzle.

In spite of all these things : in spite of soothing syrups and woven undershirts and all the other devices of ingenious inventors who have spent years in getting up appliances for ameliorating the condition of babies, the modern infant persists in staying awake and howling with a persistency that is disgusting and disreputable.

The cause of this wicked disposition is not clearly

apparent ; if it were, something might be done in the way
of procuring legislation to correct it. There are persons
who attribute it to the force of original sin. The baby
being small, and yet having as much of this dreadful heir-
loom as a grown person, has greater pressure to the
square inch, and he is compelled to yield to it. This
theory will seem a little strained when we recur to the
excellent conduct of the infant Moses, and remember that
he was subjected to the same pressure, but succeeded in
resisting it. The modern milkman may be partially responsible, for even a totally depraved baby may be forgiven
for screeching if an undue predominance of cold water in
its diet awakes a pain more intense than any baby knew
aforetime, when milkmen were guileless and the pump
was not their chief coadjutor.

The probability, however, is that as the human race
grows older, and more refined, and more fastidious, it
also becomes more nervous, and that, consequently, the
babies start in life with nervous systems much more delicate and more acutely sensitive than those that belonged
to their predecessors. If this is the case, it is difficult to
perceive precisely how the uproariousness of the average
baby is to be subdued in any general and effectual
manner, unless by the use of positive force.

The properly-trained Indian baby never howls. The
reason is that when it begins its career its mother sup-
presses its very first outbursts by taking its nose between
her forefinger and her thumb, and holding her palm over
its mouth. Then it cannot cry without peril of bursting,
and after a few ineffectual attempts it abandons the business in despair, comprehends that silence is one of the

conditions of existence, and thenceforth it hides its sorrows and nurses its grief in secret. It is not by any means saddest when it sings.

Extremes are very sure to meet. We may be approaching the day when the highly-civilized parent will be compelled to adopt the method of the wholly savage aborigine in compelling the average baby to refrain its ululations.

These reflections are born of certain recent observations of the conduct and misconduct of the babies who owe allegiance to my neighbours, the Magruders.

The Magruders have twins, and although that fact was known to most persons living in the village, it was not known to Mr. Partridge, their next-door neighbour, when he came home from a summer's sojourn at the sea-side.

Upon the first night of his arrival, he was awakened about one o'clock by some unusually loud caterwauling, apparently in Magruder's yard. He rose, went to the window, and ejaculated " Scat!" several times, but without effect. The noise continued. Then he fumbled around in the closet for an old boot, and projected it at the spot where he thought the cats were. There was a momentary lull, but in a minute or two the screeching became more vociferous than ever. Partridge went for another boot, and hurled it with terrific force into Magru·der's yard, and then he followed it with another, and then the noise became a positive shriek. Partridge was gradually getting excited, and dashing into the closet he scooped up all the boots on the floor, and the bootjack, and after flinging them over Magruder's fence in quick succession, but without stopping the serenade, he danced

around in a frenzy and fired off everything he could lay
his hands on.　Mrs. Partridge's gaiters, the soap-cup, the
towel-rack, the pomatum-jug, the cologne bottle, the foot-
stool, Mrs. Partridge's hoops, the hair-brushes, the wax
fruit, the hymn book, and the plaster image of little
Samuel saying his prayers, with a stubby-nosed angel in
a bolster-case watching him—all of these things were
hurled furiously at the unseen cats; and still the duet
proceeded.　At last, when all the available material in
the room, excepting the bedstead and Mrs. Partridge, had
been flung away, Partridge rushed downstairs for his gun,
and then emptied both barrels into Magruder's dining-
room shutters.　Then Magruder appeared at the back
window, and exclaimed :

"What in the thunder is the matter ? '

"Matter?" shouted Partridge, "why, I'm trying to
stop those cats in your yard."

"What cats ?" inquired Magruder ; "I don't see any
cats."

"But you can hear 'em, can't you ?　They've been
yowlin' around down there for the last two hours like
fury.　There they go.　Don't you hear that ?　Just listen
to that, will you ? "

"Partridge, you certainly *must* be intoxicated.　Cats !
Why, good gracious, man, those are the twins over here
in our room.　They were born last Friday ?　Didn't you
hear about it ? '

"And I don't want to hear about it now," said Partridge, as he closed the window savagely, and went to bed.

Magruder bought a coach for each of the children,
when they were old enough to go out, and he bought a

trained goat, which pulled one of the coaches, while the nurse-girl pulled the other. But one day the goat met another goat, that differed from him in politics or religion, or something, and each undertook to convince the other by jamming him in the skull. Every time Magruder's goat would rear up, preparatory to making a lunge forward, Magruder's baby would lurch over backwards, and when Magruder's goat struck the other goat, the concussion would shake the milk in the baby's stomach into butter.

And sometimes the other goat would aim at Magruder's goat, which would dodge, and then the other goat would plunge headforemost into the coach, and mash the baby up in the most frightful manner. And in the midst of the contest a couple of dogs joined in, and Magruder's goat backed off and tilted the coach into the gutter, and the dogs, biting around kind of generally, would snap at the goat and cause it to whirl the baby around just in time for the bite. Until at last the goat got disheartened and sprang through the fence, leaving the coach on the other side, and it struggled frantically to escape, while the other goat crowded up against the baby in order to avoid the dogs, and finally knocked the baby out, and butted the coach to splinters.

They say that the way Mrs. Magruder eyed Magruder that afternoon, when they brought the baby home, mutilated and dishevelled, was simply awful to behold; but she didn't speak to him for a week, and he had to soften her down by buying her an ostrich feather for her winter hat. The goat is still at large. Anybody who wants him can have him free of charge. Magruder

"Brought the baby home mutilated."—*Page* 91.

doesn't recognize him when he meets the animal upon the street.

Magruder is enthusiastic upon the subject of the twins, and he is occasionally imprudent in expressing his feelings. A few months after the birth of the children, the whole town, one night, was aroused by a succession of shouts, followed by a firing of pistols and the springing of a watchman's rattle. In a few moments the entire population was in the street, and everybody hurried to the place from whence the noises came. When they reached Magruder's house they saw Magruder leaning out of the window turning a rattle furiously and halloaing at the top of his voice, while every now and then he would brandish his revolver and fire it half-a-dozen times. The policemen felt certain that burglars were in the house, and while they were bursting open the back window to capture the thieves, a rumour spread that the house was afire. In two minutes the engine was on the ground, a ladder was raised, and they had a stream playing through the third story window.

As the policemen forced the kitchen window, the firemen kicked open the front door and rushed in, followed by the crowd. Magruder met them on the stairs, and the Mayor of the town said :

"Magruder, what on earth is the matter?"

Magruder danced about for a moment, and then he shouted :

"Come in, come right in, gentlemen, and see it."

"See it ! see what ?" asked the Mayor.

"Why, the baby, one of the twins ! Got a tooth ! just got its first tooth ! Go right up, and look at it for your-selves.'

"Mr. Magruder," said the Mayor, sternly, "do you mean to say that you have created all this disturbance for such a trivial reason ?"

"Trivial ! I don't understand you. Why, man, the child actually has a tooth !"

The Mayor turned away, and went out in silent disgust, and the crowd followed him.

Good judges estimate that that tooth cost Magruder about four hundred dollars for damages, and Mrs. Ma-gruder intimated to a friend that the appearance of sub-sequent teeth would be concealed from him until he was perfectly sober.

There came a time, however, when Magruder had rather more of the twins than he wanted. One day he and Mrs. Magruder went to the railway station to start upon a journey to Chicago. They engaged berths in a sleeping car, and they had the twins with them. A few moments before the hour of starting, Mrs. Magruder asked Mr. Magruder to hold the children for a moment, while she went to the waiting-room in the station to get a shawl that she had forgotten.

She must have made a mistake about the time, for before she returned the train started, and Magruder was in a state of wild despair. Pretty soon the babies began to cry, and then—no words can describe his misery.

All the passengers stared at him, and, as he dandled the babies upon his knees, the perspiration streamed from every pore. This kind of thing continued until nightfall, when Magruder put the children into a berth and tried to soothe them to sleep. But they were hungry, and they cried harder every moment. And while Magruder sat there beside them the long, long night, the passengers in the other berths groaned, and growled, and made savage remarks, and uttered the most uncharitable prophecies concerning the ultimate destination of the Magruder family.

By the time morning came, Magruder was almost insane, and the twins were on the verge of starvation. He had nothing to give them but cigars and the bay-rum which he carried for his hair, and he knew those were not healthy. The first time the train stopped, he bolted out and bought a pie. When he returned, one of the twins had tumbled off the seat and had a broken nose ; but he stuffed them both with the pie until they were deathly sick, and then Magruder was in a worse case than ever.

Finally, he reached Chicago in a condition of complete demoralization, and then he had to sit in the station with the babies for eight hours, lest he should miss Mrs. Magruder, who he knew would come in the next train.

And she did come, but when Magruder saw her he did not greet her warmly. He arose and went out into the fresh air in order to calm his feelings, so as to avoid an exciting conjugal scene in a public place. Then he hired a cab, and, placing his family in it, they drove to an hotel.

The next time he goes upon a journey, Mrs. Magruder will remain at home with the offspring.

The Glee-Club Tournament.

WITH A FEW THOUGHTS RESPECTING THE NOCTURNAL SERENADE.

OUR forefathers unconsciously did us a great injury when they clothed the nocturnal serenader with an air of romance and poetry, and fixed in the traditions of the race the theory that a musical performance, such as he offers, is a thing to be desired. In the old, old times, there may have been some justification for this doctrine. Musical instruments were scarce ; musical skill was rare; the piano had not been created, and the world had yet to note the birth of the monster who was to invent the bass drum. When there was very little music of any kind to be had, that person was excusable who found satisfaction in having his or her midnight slumbers disturbed by the tinkling of a lute beneath

the chamber window.   There was reason for the decla·
ration that

> " The gentlest of all sounds are those full of feeling
> That soft from the lute of some lover are stealing."

The listener felt a glow of gratitude to the enthusiastic
young man who turned out in the cold in doublet and
thin tights, and performed for an hour or two, while the
dew on the grass sent spasms of rheumatism up through
his legs.   And it is not surprising that lovers found this
the most certain method of capturing the female heart.
The charmer, being sleepy, could not readily determine if
he sang flat ; the night being dark, she could not witness
the distortions of his face consequent upon his efforts to
reach the high notes ; there was nothing to detract from
the romantic interest of the occasion, while a certain
sympathy, the prelude to affection, was born of her knowledge that the singer was taking a great deal of trouble
for her sake.   Those were the days when the nocturnal
serenade had a basis of wisdom and strong good sense.
But those days have passed, and the serenader is still
here.

We live in an age when no man can inhabit any
community without having next door a girl with a piano.
If he cannot satiate himself with her music, he can
hammer some out of his own piano, or he can haunt the
opera house and concert room.   Somewhere, under some
conditions, he can obtain during waking hours enough
music to last him until next morning.   The nocturnal
serenader, therefore, is not a necessity.   He is, in fact,
an intolerable bore.   He supplies something that nobody

" A boot or a pitcher of water hurled at the minstrel."—*Page* 100.

wants, and he forces it on us at a time when we want nothing of any sort but peace and quietness. Moreover, he comes no more in the guise of a solo singer who picks out soft accompaniments upon a lute. If he did appear in such a form, we might have redress. A boot, a cake of soap, a pitcherful of water hurled at such a minstrel would convey clearly to his mind the impression that the audience was ready to have the performance brought to a conclusion ; and if he did not catch the idea, we would call a policeman.

But the modern serenader always comes with a squad. If he is affluent or especially enthusiastic, he brings a brass band, special care being taken to entrust the bass drum and cymbals to men of enormous muscular power, who are convinced that they are the only musicians who are really of any importance as contributors to the harmony. At midnight they range themselves upon the pavement beneath the victim's window and begin :

> " So swells each windpipe ; ass intones to ass,
> Harmonic twang of leather, horn, and brass."

The serenaded man bounces from bed with a dire feeling that Daniel's prophecy concerning the end of all things is being fulfilled, and when he recovers his senses he remembers with indignation that he has perhaps to catch an early train and to perform duties for which the loss of sleep will unfit him. Meantime, several hundred other families in the neighbourhood are awakened by the racket ; good men objurgate, sick people moan and sigh, multitudinous babies rend the air with wild and piercing shrieks, innumerable dogs fill the night with ululations, and a quiet neighbourhood is suddenly transformed into a Pandemonium. But the remorseless bass drummer vies with the cymbal player in the vigour of his blows, the cornet utters fiendish blasts, and the E flat horn, mayhap, plays flatter than its inventor ever intended it should.

This is bad enough. There are few things which are worse than the nocturnal brass band ; and one of the few is the nocturnal glee club. It is·the common failing of man to believe that he can do in the best manner the very thing for which nature has specially disqualified him. One of the most frequent forms of delusion is that which induces a man who can't sing to feel assured that he can. When a young man with a voice like a crow, and an ear that is large enough for everything but music, has such faith, he inevitably drifts into a glee club composed of others like him. Here he is either placed among the basses, where he produces a noise similar to that which proceeds from a bark-mill in active motion ; or he is pushed in among the tenors, where he tries to sing falsetto through his nose ; other misguided youths meanwhile roam about the scale in futile efforts to discover the soprano and contralto parts.

When the club, by long practice, has fitted itself for its evil work, it selects some unfortunate fellow-creature, and determines to serenade him. Then, in the most solemn stillness of the night, it wakes the echoes of a quiet street with a diabolical congregation of discords, the refrain of which, perhaps, in bitter mockery, implores the aroused and enraged listener to " Slumber on in sweet repose," the basses growling while the tenors enlarge

their nostrils in malignant efforts to make themselves disgustingly vociferous.

If such serenaders as these had lived in the old, old
times, when the wrath of man expended itself in vindictive
action, we should have had less poetry upon the subject,
and the coroners of the period would have had more
business. Unhappily, modern society is constructed in
such a manner that a jury will refuse to acquit a serenaded
person who fires handsful of bullets into a boisterous glee-
club. Thus there is no defence for the peaceable citizen
but through the instrumentality of the law; but the law
ought to give him a remedy. One of the first rights of
man is the right to peace and quietness at night ; and
when we are completely civilized, the fact will be recognized, and the officers of law will consign to a dungeon a
bass drummer or a nasal tenor who ventures to trespass
upon the repose of the sleeping citizen.

These remarks may serve as an introduction to a brief
narrative of two glee-club experiences, in both of which
that form of vocal organization really did obtain something
like retributive justice.

Soon after the Orpheus Glee Club of the village of
Blank was formed, a proposal was made that a serenade
should be given to Miss Peterson, a young lady who was
admired by all the members, but for whom the president
was known to have a specially tender feeling.

The proposal was agreed to, and for two or three
evenings the club practised with such energy and assiduity
as to excite strong discontent among the people who lived
in the vicinity of the club-room.

Upon the appointed night, precisely at twelve, the

club sallied forth. It carried neither lamp nor music, the members feeling confident that they could depend upon memory to enable them to go properly through the programme.

After a rapid walk, the residence of Miss Peterson was reached, and the club halted upon the pavement in front of it. The windows showed no light of any kind, and the club rejoiced to think that the lovely Peterson would be awakened sweetly from her slumbers by the harmony which it would forthwith produce. The first and second tenors ranged themselves together, while the first and second basses took their appropriate places.

The leader gave the pitch in a low voice, and the club dashed gallantly into " Sweet be thy slumber, darling." There were four verses, each ending with a chorus. When the piece was concluded, every eye in the club was raised to the windows, to catch the first glimpse of the head of the enchanting Peterson. But she did not appear. There was nothing to indicate that anyone in the house had heard the music so-called.

" We must put on a little more pressure," said the leader. " They don't seem to hear us."

So the club tuned up, and presently emitted the words of the song: "Star of the evening, beautiful star." The singers filled their lungs bravely, and emptied them vigorously, the tenors trying to drown out the basses, and the basses growling away in such a manner that the tenors hardly considered they had fair play.

As the final cadence died away upon the midnight air, the club looked to the windows with eager expectation, feeling sure that Miss Peterson would give some

token of delight. But, strange to say, the windows remained closed ; and no one appeared.

"Maybe she sleeps in a back room," suggested Philpott, one of the tenors.

"No," said the president ; " her little brother told me
that her room was that one, there, in the front."

"She must be a very sound sleeper, then," said the
leader. "Let's give her a roaring song, *fortissimo*, and
see if we can't get her up."

Then the club, taking the pitch, plunged into, " Hail,
happy Morn ;" and sang with such vehemence, that it
might have been heard miles away. While the performance was proceeding, the singers heard the noise of the
lifting of a window-sash, and their eyes involuntarily
sought the house. But no ; it was a window of the house
next door on the right. From this a head protruded,
listening. When the music was hushed, a voice said :

"Halloa there ! What are you fellows about ? "

"Singing."

"What for ? "

"Serenading Miss Peterson."

"Who ? "

"Miss Peterson."

The man at the window gave a short laugh and with
drew. But Miss Peterson was yet to be heard from.

"I don't understand it," said the president, somewhat
mystified, " she must have heard us."

"Mighty queer," said Philpott, "most women are so
fond of serenades, too."

"Let's quit and go home," remarked Quigg, one of the
basses.

"Oh, no," quickly rejoined the president. "We ought to give her one more chance. Try her with 'Row, Brothers, Row!' and sing it loud."

The club put all its strength into the song, and in the midst of the harmony another window was heard opening. A moment later an old boot descended among the singers. They stopped. The missile came from a house upon the left

side of Peterson's. Before the president could express his indignation respecting the boot, a voice said :

"Why don't you vagabonds shut up and go home? It's an outrage for you to be howling out there at this time of night."

"Mind your own business," replied the president. "We're not troubling you. We're serenading Miss Peterson."

"Who?"

"Miss Peterson. Go to bed and hush."

This man also laughed, and said something to another person who was heard to laugh too. The club began to feel angry; especially as none of the Peterson family appeared to pay the smallest attention to the serenade.

"One more, and then if she don't come we'll stop," said the president.

The man at the window laughed again and remained to listen. The club began to sing, "Angels Watch Over  Thee!" and it sang with the loud pedal on. But the chorus of the eighth verse died away, and still the bewildering Peterson failed to signify her delight.

"Give her another one, boys," said the man at the window. "Maybe you haven't sung anything she likes."

The club was annoyed by the remark, but it scorned to notice such impertinence.

"I wonder what can be the matter," said Philpott.

"Maybe we've got the wrong house," exclaimed Quigg.

"Oh, no! I know the house well enough," replied the president.

"Well, it's very queer," said the leader.

"Is there a door-plate on the door?" asked Quigg.

"Certainly," replied the president, "don't you see it. That white thing there."

"Strike a match, and let's look at it," said Philpott.

The leader went up the steps, followed by the club. He struck a match. Then every member of the club saw a placard upon which was written in large letters the legend :

"THIS HOUSE FOR RENT."

The shock was so great that for a moment nobody spoke.
Then Philpott said softly ·.

"By George, they have moved!"

The man
at the win-
dow then observed :
"She heard you
were coming, boys,
and she packed up
and fled; she has gone into the country for the summer.
Probably she will never come back until she hears that
you have disbanded."

If the club had followed its impulses it would have

reduced that man to mincemeat at once. But it walked
sadly away, and each man went to his own home.

At the next meeting, a bye-law was adopted providing
that no serenade should be undertaken unless an understanding should first be had with the person to whom the
compliment was offered.

A few months later, what was called "A Glee-Club
Tournament" was held in the village, and five or six
other clubs joined the Orpheus in a singing contest for a
prize.

The performance need not be described. It will be
sufficient to say that the memory of that night of horror
will linger long in the minds of the peacefully-disposed
inhabitants of the town. A committee of expert musicians
sat in judgment upon the efforts of the contestants, and
its opinions were given a week later in a formal report, of
which the following is the conclusion :

THE REPORT.

"If the prize had been offered tor originality in the
treatment of the given themes, we should have no difficulty
in deciding to award it to the Orpheus Club. The method
of this organization is wholly new to us. The manner in
which the tenors kept two beats ahead of the voices that
carried the air was of itself surprising, but not more so
than the evident belief of the singers that successful tenor
singing is achieved by closing the mouth and emitting
shrill sounds through the nose. The basses, on the other
hand, seemed each to compose his own part as he went
along, thus making the harmony as peculiar as it was
amusing. Our prejudices have always been in favour of

a bass that afforded a full, deep, resonant tone, but if the theory of the Orpheus Club is correct, a bass voice in action should bear a close resemblance to the sound made by a boy who rattles a stick along the palings of a fence. Add to this the fact that the members of the club have no more accurate notion of time than if all of them had been born and educated in eternity, and we reach the conclusion that the Orpheus Club is hardly entitled to the prize.

"In considering the performance of the Apollo Club, we encounter a formidable difficulty at the outset. We are unable to determine precisely what it was they sang. In the programme, 'Bright and Cheery was the Morn' was allotted to them, but while part of the Committee think that the music really sung was that of 'Old Hundred,' and while another part insist that it was a distorted fragment of Wagner's music, the remainder of the Committee insist that it was really a combination of the two, with here and there brief snatches interpolated from 'Bright and Cheery was the Morn.' The Committee deeply regret the presence of this element of uncertainty, because they are unanimous upon almost every other point. They are confident that the club would become very efficient if it would secure a body of new members who have good voices and know how to sing, and would promptly expel every person at present belonging to the organization, with the exception, perhaps, of the leader, who ought to be retained either as a curiosity, or as a student who needs to learn that the mere frantic brandishing of a stick, without regard to rhythm or time, may be profitable as a muscular exercise, but certainly is not valuable in a musical sense.

" The Cecilian Club has the gift of power to a remarkable degree. If the purpose of the organization were to produce war-whoops, to vend vegetables and fish in the public streets, or to do duty as a fog-signal upon the coast ; or, indeed, if the emotions of the human soul could be expressed in ear-piercing yells, the club would have opening out before it a bright and beautiful future, in which success would surely follow as the reward of earnest effort. But the Committee, wrongfully, perhaps, have yielded to a conviction that when eighteen stalwart young men, each with a capacity for pouring forth from their lungs six hundred cubic feet of air a minute, sing ' Hush Thee, my Baby,' with such vehemence that the refrain may possibly be heard in Peru, the spirit of the composition somehow is missed, and the sentiment suffers irreparable injury. We may err in proffering advice, but we feel it to be our duty to suggest that this club will give pleasure in exact ratio with its diminution of lung-force. And, perhaps, it will afford most satisfaction when it learns to sing so that it cannot be heard by anybody without an ear-trumpet.

" Of the singing of the Orion Club we speak with mingled indignation and regret. Our fathers died for this country. The blood of patriots has made it free. Its soil has been bedewed with the tears of the widows and orphans whose loved ones perished in the struggle to secure our liberties. We have reared a fair fabric of government, and declared our purpose to protect the people in the enjoyment of their rights. And yet we seem to have failed utterly to secure popular happiness and peaceful repose, because we are confronted with the possibility that such organization as the Orion Glee Club may prowl around over our beloved land, rending the air of liberty with shrieks and howls, and assailing the ear-drums of the children of freedom with a diabolical con-gregation of noises of which a Pawnee Indian, charged full with fire-water and crazed with delirium, would be ashamed. Of course, we cannot award it a prize ; but we recommend the people who live in the town in which it exists to offer it a large pecuniary inducement to disband.

"As for the Mozart Club, its performance was uni-formly of a kind that would have hurried Mozart to an earlier grave if he could have heard it. Its grace notes were disgraceful. It took all the *andante* passages rapidly, and the *lento* passages quickly. When there was a *slur* it sang *staccato*, and where light and vivacious treatment was demanded, it sang as if it were working off a dirge at a funeral. The ascent of the scale by some of the singers, when the music descended, we attribute to the circumstance that some of them held their note-books upside-down. The leader beat eight kinds of time within seven minutes, and the tenors persistently followed the air, while the basses, it is believed, were singing the wrong piece, or else were trying to introduce variations of the original music.

"Upon the whole, therefore, we decline to award the prize. Where all were so bad, where all displayed ignorance of music quite as dense as that of a deaf and dumb man concerning eloquence, we cannot conscien-tiously give to either a reward of merit. We shall make our experience the basis of an immediate demand upon

the legislature for the passage of a law making member-
ship in a glee club punishable with death, unless a genuine
acquaintance with music is obtained beforehand."

When the clubs read the report they were discouraged,
but all of them remain in a condition of boisterous
activity, and the legislature has not yet done its duty.

Mr. Fisher's Bereavements.

HE wife of my neighbour, Mr. Archibald N. Fisher, was attacked some years ago by a very dangerous malady, from which there was, from the first, very little hopes of her recovery. And one day when Mr. Fisher came home, they communicated to him the sad intelligence that she was no more. When the first outbreak of grief had subsided, he sent an order to the undertaker for a coffin, he tied crape on the door-knob, he sent his hat around to the store to have it draped in black, he advertised the death in the papers with some poetry attached to the announcement, and he made general preparations for the funeral. Then he sat down in the parlour with his great sorrow, and his friends tried to comfort him.

8

"It's no use," he said; "I'll never get over it. There never was any woman like her, and there never will be again. I don't want to live without her. Now she's gone, I'm ready to go any time. I'd welcome the grave. What's life to a man like me? It's a void—an empty void; that's what it is; and there is no more happiness in it for me.'

"You must try to bear up under it," said Dr. Potts. "These afflictions are meant for our good. She is now an angel."

"I know! I know!" said Mr. Fisher, sobbing, "but there's no comfort in that. An angel is no use to me. Angels don't make your home happy. They don't sew on buttons and look after the children. I'd rather have a woman like Mrs. Fisher than the best of them."

"But," said Dr. Potts, "you must reflect how much happier she is now; you must remember that our loss is her gain."

"Well, I don't see it," replied Fisher. "She was happy enough here, bustling around, making things lively, quarrelling with me sometimes, bless her dear heart, when I annoyed her, and scolding away all day long at the children and the hired girl, making music in the house. Who's she going to scold now, I'd like to know? How's she going to relieve her feelings when she gets mad? Flying around in a night-gown with wings on behind her shoulder blades. And what I say is, that if Henrietta had her choice, she rather be home here tending to things, even if every day in the week was a rainy wash-day. Now I know she would."

"You take a gloomy view of things now," said Dr.

Potts. " After a while the skies will seem brighter to you."

" No, they won't," said Mr. Fisher. " They'll grow darker until there's a regular awful thunderstorm of grief. I can't live through it. It'll kill me. I've a notion to jump into Henrietta's grave and be buried with her. I've got half a mind to commit suicide, so I can———"

Just here the doctor came downstairs and into the parlour, with a smile on his face. Mr. Fisher saw it, and stopping abruptly, he said :

" Dr. Burns, how you can smile in the midst of the awful desolation of this family, is more than I can understand, and I don't———"

" I've got some good news for you, Mr. Fisher," said the doctor.

" No, you haven't," said Fisher. " There can be no more good news for me in this world."

" Mrs. Fisher is alive."

" What ? "

" Mrs. Fisher is alive," said the doctor. " She was only in a condition of suspended animation after all. She'll be perfectly well, I think, in a few days."

Mr. Fisher wiped his eyes, and with a frown upon his face put his handkerchief in his pocket, and said :

" You don't really mean to say Mrs. Fisher's going to rise up from her bed, and remain alive ? Going to remain here with us ?

" Precisely ! and I congratulate you heartily."

" Oh, you needn't congratulate *me*," exclaimed Fisher, rising and looking gloomily out of the window. " This is a pretty piece of business ! But it's just like Henrietta. She

always was the contrariest woman in the state! Who's
going to pay the undertaker's bill, I'd like to know? She
can just do it herself; and the advertising, and that
poetry, and the crape, and all the things! I never heard
of such foolishness! It makes me mad for women to be
carrying on so! Hanged if I'm going to——"

Just here the boy came in with Mr. Fisher's hat, with a
weed around it, and Fisher, giving the hat a savage kick,
said to the boy:

"You miserable little scoundrel, get out of here, or
I'll break your neck."

Then the company adjourned, and Fisher, taking the
crape off the door-knob, went around to see the undertaker.

But Mrs. Fisher did not get well. Two or three days
later she suffered a relapse, and within a week she passed
peacefully away. Upon the same day one of Mr. Fisher's
fellow-townsmen, Lucius Grant, lost his wife, and the
interments were made in the cemetery upon the same day,
and at about the same hour.

As the two funeral parties were coming out of the
burying ground, Fisher met Grant, and clasping each
other's hand they indulged in a sympathetic squeeze, and
the following conversation ensued:

Fisher—" I'm sorry for you. It's an unspeakable loss,
isn't it?"

Grant—" Awful. She was the best woman that ever
lived."

Fisher—" She was indeed. I never met her equal.
She was a good wife to me."

Grant—" I was referring to my wife. There couldn't
be *two* best you know."

" They indulged in a sympathetic squeeze."—*Page* 116.

Fisher—" Yes, I know.   I know well enough that your wife couldn't hold a candle to mine "

Grant—" She couldn't, hey ?   Couldn't hold a candle. Why she could lead Mrs. Fisher every day in the week, including Sundays, and not half try !   She was an angel."

Fisher—" Oh, she was, was she ?   Well, I don't want to be personal, but if I owned an angel as bony as an omnibus horse, I'd kill her if she didn't die of her own accord."

Grant—" Better be bony than wear the kind of a red nose that your wife flourished around this community. It'll burn a hole through the coffin lid.   And you pretend you're sorry she's gone.   But you can't impose on me ! I know you're glad enough to hurrah about it."

Fisher—" If you abuse my wife, I'll knock you down."

Grant— " I'd like to see you try it."

There would have been a hand-to-hand combat be- tween the two disconsolate widowers, if the friends of the parties had not interfered at this juncture. Grant's friends thrust him in a carriage, and drove away, while Fishei was put in the carriage with Rev. Dr. Potts, and he spent the time consumed by the journey in giving expression to his sorrow for the loss of his wife.

" Doctor," he said, " in one respect I never saw her equal.   I've known that dear woman to take an old pair of my trousers, and cut them up for the boys.   She'd make a splendid suit of clothes for both of them out of those old trousers, get out stuff enough for a coat for the baby, and a cap for Johnny, and have some left over for rag-carpet, besides making handkerchiefs out of the pockets, and a bustle for herself out of the other linings.

Give her any old garment, and it was as good as a gold mine. She'd take a worn-out stocking and make a brand new overcoat out of it, I believe. She had a turn for that kind of economy. There's one of my shirts that I bought in 1847, still going about making itself useful as window curtains and panta- lettes, and plenty of other things. Only last July our gridiron gave out, and she took it apart, and in two hours it was rigged on the side of the house as a splendid lightning-rod, all except what she had  made into a poker and an ice-pick. Ingenious? Why, she kept our family in buttons and whistles out of the ham bones she saved, and she made fifteen chicken-coops from her old hoop-skirts, and a pig-pen out of her used-up corset bones. She never wasted a solitary thing. Let a cat die around our house, and the first thing you knew Mary Jane'd have a muff and set of furs, and I begin to find mince-pies on the dinner-table. She'd stuff a feather bed with the feathers that she'd got off of one little bit of a rooster. I've seen her cook potato parings so's you'd think they were canvas-back duck, and she had a way of

doctoring up shavings, so that the pig'd eat 'em and grow
fat on 'em. I believe that woman could a built a four-
storey hotel, if you'd a given her a single pine board ; or a
steamboat out of a wash-boiler ; and the very last thing
she said to me was to bury her in the garden so's she'd be
useful down below there, helping to shove up the cab-
bages. I'll never see her like again."

When the mourners all got home, Mr. Grant tied
crape upon all his window-shutters, to show how deeply
he mourned, and as Fisher knew that his grief for Mrs.
Fisher was deeper, he not only decorated his shutters,
but he fixed five yards of black bombazine on the bell-
pull, and dressed his whole family in mourning. Then
Grant determined that his duty to the departed was not

to let himself be beaten by a man who couldn't feel any
genuine sorrow, so he sewed a black flag on his lightning-
rod, and festooned the front of his house with black
alpaca.

Then Fisher became excited, and he expressed his
sense of bereavement by painting his dwelling black, and
by putting up a monument to Mrs. Fisher in his front
yard. Grant thereupon stained his yellow horse with
lampblack, tied crape to his cow's horn, daubed his dog

with ink, and began to wipe his nose on a black handkerchief.

These little indulgences in generous rivalry lasted for
nearly a year ; and it is impossible to say what would
have been the result of the contest, had not Fisher, in the
midst of his sorrow, suddenly discovered in his heart a
deep affection for a Miss Lang, a young lady who happened to be visiting one of Fisher's friends. Fisher
began to pay her attention, and as he did so, he gradually
removed the manifestations of his grief for the dear
departed.

A year later they were married, and this made Mr.
Grant so angry, that he went around to the widow Jones's,
and proposed, and was accepted on the spot.

Miss Lang was the fourth woman to whom Fisher has
been married; and this fact was the cause of a very
unpleasant incident.

Parker had been out in California for nearly thirty
years ; but last winter he came on East and paid a visit
to his old home. Among other acquaintances of former
days he met Mr. Fisher, and Fisher mentioned that he
was sorry his wife was out of town as he would like Parker
to see her.

"And how is she?" asked Parker. "I remember
her well. Mary Jones she was before you married her.
Splendid woman ! And how is she anyhow?"

"I am sorry to say Mary is dead ; been dead more
than twenty years."

"Oh, I beg pardon," said Parker. "Excuse me for
stirring up old griefs. But how is your second wife?
Fine-looking woman, I'll bet, Fisher! You were always

the awfullest man at falling in love with pretty women I
ever saw. What is she? Brunette, I venture to say. Are
you going to introduce me to her?"

·"It's not—not a pleasant subject to discuss—but—but
—my second wife was laid away in the grave more than
fifteen years ago."

"You don't say? Oh! I know, of course—your second
wife, of course, dead ; I forgot about it. Did I say your
second wife? I meant your *third* instead of your second.
And how is *she?* Fisher, I must know that woman.
Introduce me, will you? Hang me if I don't stay in town
until I know her.'

"That will be impossible, Mr. Parker. My third wife
has been an angel ever since 1865."

"Well, now, I declare it's too bad; I had no idea—of
course, I didn't mean anything. Less see, it's ten years
since 1865, ain't it? Ten, yes. Well, now, old fellow, you'll
forgive me for tearing up your feelings that way ; but I'll
make it all right by asking how in thunder is your present
wife—your fifth?'

"Mr. Parker, you are mistaken again. I have no fifth
wife. I——"

"Well, then, your sixth. How is she? Pardon me,
old boy, for saying that you have been going it. Six wives
in thirty years, and here I am not married yet. Now
how *is* Mrs. Fisher No. 6?"

"Mr. Parker, the lady with whom I live at present is
my *fourth* wife. I don't like the tone in which you speak
of this subject."

"Don't like it! Well, it seems to me, Fisher, that
for a man who marries them and buries them as fast

as you do, to talk about sensibility upon the subject is a little more than ridiculous. I don't care how your wife is, or when you get another one. But if you take my advice, you will have your undertaking business done by contract at wholesale rates."

Then Mr. Parker took the earliest through-train for California.

Mr. Coombs, the Undertaker.

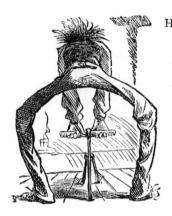

THERE is a certain oddity about the fact that when death overtakes a human being, man undertakes him. It is equally odd that while to every mind the word "undertaker" suggests one who is eager to "talk of graves, and worms, and epitaphs," the dictionaries define an undertaker as "one who under takes," making no reference to his claim to be considered purely as a funereal functionary. Precisely why this personage, of all those who engage in undertakings, should be distinguished as *the* undertaker, has been a puzzle to many; but the explanation probably may be found in the primary signification of the word "undertake," which is, of course, to *take under,* the duty of the undertaker being to perform that service for those who are ready for the grave.

Mr. Samuel Toombs, the leading undertaker of the village of which I write, had originally been a physician in a town of Iowa, but he was compelled to leave the place because of a difficulty that he had with some of his patients.

The doctor, it seems, had a large tank placed on the top of his house, from which to supply his bath-room, and so forth, with water. The water had to be pumped up about fifty feet from the cistern in the yard, and the doc-tor found it to be a pretty good-sized job, which would cause him constant expense. So, after thinking the matter over very carefully, one day an idea struck him. He built a room over the cistern, and put the word "Sanitarium" over the door. Then he concealed the pump machinery beneath the floor, and he rigged up a kind of complicated apparatus, with handles, and hinges, and a crank, so that a man, by standing in the middle of the machine and pulling the handle up and down, would operate the pump.

Then the doctor got out circulars and published ad-vertisements about "Toombs's Patent Health-Lift," and he secured testimonials from a thousand or so people, who agreed that the Health-Lift was the only hope for the physical salvation of the human race. Pretty soon people began to call to see about it, and Toombs would rush them out to the "Sanitarium," and set them to jerk-ing the handles. And when a customer had pumped up fifty gallons or so, Toombs would charge him a fee, and tell him that three months of that sort of thing would give him muscles like a prize-fighter.

He would push the project among his patients. If a man was bilious, or had the toothache, or was afflicted with rheumatism, or croup, or yellow fever, or cholera morbus, Toombs would turn him at the Health-Lift, and get a fee each time. The thing became so popular that he had to enlarge his tank, and put in a smaller pump; and he not only got all his pumping done for nothing, but the people who did it paid him about fifteen hundred dollars a year for the privilege. It began to look like an uncommonly good thing, and everybody was contented and happy.

One day, however, old Mr. Maginnis, who had been practising at the Health-Lift every day for months, in order to cure himself of indigestion, jammed the handles down a little too hard, and broke the board upon which he was standing. As the board gave way, it plunged Mr. Maginnis into the cistern, and just as he was sinking for the third time, Toombs fished him out with a crooked nail in the end of a clothes-prop. As soon as the water was drained out of him, Maginnis said :

" I didn't know you had a cistern under that floor. What did you do that for ? "

" Why, to keep the air moist. It is healthier than dry air."

" It looked to me as if there was some kind of a pump under there."

" Oh, no ; those are only the levers of the Lift."

" Mighty queer," said Maginnis, thoughtfully. " If that isn't a pump, then I don't know one when I see it."

So a few days later Maginnis came around with a lot of other patients, and found the doctor out. They deter-

mined to investigate. They pulled up a couple of boards, and ascertained the facts about the pump. Then they cross-examined Toombs' servant-girl, and learned about the truth, and then they went home mad. A consultation was held, at which every bilious and rheumatic individual, who had been working the doctor's pump, used violent language, and talked about murder and sudden death. Finally they resolved to prosecute Toombs for damages, and for obtaining money under false pretences.

Toombs concluded to fly, in order to save trouble ; so he came east, and finding that there was less risk and more money in burying people than in slaying them, he resolved to begin business as an undertaker.

He has had some curious and interesting experiences, and not the least curious was that afforded by the celebrated Cadwallader case.

In the town there are two families of Cadwalladers, and at one time the head of each was named Henry.

One Henry was a store-keeper, and the other was a butcher, and neither was related in any way to the other. About the middle of June, the butcher died rather suddenly ; but somehow the impression got out around town that it was the other Henry. Late one evening a waggon drove up in front of the living Cadwallader's house, and a man rung the bell. Cadwallader was in bed. He arose, opened the window, and shouted :

" Who's there ? "

" I ; Toombs ! "

" Toombs ! Who's Toombs ? What d'you want ? "

" Why, I've just run around with a load of ice for the old man. Let me in, so's I can fix him."

" Dunno what you mean. Nobody around here wants fixing with ice. We're temperance people."

" No, no ; I'm the undertaker. I have brought it around to pack the deceased man in. Hurry up, sonny. I want to get done and go home."

" What deceased man ? "

" Why, Cadwallader. Don't you know, if he isn't laid in ice, he won't keep ; and that will afflict his family like thunder."

" I guess you've struck the wrong house."

" Isn't this Henry Cadwallader's place ? "

" Yes."

" Well, then, he's my man. I've got a coffin in here that'll fit him like a glove, after we've frozen him up a while. Le' me in 's quick as you can, and I'll show you the silver-plated handles and the mahogany trimmings of the coffin. A duke don't want anything more gorgeous than they are."

While Toombs was speaking, another man came up and rang the bell, and Cadwallader asked him what *he* wanted.

" Want to see Mrs. Cadwallader about the tomb-stone.'

" Tombstone ! This is getting solemn. What tomb-stone ? "

" Old Cadwallader's. Mr. Mix sent me round to ask whether he should cut the name ' Henry Cadwallader' in a straight line or a curve, and whether she wants to put on the stone a broken rosebud or a torch upside down. You tell the widow to take my advice, and go in on the rosebud and the straight line. It's cheaper, and 'twon't make any difference to the deceased."

9

"I'll mention it to her. When is the tombstone to be done?"

"Wednesday, right after the funeral. Weighs about a ton. Mix says Mrs. Cadwallader probably wanted it heavy, so's to be sure it would hold Henry down. He will have his fun."

During the conversation, and while Mr. Toombs was removing his funeral appliances from the waggon, a third man arrived. He asked for Mrs. Cadwallader.

"What do *you* want?" asked Mr. C.

"How's the widow takin' it? Hard?" he asked.

"Not so very."

"Well, you tell her, for me, not to go on about it. Plenty of fish in the sea 's good as any ever caught. Tell her the company's all right. It'll pay her in full, and then she can get on her feet again."

"What company do you mean?"

"Why, the Hopelessly Mutual. I'm Benjamin P. Gunn, the insurance agent. Took his risk in January. Thought maybe the widow might be suffering from grief, and I'd call to cheer her up. I'm coming to the funeral and I'll see that Henry's stowed away as snug as a bug in a rug."

Cadwallader came down and explained the matter, and got things straightened out a little. On the day of the dead Henry's funeral he thought he would go to it, in order to ascertain how it felt to attend the obsequies of Henry Cadwallader. It turned out that some of the live Henry's friends, who didn't know where he lived, were at the house of the dead man, thinking that it was the storekeeper's funeral. When the latter came in, Mr. Jones met him, and said to him :

"Heaven and earth, Cadwallader! how d' you get out of that coffin?"

"I never was in it."

"What! I've been crying like a baby about you, in the parlour there. Not dead! Now, see here, Ca'wallader; this is not the square thing! Blame me if I haven't wasted an enormous amount of sacred emotion over you, and now you go back on me. Is that treating a man right?"

"I dunno. Seems to me so."

"Well, hang me if it seems so to me. If you advertise that you are going to be buried, why in the name of decency don't you stand by your contract like a man?"

"Let me explain——"

"No, sir; no apologies. This finishes you, as far as I am concerned. When I die, I die. I don't invite my friends to see me interred, get them to cry, and then come shuffling around with some shabby excuse about not being dead! I'd rather pick a man's pocket at once than trample on his feelings that way!"

And as Mr. Jones shouldered his umbrella and marched

off home, Cadwallader went also, a little gloomy because
he felt that if he had been a thoroughly conscientious
man, who understood his duty to society, he would be a
corpse. He talked of applying to the legislature at the
next session for permission to change his name.

Mr. Toombs is a single man ; but he came very near
once to marriage—or, at least, he thought so. It appears
that Mr. Bungay, the real estate agent, some years ago
suspected that Mrs. Bungay didn't care as much for him
as she ought to. So one day he went up to the city, after
leaving word that he would be gone two or three days.
While there, he arranged with a friend to send a telegram
to his wife at a certain hour announcing that he had been
run over on the railroad and killed. Then Bungay came
home, and slipping into the house unperceived, he
secreted himself in the closet in the sitting-room to await
the arrival of the telegram, and to see how Mrs. Bungay
took it. After a while it came, and he saw the servant-girl
give it to his wife. She opened it, and as she read it, she
gave one little start. Then Bungay saw a smile gradually
overspread her features. She rang for the girl, and when
the servant came, Mrs. Bungay said to her :

" Mary, Mr. Bungay's been killed. I've just got the
news. I reckon I'll have to put on black for him, though
I hate to give up my new bonnet for mourning. You just
go round to the milliner's and ask her to fetch me up
some of the latest styles of widow's bonnets, and tie a
bunch of crape on the door, and then bring the undertaker
here."

While Mrs. Bungay was waiting she smiled continually,
and once or twice she danced around the room, and stood

in front of the looking-glass, and Bungay heard her murmur to herself :

"I ain't such a bad-looking woman, either. I wonder what Lemuel will think of me ?"

"Lemuel !" thought Bungay, as his widow took her seat and sang softly, as if she felt particularly happy. "Who's Lemuel? She certainly can't mean that infamous old undertaker, Toombs ! His name's Lemuel, and he's single ; but it's preposterous to suppose that she cares for him, or is going to prowl after a husband so quick as this."

While he brooded in horror over the thought, Mr. Toombs arrived. The widow said :

" Mr. Toombs, Bungay is dead ; run over by a loco-motive."

"Very sorry to hear it, madam ; I sympathize with you in your affliction."

" Thank you ; it is pretty sad. But I don't worry much. Bungay was a poor sort of a man to get along with, and now that he's gone I'm going to stand it without crying my eyes out. We'll have to bury him, I s'pose, though ? "

" That is the usual thing to do in such cases."

"Well, I want you to 'tend to it for me. I reckon the coroner'll have to sit on him first. But when they get through, if you'll just collect the pieces and pack him into a coffin, I'll be obliged."

" Certainly, Mrs. Bungay. When do you want the funeral to occur ? "

" Oh, 'most any day. Perhaps the sooner the better so's we can have it over. I don't want to spend much money on it, Mr. Toombs. Rig him up some kind of a cheap coffin, and bury him with as little fuss as possible. I'll come along with a couple of friends; and we'll walk. No carriages. Times are too hard."

"I will attend to it."

"And, Mr. Toombs, there is another matter. Mr. Bungay's life was insured for about twenty thousand dollars, and I want to get it as soon as possible, and when I get it I shall think of marrying again."

"Indeed, madam !"

"Yes ; and can you think of anybody who'll suit me."

"I dunno. I might. Twenty thousand you say he left ?"

"Twenty thousand ; yes. Now, Mr. Toombs, you'll think me bold, but I only tell the honest truth when I say that I prefer a man who is about middle-age, and in some business connected with cemeteries."

"How would an undertaker suit you ?"

"I think very well, if I could find one. I often told Bungay that I wished he was an undertaker."

"Well, Mrs. Bungay, it's a little sudden ; I haven't thought much about it ; and Bungay's hardly got fairly settled in the world of the hereafter; but business is business, and if you *must* have an undertaker to love you and look after that life insurance money, it appears to me that I am just about that kind of a man. Will you take me ?"

"Oh, Lemuel! fold me to your bosom !"

Lemuel was just about to fold her, when Bungay, white with rage, burst from the closet, and exclaimed :

"Unhand her, villain ! Touch that woman, and you die ! Leave this house at once, or I'll brain you with the

poker! And as for you, Mrs. Bungay, you can pack up
your duds and quit. I've done with you. I know now
that you are a cold-hearted, faithless, abominable wretch!
Go, and go at once! I did this to try you, and my eyes
are opened."

"I know you did, and I concluded to pay you in your
own coin."

"That's absurd; it won't hold water."

"It's true, anyhow. You told Mr. Magill you were
going to do it, and he told me."

"He did, hey? I'll knock the head off of him."

"When you are really dead I will be a good deal more
sorry, provided you don't make such a fool of yourself
while you're alive."

"You will? You will really be sorry!"

"Of course!"

"And you won't marry Toombs? Where is that man Toombs? By George, I'll go for him now! He was mighty hungry for that life insurance money! I'll step around and kick him at once while I'm mad. We'll talk this matter over when I come back."

Then Bungay left to call upon Toombs, and when he returned he dropped the subject. He has drawn up his will so that his wife is cut off with a shilling if she employs Toombs as the undertaker, and Toombs is still a lonely bachelor.

The Shoals Lighthouse.

A SERIOUS STORY.*

WELL, Bessie, so the time has come at last."

"No, Tom, not quite yet. This is only the twenty-third, you know. Two more days; then Christmas, and then our wedding."

"Oh, well," replied Tom, "the great event is so near, that after our long waiting the two days seem as nothing."

---

* It may interest some one to learn that the principal incident of this story occurred precisely as it is here narrated.

"A great many wonderful things may happen in two days, Tom."

"Yes, but nothing can happen to separate us, Bessie. You are mine and I am yours. Our lives join together now, and no man may part them asunder."

"Oh, I hope and believe there may be nothing to interfere with our happiness," said Bessie. "The sky is very bright for us now, and I cannot conceive of any calamity which could befall us before our wedding."

"Of course not," replied Tom. "Don't think of such a thing. It will be good-bye to you to-day, good-bye to-morrow, and then no more farewells for ever, for we shall be man and wife. But maybe I won't be here to-morrow, though, until late in the evening."

"Why?" asked Bessie.

"Because I think I shall go duck-shooting over at the Shoals with Jan Eckels, and it is hardly likely I shall get back before supper time."

"Who is Jan Eckels?" inquired Bessie.

"Why, a young Norwegian, a fisherman who lives on Star Island. He says the gunning around there is splendid now, and he is going to take me over in his boat in the morning."

"Isn't it a little dangerous out on the open sea at this season, Tom?"

"Not a bit, when the weather is fine. Jan is a first-rate sailor, and we won't go, you know, if there is danger of a storm. I will be around to-morrow night early, Bessie, for certain."

"I hope so," said Bessie. "But, Tom, dear, for fear

you shouldn't get back in time, I've half a notion to give
you your Christmas present now. Shall I."

"You might as well, Bess. I have yours in my pocket
now. Let's exchange to-night."

Bessie bounced out of the room and returned presently
with a tiny morocco box. Tom took from his pocket a
case, from which he removed a beautiful locket and chain,
which he fastened upon Bessie's neck.

"Oh, Tom! isn't it beautiful? I can't tell you how
much I am obliged to you. It is the very thing I wanted.
It was very, very kind of you to find out what I wished.
And now let me give you yours. Hold out your hand,
sir! There!"

And Bessie placed upon her lover's finger a dainty
amethyst ring.

"It's magnificent," exclaimed Tom; holding it at a
distance and admiring the stone.

"And I have had an inscription placed inside," said
Bessie,

"'*From Bessie Archer to Thomas Freeborn,
Christmas,* 186-.'

"It is the last thing Bessie Archer will give you, Tom.
Before present-giving times come round again, I shall be
Bessie Freeborn."

Then the good-nights were said in that sweet old
fashion which all true lovers know, and so they parted,
each with a soul full of pure happiness in the present, and
of tender hope for that blissful future which seemed so
close at hand.

Tom Freeborn, the son of a widow, whose only child

"It's magnificent," said Tom.—*Page* 139.

he was, and who loved him with such deep affection that she was almost jealous of the fair girl who had come to share his heart, returned to his home and began his preparations for the morrow's expedition. Bessie Archer, the only daughter of a wealthy banker, and a woman whose lovely face was but the outward sign of the purity which crowned her character, retired to rest, to wait amid pleasant dreams the morrow which would bring her nearer to the consummation of her happiness.

The town of Portsmouth, New Hampshire, in which these persons lived, lies close upon a river which flows in tortuous course until, a mile or two below the wharves, it empties into the sea. Twelve miles beyond, out in the ocean, lie the Isles of Shoals, a group of small islands, some of which are inhabited, one of which uprears a light-house boldly from its cliffs, and others of which have no signs of a man's presence, but are the resort of the wild geese, and swans, and ducks, of the white owl and the sea-gulls, the fish-hawk and the stormy petrel.

From the little settlement upon the rocky hill of Star Island came Jan Eckels on that bright December morning in his open boat, containing two masts, as is the fashion in that region with the craft of the fishermen. He belonged to a family of Norwegians, many of whom are found upon the islands and upon the mainland in the vicinity; and he handled his little shell of a boat with the dexterity of one who had spent his life upon the water.

Tom was waiting for him at the wharf when he arrived, but as the tide was running swiftly up the channel and was nearly at the flood, Jan determined to wait for it to

turn rather than to try to beat down the crooked stream
against it. So, when the two sportsmen finally set out
upon their journey, it was after ten o'clock, and two hours
more would elapse before they could reach Duck Island,
their destination. But the day, though cold, was clear
and beautiful, and the wind as it filled the sails and swept
the boat over the rough waters gave them no discomfort,
for they were warmly clad and well used to such expo-
sure.

There was splendid sport at the island. Freeborn

and Eckels landed in a small cove where the surf did not
beat, and, fastening the boat's painter to a rock, they took
up their guns and started for the eastern shore. All the
afternoon they tramped about over the rugged and
broken surface of the place, creeping behind first one
boulder and then another as they approached the game,
until, when the sun approached the horizon, they counted
up a goodly number of black ducks and three or four

superb swans. As they were looking over the trophies of their sport and placing them in the bags, Eckels said:

"We had better hurry, Mr. Freeborn. It looks pretty dark yonder, and I'm afeard we'll have a squall."

"Not much of a one, I hope," replied Tom, beginning to move toward the boat. "I don't care to get a wetting such a cold night as this. We should freeze to death."

"We must make good time then," said Eckels, "for it's going to rain, certain, and I'm afeard of a big blow."

They reached the boat, and tossed the game and the fowling-pieces into it, and then, jumping in themselves, Jan hastily raised the sails, and they started toward Portsmouth. The wind blew strongly from the north-west, and the clouds came scurrying thick and fast overhead, becoming blacker and blacker every moment, while the surface of the sea was covered with the white-caps, the great waves rolling in mightier masses each moment as the wind grew fiercer.

"I'm afeard we won't make it," said Jan, with a scared look upon his face. "There'll be a gale before we reach the harbour, and then take care! We'll have trouble, Mr. Freeborn."

"Well, let's drive ahead and do our best," replied Tom, gloomily.

"Look!—look there!—there it comes, sure enough!" shouted Jan. "The squall has got us!"

Tom did look, and far out upon the sea he could perceive the waves in fearful tumult, while above them a dense white cloud swept forward with terrible velocity. In a moment they were blinded by the storm of snow which dashed into their faces, and while the wind roared about their ears with a shriek such as might have come from the lips of a host of maddened fiends, their boat was tossed about in the angry billows with such violence that it seemed as if it must go to pieces. But Jan clung to the helm, and desperately strove to guide the craft, and he still showed in his face that he had a brave hope of weathering the storm. He was about to say a cheerful word to Tom, when the handle was wrenched from his grasp, and as he caught it again, a cry of agonized despair reached Tom through the noise of the tempest.

"The rudder is gone!" shrieked Jan; " we are lost! we are lost!"

The boat, no longer controlled by the helm, whirled around with her broadside to the wind, and in an instant there was a crash as both masts were swept over the side, one of them striking Jan's arm in its descent, and wounding him severely. But the staunch little ship did not capsize. She was built for rough work, and she remained upright. Jan sank upon the floor in utter helplessness, and cried like a child. He could do nothing in his crippled condition, even if there was anything to be done. But the waves now and then swept over the boat, and she was gradually filling with water, so Tom, after placing Jan upon one of the thwarts, went to work to bale the water out as fast as possible. While he was thus busy, a cry from Jan caused him to look up ; they were hurrying past the White Island lighthouse, and they were so close to it, that through the dusk they could see the keeper upon the shore making frantic gestures to them. But, alas! no help could come to them.

They dashed by at frightful speed, and in a moment

the tall shaft of the lighthouse was but a white speck amid the gloom. The air became colder; each wave that dashed into the boat covered the unhappy men with a sheet of ice, and the spray hurled upward by the sea in its fury fell upon them in icy particles which stung their frozen faces until the agony became almost unendurable. Tom kept his blood in active circulation by his exertions to relieve the boat from the water. But Jan—before the lighthouse was an hour behind, Jan suddenly fell prone upon the boat's floor, and lay there motionless. Tom leaped to his side and tried to lift him. He wore an icy coat of mail from head to foot; his arm was pulseless, his eyes were set in a stony glare, and his breathing had ceased. His soul had gone out from the midst of that wild and terrible tumult of the elements into the land of everlasting peace.

The tears came into Tom's eyes as he looked down upon the face of his dead comrade, and he broke forth into loud lamentations. But he could not pause from his labour to indulge in mourning. The boat was filling each moment, and nothing but desperate exertion remained between him and certain death. The boat itself was now cased in ice and sank deeply into the water, and Tom perceived that he must bale more rapidly or be swallowed up in the angry sea.

Onward and onward he hurried before the pitiless blast, the gale seeming to increase in fury every moment. He saw the light on Cape Cod as he went swirling by in the darkness, and he knew that he had come nearly a hundred miles upon that frightful voyage. Where would it end? He did not dare to think. He must work—

work desperately, savagely, with every energy of soul and body. And so with fierce, unceasing toil, which seemed too terrible to be endured much longer, with now a thought that it would be better to stop and let the end come, then with a remembrance of Bessie and of the blessedness of life, and with hope of rescue and salvation, he struggled on until daylight came; and as the gale died away, little by little, the sun came out and looked down upon a floating mass of ice, bearing up a corpse that lay statue-like upon its frozen bier; and a man, haggard and pale, and covered, like his lost companion, with a glittering shroud.

Utterly worn out with his awful battle with fate, Tom looked about him to see if any help might be near. He espied a barque far ahead, and lying right in his course. He ceased baling, and tying his handkerchief to an oar, and holding it upward, waved it to and fro. The signal was seen. The barque went about and stood straight for him. The boat swept closer and closer, and Tom's heart was filled with a great and eager hope of rescue. The boat dashed beneath the bows of the vessel, and coursed along its side. A rope was thrown to him by a sailor. He clutched it frantically and held it fast. The boat swept away beneath him, and he plunged into the sea. " He is lost," was the cry that reached him from the deck.

Not so. He thrust his arm through the loop in the rope, a sturdy pull from the sailor tightened the slip-knot, and in a moment he lay upon the deck; while Jan, in his icy tomb, went hurtling far, far out to sea, and to burial beneath the rolling billows.

A great dread filled two hearts in Portsmouth on the

night of the storm, when hour after hour passed, and Tom did not return. Bessie was very hopeful though, for she thought her lover might have returned too late to visit her, and had gone home. But his mother spent the night in agony, fearing the worst, and yet half believing that her boy and his companion had landed upon one of the islands and remained there, rather than to attempt the passage of that raging sea.

In the morning Bessie called early at Mrs. Freeborn's, and was greatly alarmed to find that Tom was not at home. Both women then sought Bessie's father for advice, and he instantly dispatched a boat to the islands to discover if Tom and Eckels had spent the night there.

Four or five hours elapsed before the messenger returned; and meantime Bessie and Mrs. Freeborn endured torture, for they were certain Tom would have come back early in the morning, if he had been detained at the Shoals. And when the boatman at last presented himself, he had a sad, sad story to tell. He had talked with the keeper of the lighthouse, who said that a terrible squall struck the islands late yesterday afternoon, and that while he stood upon the rocks of the shore he had seen Jan's boat go flying past in the tempest with masts and rudder gone, with Jan sitting motionless upon the thwart, and with Tom desperately striving to keep the boat from sinking. There could be no doubt, the keeper said, that they were lost. No boat could live in such a sea, and this one was a wreck when it reached the lighthouse.

A wild cry of anguish came from Bessie's lips at this recital, while Mrs. Freeborn gave herself up to frantic grief. The two women, somewhat estranged before, were brought close together by their common sorrow. Both had dearly loved the poor drowned lad, and both were stricken with the same intense and overwhelming anguish. And as Bessie strove, amid her own suffering, to comfort the woman who was thus left desolate in the world, the flame of a new affection was kindled between them, and the mother loved the girl because her son had loved her: while Bessie felt that in Tom's mother she could find the only person in the world who could give her fullest compassion and sympathy in her great misery.

And so these two became fast friends. Bessie was often at Mrs. Freeborn's house; and as the weeks and months passed away, and no tidings came of poor Tom, all hope faded out of their hearts, and they gave up for ever the expectation of seeing him again. But they talked to each other of him, and in the rehearsal of his characteristics, and the recital of the events with which each was familiar in his life, they found strong consolation in their communion with each other.

A year passed away. Christmas came again, with its solemn memories, and brought no joy to Bessie or to Mrs Freeborn. Then another year came and went ; and the two women, one grey and haggard, with deep furrows upon her brow, and with the story of a great sorrow written upon her face ; the other still wearing the bloom of youth, still beautiful and full of physical grace and vigour, but grave and sad with the memory of the affliction which was ever fresh in her mind—these two were yet companions. But, a month afterwards, Mrs. Freeborn died, suddenly, while Bessie was absent from home ;

and ere she had recovered from the shock caused by this intelligence, her father's firm failed, and he came home to her one night a beggar. Mrs. Freeborn had intended to give Tom's inheritance to Bessie; but, alas! she died without making a will, and her relatives took all of her property.

After trying in vain for several months to obtain employment, Mr. Archer accepted an appointment as keeper of the lighthouse on White Island, and there upon that narrow rock, far from the great world, and almost isolated from humanity, the two established their home. In this lonely spot the summer and autumn passed, and during the pleasant weather Bessie would often seat herself upon the shore, where the light-keeper on that fatal night had seen Jan's boat coursing through the torrent, and try to picture to herself the dreadful scene. And never did the wind howl about their little dwelling, or the roaring sea hurl its mighty surges against the lighthouse and the barrier of rocks around it, but Bessie would think of the storm that swept away her darling, and of the horror of that death amid the seething waves.

Winter came, and with it many a furious war of the elements, during which Bessie's heart sometimes was filled with fear lest even they, upon that tiny spot of earth and stone, might be submerged by the mountain waves which rolled in awful volume against the shore. The weary days and nights went by, and Christmas-eve came again, bringing with it the most terrible gale that the Archers had ever encountered since their hermitage began. The sea was a boiling cauldron in which the waters were flung wildly to and fro, the white crests which crowned the waves being merged in one weltering mass of foam that shone strangely out from the black darkness of the night. The lantern overhead in the lighthouse shot its red and white light far out over the waters, warning mariners to avoid the treacherous rocks which here lurk close beneath the surface ; and against the thick glass which surrounded the light, swarms of birds, fleeing before the howling storm, were dashed and fell crushed and dead among the boulders beneath. The wind shrieked and screamed so fearfully about the low hut at the foot of the tower, that the two occupants could scarce hear their own voices even when they spoke in loudest tones.

"It is an awful night, Bessie," said Mr. Archer. "Heaven help any poor sailors who are caught in this neighbourhood in such a storm. It will be certain death for them."

Before Bessie could reply, a dull thud was heard outside above the roar of the tempest. Then another and another.

"They are signal guns!" exclaimed Mr. Archer, leaping to his feet. "Hark! there they are again! They are firing rapidly, and the vessel is evidently close at hand!"

The two rushed to the window and looked out. Nothing could be seen but the thick gloom and that ghastly white surface of the restless sea. Again the guns were heard, and then the sound ceased. Bessie and her father sat silently for awhile before the fire, each thinking of the horrors which the morrow's sun might reveal to them, and at last Mr. Archer said :

"She has gone ashore, I fear, either on Duck Island

or on Smutty Nose. It is the latter, I think, or we should not have heard her guns so plainly."

And Bessie clasped her father's hand tightly, and thought how poor Tom had braved such a tempest and had gone down into the fathomless depths to which these unfortunate men even now were sinking. Sleep was impossible on such a night, and Bessie kept watch with her father, who must remain awake to charge the lamps every hour with fresh supplies of oil.

It was after midnight when the guns were heard, and Bessie sat by the fireside until the early dawn, when her father ascended the tower to extinguish the lights. Mr. Archer had been gone but a few moments, when he came running down in extreme agitation. As he entered the room, he exclaimed:

"Bessie, let us go out to the beach quickly. I think a body has been washed ashore. I saw it from the lantern. Come!" And the two hurried through the doorway.

The rain had ceased, and the wind, though blowing strongly from the west, had lost much of its violence. They ran down the pathway to the spot where Bessie had so often stood and imagined Tom's terrible journey, and there, as Mr. Archer had supposed, lay the body of a drowned sailor. He had lashed himself to a spar, and had probably remained afloat for some time; but the pitiless waves had swept over and over him until he had ceased to breathe, and then they had cast him from their deadly embrace upon this morsel of kindly mother earth for Christian burial. He was a tall, manly fellow, with bronzed and rugged face, strong arms, a flowing beard, and dark-brown hair. Mr. Archer cut away the lashings,

and they carried him up to the house and placed him
before the fire. They determined to attempt his resusci-
tation, although they had little hope of effecting it, for the
sailor had probably been in the water, dead, for several
hours.

While Mr. Archer breathed into the man's lungs,
Bessie determined to chafe his hands. She seized one of

them for the purpose, when a loud exclamation from her
attracted her father's attention. Bessie was examining an
amethyst ring upon the man's finger, while her face grew

pale as death. She drew the ring away and looked upon the inside of it ; then she gazed steadfastly for a moment in the sailor's face, and with a faint cry swooned away. Mr. Archer picked up the fallen ring from the floor and read the inscription in it. It was this—

> " *From Bessie Archer to Thomas Freeborn,*
> *Christmas,* 186—."

This, indeed, was Tom, come back in this strange and dreadful fashion, and led—by what mysterious fate?—to the very feet of the woman he had loved. And when Bessie had recovered herself, she and her father went to work again with renewed earnestness, both with eager hope ; but Bessie with a mighty longing in her heart, which was too overpowering for language.

Half an hour passed, and Mr. Archer thought he perceived a convulsive movement of the chest. They redoubled their exertions, and presently the breast heaved slowly and painfully, and a sigh escaped from the lips. In a few moments the spark of life which had been so nearly extinguished was rekindled, and the patient was carried to the bed, where, after a few draughts of brandy, consciousness returned, and Tom, suffering intensely, lay moaning and sighing, too feeble to look upon those who had saved him. Then he fell into a deep sleep, and before he awoke Mr. Archer sent for assistance to Star Island. He feared the shock would be fatal if Tom should see and know him or Bessie while he was so ill.

But careful and tender nursing soon gave him strength, and in a few days Mr. Archer entered the room. Tom in-

stantly recognized him; but even his great surprise did
not keep back the words that came first to his lips: "Is
Bessie still alive?" And then Mr. Archer sat beside
Tom and told the whole story of his failure, their life at
the lighthouse, and his rescue; and when Bessie entered
at his summons, he went out and left those two alone in
their great joy. It was too sacred an occasion for the
presence of another. It was the blissful ending of a long
night of pain and sorrow and bereavement, the dawn of
a day of happiness and peace.

Tom had a very extended story to tell of his adventures, but we must make it a brief one here. The vessel
which rescued him from the boat was a whaler, outward
bound for the Pacific, and he remained upon her for nearly
two years. She was driven ashore near Cape Horn, and
wrecked as she was coming home, and Tom and the other
survivors were left upon the desolate coast in a most forlorn condition for several months. Finally, they were
taken off by a brig bound for Liverpool, and when that
port was reached, Tom found a vessel that was about to
sail for Portland, Maine. He shipped with her as a
sailor before the mast, and just as she was about to
end her voyage, she was caught in the great storm,
and driven on Smutty Nose Island. Tom said he
knew the locality at once, and determined to try to
save himself by lashing himself to a spar. He became
unconscious in the water, and awoke to find himself
saved.

Before another Christmas came around, Tom and
Bessie were married; and with his mother's fortune,
which he claimed and secured, he gave to Bessie and

her father a comfortable home, where they lived together in such complete felicity as is surely granted when from a great tribulation the soul comes at last into the full fruition of its hopes and to the serenity of perfect rest.

The Tragedy of Thompson Dunbar.

CHAPTER I.

THE ELOPEMENT.

SALT LAKE CITY; the Mormon capital! Let us look at it. It lies deep in the valley, in a valley which is six thousand feet above the level of the sea. To the right, to the left, to the north, the south, the east, and the west, mountains!

Some near, some far. Some mighty, some dwarfed by contrast with the greater. A serrated chain of hills filling the whole horizon and outlining their dusky summits clearly against the pure blue of the sky. From among them the Twin Peaks rise, boldly and grandly, seventy-five hundred feet above the valley, and stand in hoary grandeur, their snow-clad tops the reservoirs from which the plain draws inexhaustible supplies of cold and limpid water. The plain itself, a wide stretch of sandy earth, partly cultivated, but almost wholly covered upon this August day with myriads of gleaming golden sun-flowers, which to him who takes a bird's-eye view, seem a garb altogether glorious. Lying in the midst of it, the city.

America has no other like it. Surveyed from a distance it wears a distinctly Oriental appearance. So we of the Far West who have only dreamed of the East imagine how Damascus may look. White houses shin-ing amid rich masses of green foliage. A dome, a tower, a spire, that may answer for a minaret, deep gardens, buildings with flat roofs, a faint mist of dust marking the line of a travelled street, a sky of more than Oriental softness overhead, and an atmosphere so pure that to breathe it is luxury, and to look through it is to gain such power of vision that the peaks of the Wasatch range, twenty miles away, seem within reach of the pedestrian who has five minutes to spare.

In the city there are broad streets covered with gravel. Upon each side where the gutter should be, there is a stream of pure and delicious water hurtling fiercely along with the impetus gained at the top of the Twin Peaks. The dwellings of stone, of wood, of adobe or sun-burned bricks, are far apart and enshrined among mighty trees. Shops, here and there, thrust themselves out to the edge of the footway, and offer their wares to the passers-by.

It is a queer throng that is thus tempted. Such a one as no other street in this broad earth can gather. Here is a Mormon saint, a patriarch with twelve wives, and so many children that he is compelled to refer to his memorandum book for a list of them. Stout, rugged, coarse in nature and feature, he is of the kind that found his valley a wilderness and transformed it into a luscious garden. There is a Utah Indian, clad perhaps in a stove-pipe hat, a blanket, and buckskin breeches. He wears huge earrings, long straight hair, thick, and as black as midnight. Here is a Mexican—dashing along at break-neck speed, upon a shaggy pony. He wears a dress as picturesque as that of a Greek, and he is as fine a horseman as the Arabian desert knows. There go two army officers, wearing blue coats, and looking as if they were in authority. They hie to the camp upon the hill side, from whence the guns that they control can level the city in a day. Gentile miners, with fierce whiskers, broad hats, trousers tucked in boots, and pistols thrust in belts, swagger about in search of firewater; Mormon policemen, quiet, reserved, but keen as hounds, stand upon the corners. Huge waggons drawn by six, and eight, and ten mules come lumbering down the street, bringing from outlying settlements of the saints the tithes for the Prophet's storehouse. Hurrying past them, dash graceful and elegant pleasure carriages such as Hyde Park might be proud of. But where are the women? Of men there are enough. Now and then a Gentile woman passes, but not often ; and the Mormon women appear still less frequently. It is Orientalism in the extreme Occident. There is the polygamy of Turkey with an approach to the custom which keeps the woman under a veil. It is a strange city, a new city, born within the last half century ; a city of its own kind ; a city that is as striking, as novel, as interesting, as unprecedented to the view of the American who lives east of the Rocky Moun-tains, as it is to that of the citizen of London.

To begin with. We have to do with a large white adobe structure, which stands upon the eastern edge of the town, in the midst of a garden, wherein are trees that overtop the roof, and grass that is gemmed with flowers. It is Mrs. Ballygag's Boarding School for young ladies. Two young men meet at the gate. We recognize them as young Mormons. One is Thompson Dunbar; the other is Arbutus Jones. Arbutus is speaking.

"Yes, sir; I shall marry them; clean out the school. I have had a special revelation; the entire senior class has been sealed to me, and I am going to marry the two other classes so as to make a complete job of it."

"But the senior and junior classes have engaged themselves to me," replied Dunbar. "I proposed to them yesterday, and they said that they could love me alone."

"Can't help that," said Jones; "I have arranged the matter with the Prophet and the parents. The entire concern has been offered me in marriage, and I am now on my way to see Mrs. Ballygag, and to get her to wind up the term and graduate them at once."

"This is maddening!" exclaimed Dunbar. "Jones, the affections of those classes have been given to me— their young hearts are mine. What right have you to come in and trample rudely upon the holiest emotions of your fellow-creatures?"

"The best of rights, in this case," said Jones. "It has been revealed to me that my duty is to annex this boarding-school. It is a sacred obligation. There is not a bit of use, you know, Dunbar, in your kicking against the decrees of the church."

"But you don't want the whole thirty-two of them?"

"Yes, sir; I want them all. I claim them as my bride."

"I love them all dearly," said Dunbar; "but sooner than have any fuss I'll let you pick sixteen, if you'll leave me the rest."

"No; I shall take them all. But I don't know; maybe, I might agree to leave you the one with warm hair and freckles. My heart, somehow, doesn't throb wildly for her."

"Never!" exclaimed Dunbar.

"Oh, very well, then. Let her alone. I'll pool her in with the rest."

The eye of Thompson Dunbar flashed fire. Stepping up to Arbutus Jones, he whispered fiercely in his ear:

"You think you will marry this school. Never! never! I swear it! My faith is pledged to the women of my love, and they shall be mine. Mark what I say! I shall make them my wife!"

Arbutus Jones opened the gate, and, turning away with a light laugh, he said, "Dunbar, don't talk like an idiot," and then he walked up to the porch, pulled the door-bell, and called for Mrs. Ballygag.

Thompson Dunbar sauntered sadly down the street, meditating upon his plans. Secretly he entered his office, and writing thirty-two letters, he dispatched them through the post, and then went towards the livery-stable.

Midnight came. Dark, cold, and silent. The belated wayfarer, walking into town, was startled to perceive, rushing by him in the gloom, a man, who seemed to be carrying a coil of rope upon his arm. Behind him eight carriages proceeded slowly, and with little noise.

" A midnight funeral procession," the traveller thought. The man stopped in front of Mrs. Ballygag's mansion. The carriages halted by the kerbstone, a hundred yards below. The man opened the gate noiselessly, and walked quickly around to the side of the house. He uttered a low whistle, and a sash in a second-story window was carefully raised. He flung toward it the end of a rope, which was seized and hauled until a ladder of rope stretched from the window to the ground.

" Come, dearest," said Thompson Dunbar, in a loud whisper. " Do not be afraid. I will catch you if you fall." Then the form of a lithe and graceful girl emerged from the window, and glided slowly, but easily down the frail ladder. Then another descended. Then another, until thirty-two lithe and graceful girls had reached the ground. As they came, Thompson Dunbar clasped them one by one in his arms, and kissed them fervently, pointing the way to the carriages.

The last one whispered in his ravished ear that the thirty-two trunks were standing, ready packed, in the chamber above, and that Thompson had better see to getting them down. But the idea did not seem to strike Thompson. He asked himself what love had to do with trunks? He thought how little pure affection cares for material things. He knew that he was ready to die for his darlings. That would be heroic. But to carry thirty-two trunks down a rope-ladder, he considered, in the strictest sense, a prosaic performance. Did Romeo shoulder Juliet's trunk? Did Paul take Virginia upon one arm, and her trunk upon the other? Did Petrarch interrupt his sweet converse with Laura with struggles with her luggage? He thought not. Let the trunks remain as a souvenir with Mrs. Ballygag. He gloated over the thought that she and Jones would weep tears of anguish and helpless rage over those leathern receptacles.

He went toward the carriages. They were all filled, and the doors were closed. He mounted upon the seat with the driver of the foremost one, and said :—

"Drive like mad, now! Forty dollars extra for you, if you reach Ogden by daylight!"

The vehicles dashed onward swiftly through the night. Over rough roads, down through cañons, through dense forests, over mighty hills, along the brow of more than one precipice ; scaring the fox and the rabbit that lay in the path ; waking the echoes of the passes, and defying the winds which blew in gusty blasts from the mountain tops.

It was a long and difficult ride. It would have been tedious for Thompson and his bride, but for the thought that each moment brought them nearer to the wedded bliss which is the holiest joy that has ever sweetened human life.

The day was faintly breaking over the summits of the Wasatch range when the procession entered Ogden. Thompson ordered his companion to drive at once to the house of Bishop Potts. The Bishop's dwelling showed no signs of life. He was asleep with his family—at that early hour. Thompson rang the door-bell fiercely. The Bishop's grey head was thrust from the window.

"Who is making all that racket down there?" he said "What's the matter? What do you want?"

"It's I, Thompson Dunbar! I've run over from the

city to be married. Hurry down and perform the ceremony, please."

"Can't you get married at some less unearthly hour.
than this? I've been up all night with the twins and
sixteen others of the children, and four of Mrs. Potts have
not had a wink of sleep, and here you come routing us
out just as we are dozing off! I'll marry you after breakfast. There is no hurry about it, I reckon."

"But there *is* a hurry though. I've eloped with Mrs.
Ballygag's boarding school. It loved me, and they
wanted to marry it to another man, Arbutus Jones, you
know; so it fled with me. We are bent on instantaneous
consolidation!"

"How many of her are there?" asked the Bishop.

"Only thirty-two."

"And you're single?"

"Yes."

"Very well. That'll do to begin with, but a man
of your standing must disembowel a couple more
boarding schools if you want to hold your own in the
church! I'll come down and see what I can do for
you."

Thompson helped his bride to alight, and a most charming picture she presented, standing there in a row in the
early morning light, blushing with modest joy beneath the
smiles and caresses of her devoted lover. While she
waited for the Bishop she engaged in a simultaneous
arrangement of her back hair. Thompson thought she
had never appeared so lovely as when, holding the front
strands in her mouth, the whole thirty-two of her twisted
up her tresses, and inserted her combs in them.

A moment later the front door opened, and the Bishop appeared in dressing-gown and slippers.

Mr. Dunbar ushered the bride into the Bishop's drawing-room, and seated her upon the sofas and chairs. Then he drew the Bishop aside.

"By the way, Bishop, what are you going to charge? What are your rates?"

"Well," said the Bishop, smiling, "where there is only one couple my regular fee is two dollars. But of course I allow a discount on wholesale transactions. I'll tell you what I'll do. Seeing that you are a young man, and evidently in earnest in your efforts to start properly in life, I'll put you the whole lot in at forty-five dollars. How's that?"

"Reasonable, very reasonable, indeed," said Thompson.

"Stand up, my dear," said the Bishop to the bride.

The bride stood up in a semicircle, while in the doorway gathered seven or eight of the Bishop's wife, to witness the impressive scene.

Thompson Dunbar then advanced, and taking from the pocket of his coat tail a quarter of a peck of gold rings he put them in his hat and handed them to the Bishop, who began the service.

"Thompson Dunbar, you take these women for your wedded wife? You promise to love, honour, and cherish?" etc., etc.

Thompson Dunbar said, "I do."

The Bishop, turning to the bride, said—

"Emma, Henrietta, Louisa, Geraldine, Polly, Mary ane, Matilda, Gertrude, Lucy, Imogene, Sally, Rebecca

Maria, Georgine. Hetty, Columbia, Martha, Caroline, Patty, Julia, Emily, Anastasia, Rachel, Sapphira, Ethelberta, Hannah, Josephine, Bertie, Mignon, Patience, Agatha, Ann Jane—you take this man to be your wedded husband? You promise to love, honour, and obey?" etc., etc.

And the bride said she did, and she would.

Then Thompson, with gladness in his eyes, and wild emotions in his bosom, took the hat from the Bishop and walked around the semi-circle of the bride, and placed the rings on her fingers. Then the Bishop pronounced them man and wife; and Thompson started around the bridal curve again to clasp her in succession to his heart.

He was just releasing himself from the twenty-sixth clasp when a wild tumult was heard in the street ; the noise of hurrying wheels, the quick tramp of horses, a crying of voices. The Bishop went to the casement to ascertain the cause of the tumult which disturbed the happy marriage festivities. Before he reached the window the door was hurled open with violence, and in rushed Arbutus Jones. Behind him was Mrs. Ballygag.

Jones was white and breathless. Mrs. Ballygag panted, and brandished in a threatening manner a protuberant umbrella.

" Stop! stop!" shouted Jones, as he projected himself into the room. " Don't go on! I forbid the marriage! these women are to be my wife! This man is a depraved villain! I command you, Bishop, not to perform the ceremony!"

"Don't you dare to do it, you grey haired old monster !" shrieked Mrs. Ballygag, menacing him with her umbrella. "You do it at your peril!"

"I think," said the Bishop, serenely, "you had better try to be calmer. Try to restrain your emotion, as the weather is too warm for violent excitement."

"Let 'em go on," said Dunbar. "It makes no difference if they get their emotional thermometers up to a hundred and ten in the shade; nobody cares."

"You don't care, hey?" exclaimed Mrs. Ballygag, "you don't care! I'll make you care if there's any law in the land. Coming round people's houses with rope-ladders in the middle of the night, stealing their poor defenceless children! I'll see if you don't care!"

"Children, madam?" said the Bishop.

"Pretty tough children, these!" said Thompson, waving his hand toward the bride.

"Yes, children," replied Mrs. Ballygag, "mere babes and sucklings. Getting married, you baggage!" said she, looking at the bride. "You're in a nice condition to think about marriage! How do you bound Nova Scotia? Tell me this instant! Don't know? I thought not! Don't know how to bound Nova Scotia—don't know that the Tropic of Capricorn is not one of the United States ; don't know that the Peloponnesian war was not fought by negroes in Canada West, and yet you consider yourselves fitted for the responsibilities of matrimony! It's simply too ridiculous to be discussed."

"I am sorry, madam, that they are ignorant of the geographical facts connected with the Peloponnesian war, but we will try to be happy while we study them up together."

"You will *never* study them together," remarked Arbutus Jones. "These ladies return at once with me."

"Certainly!" said Mrs. Ballygag; "they go back to school to-day. I shall put them on bread and water, and give them fifteen extra sums a-piece in Reduction of Compound Numbers."

"They will *not* go back, I think," said Thompson

"We'll see about that," replied Jones. "Girls, leave the room!"

"Don't go!" said Thompson.

"Attend to your own business!" exclaimed Arbutus, fiercely.

"If you speak to me in that manner again, I'll throw you out of the window!" said Dunbar.

"Lay your hand upon me and you are a dead man," replied Arbutus, drawing a revolver.

"Two can play at that game," said Thompson, quickly drawing another.

What the result might have been if the dispute had proceeded further can only be conjectured; but as soon as the weapons were produced, the bride shrieked wildly, and the whole thirty-two of her fell fainting on the floor, while Mrs. Ballygag collapsed, and embracing her umbrella, sank unconscious in the corner.

For a moment, wild confusion prevailed; but the Bishop retained his presence of mind, and running into the garden, he seized a huge watering-pot, and bringing it in, he sprinkled the faces of the bride with water until one by one she revived. Mrs. Ballygag came to without assistance, and sat up looking the picture of distress.

When all of the party were restored, the Bishop said :

"Two can play at that game," said Thompson.—*Page* 108.

"Let us have no more of these scenes! Mr. Jones, it is my duty to inform you that you have come too late. Mr. Dunbar is already married to these ladies."

"Married!" shouted Jones.

"Married!" shrieked Mrs. Ballygag.

"Married," replied the Bishop and Thompson.

"This is infamous," said Arbutus. "Dunbar, you have played me a scurvy trick. But I shall be even with you."

"You can have any satisfaction you want," replied Dunbar. "But, I say, Jones, how about that revelation? Crooked, wasn't it? Didn't reveal so very much after all?"

"We shall see!" exclaimed Jones; and then smashing his hat down savagely upon his head, he left the room.

Mrs. Ballygag began to cry.

"You have treated me shamefully," she said. "The last quarter's bills of these girls are not paid. I can't have any commencement; the reputation of the school is ruined; and I am a poor lone widow-woman, with nobody to help me!"

And Mrs. Ballygag sank down upon a sofa and sobbed violently.

Then the bride began to cry also. It was altogether too melancholy for a wedding. The Bishop drew Thompson aside.

"Dunbar," he whispered, "you'll have to do something for this woman. You must do the fair thing."

"What do you recommend?"

"Well, to tell the truth, if I were you, I'd marry her. Just throw her in with the rest, as a kind of job lot. You might as well go the whole figure, while you're at it."

"I suppose I might. I'll take her."

"I'll charge you only twenty-five cents extra for tying the knot," said the benevolent Bishop.

"You propose it to her," said Thompson.

"Mrs. Ballygag," said the Bishop, "how would you like to marry Mr. Dunbar, in with the rest? He says he is willing."

With a wild cry of joy, Mrs. Ballygag rushed forward and threw her arms about Dunbar's neck and nestled her head in his bosom.

"Do you love me, Thompson?" she asked, looking up at him.

"Well, yes; that is, of course, as it were, to a—to a —to a certain extent! Take your umbrella off my toe, please ; the pressure is too severe !"

"Then take me, take me !" she exclaimed. "I'll help you manage the girls."

The girls looked as if they were not bursting with ecstasy; but they wanted to be submissive to Thompson, and so they said nothing.

Then Dunbar took Mrs. Ballygag by the hand, the Bishop began the ceremony, and in a few moments she was made a thirty-third of him.

CHAPTER II.

THE DEPARTURE.

UPON the homeward journey most of the bride rode in the eight carriages, while the joyous groom occupied his former seat with the coachman of the foremost vehicle. The recent Mrs. Ballygag, however, was compelled by the want of room also to ride with one of the drivers. She entertained him during the journey by a cross-examination, the purpose of which was to ascertain if, in his opinion, a horse is an adverb or a preposition, and if he knew how to multiply vulgar fractions. When he remarked to her, "I ain't got no use for a hymn-book," she parsed the sentence for him, and showed him clearly how two negatives make an affirmative.

Whenever his horses were disposed to go slowly, she prodded them savagely with the ferule of her umbrella, and sometimes when the portion of the bride which was riding in the carriage beneath her laughed too boisterously, she would reach over and push her umbrella in at the window two or three times to indicate her disapprobation of such scandalous behaviour.

Altogether, it is believed that the late widow Ballygag enjoyed the trip exceedingly. But it is doubtful if the driver did ; and it is certain Thompson did not, at least, during the periods when they were passing along the edges of the precipices, and she was constantly screaming for him to come and save her from being dashed to pieces.

At last, however, Salt Lake City was reached, and the bridal party was taken at once to Dunbar's modest little cottage. When the bride had all dismounted and entered the drawing-room, Thompson whispered to the late Mrs. Ballygag that there were four of his wife to whom he had not yet been formally introduced, and he begged her to perform the ceremony. She did so, remarking at the same time to the girls—

"Your husband is a good and worthy man, and I want you to behave well towards him. I am going to keep an eye on you to see that you do it, too!"

The honeymoon passed blissfully. Thompson Dunbar was by profession a sailor, and having no ship at this time he was at liberty to devote himself wholly to domestic life. He purchased new furniture for his house. He made a contract with the calico factory for permanent supplies of dress goods, and the factory at once put in extra looms and employed more hands. He bought bonnets with a recklessness that threatened bankruptcy. He established relations with a candy manufacturer, which guaranteed him the few tons of chocolate drops that he required at lower rates than usual. In fact, he launched himself fairly and equally upon the sea of wedded life.

Wedded life! Ah, how few of us understand those words as they came to Thompson Dunbar and his bride! To how few have they so rich and beautiful a meaning! Many of us think that we have had sweet experiences within the sacred precincts of the home; but not to many of us is it given to have thirty-four souls with but a single thought—thirty-four hearts that beat as one. The man who sits down with one wife by his hearthstone, and thinks he is happy, knows nothing of the tenderer joy of him who, around a hearthstone twenty feet square, gathers thirty-

two sweet faces (the recent Mrs. Ballygag was homely),
and looks love into all of those eyes that speak again.
Such a man has a nobler affection, a loftier aim, a purer
ambition, a mightier impulse to dash into the struggle
of life and win his bread. Who would not toil valiantly
with thirty-three smiles waiting to welcome him home,
and thirty-three hungry women to nourish?

Thompson Dunbar was proud, and he had a right to
be. Never once in the early days of his married life did
anything happen to cloud his domestic sky ; excepting,
perhaps, on one occasion, when the relict of the lamented
Ballygag hid the kitten in his boot and forgot to tell him
about it ; and never did he have any doubts of the future
excepting when he reflected upon the anguish he should
suffer when his duty should call him away from those he
loved.

And the painful summons came at last. He was
ordered to join his ship at San Francisco. She was about
to sail upon a three years' cruise. Three years ! It
seemed intolerable to be separated so long from his darlings. Poor Dunbar! If he could have foreseen the
trials that were in store for him !

The hour of parting arrived. Let us draw a veil over
the scene. There are some things too sacred for the vulgar eye ; some episodes in a man's life, of which to speak
lightly were a profanation. Mrs. Dunbar clung to him, of
course. Ah, may none of us ever know the agony of such
a farewell. May we never know what a husband suffers
to whom thirty-three wives are clinging in desperate woe.

He tore himself away! He was gone ! Gone ! And
three groups of eleven each of heart-broken women sank

upon the front steps and sobbed in bitter despair. Then they flew to the windows and gazed after him, and waved their kerchiefs to him, excepting perhaps the aforetime Ballygag, who, in the violence of her emotion, waved a flannel petticoat which she had been mending.

Little did they suspect what they should endure ere they looked upon that fond face again ! Life is so full of disappointments, so full of —— But, however, let us go on.

Thompson Dunbar sailed away upon the bosom of the mighty deep. For some weeks all was well. The treacherous ocean held its powers in leash. One night there was a fearful tempest, and the gallant barque, after a prolonged contest with the elements, sank to rise no more. All on board were lost ; all save one. Lashed to a spar Thompson Dunbar contrived to sustain himself in the seething foam for four days. Upon the morning of the fifth day he was cast upon a desert island. He crawled out of the reach of the waves and fell asleep. He slumbered long, and when he awoke he released himself from the spar, and looked about him. He perceived that the island was small. It was only fifteen feet wide by thirty-eight feet long ; but Dunbar was satisfied with it. It was something for him to stand upon, to live upon.

Feeling hungry, he walked out looking to find something to eat. He discovered a bed of fine oysters in a little cove at the northern end of the island, and to his great joy he found that a huge hole in the rock contained a dozen hogsheads of rain water ! These things were so exceedingly fortunate that he felt sure of going through the regular round of desert island experiences. But ' this he was, to a certain extent, disappointed. The oysters and water remained, of course, and now and then some sociable bird would call and leave an egg, but none of the usual desert island conveniences floated ashore.

Thompson Dunbar remained upon the island for fifteen years ; but when his clothing began to wear out no vessel was wrecked upon an adjacent and handy reef, and all the crew drowned, so that he could have a fair chance at the chests which contained clothing that fitted him exactly.

And no other ship was cast ashore into which he entered and found twenty bags full of Spanish doubloons, which he gazed at with proud contempt, while the thought occurred to him how useless such dross is, especially when you are on a desert island, with no possibility of spending it.

And he did not find in the cabin of such a wreck double-barrelled guns and carpenter's tools, and canned fruits and vegetables, and such a general variety of useful and fancy articles as no ship ever included in a single cargo, excepting perhaps in cases where the purpose of the owners was to have been wrecked to oblige some Robinson Crusoe or other, and to make him fat and comfortable.

And when he felt lonely and longed for fellowship and the sweet communion of some kindred soul, it did not happen that a squad of chocolate-coloured cannibals dashed up in a canoe, and were all killed by a single explosion of a musket ; all save one, who fell at Dunbar's feet, and became his slave and his pupil and his riend.

On the contrary, Dunbar had a particularly prosaic time upon the island; eating and sleeping and walking about. After the first shock produced by his sense of isolation had passed, he surveyed the island and made a map of it. Then he took possession of it in the name of his government, and formally annexed it to the United States by hoisting a flag made of a felicitous combination of his handkerchief and his red flannel shirt. In order to put in the time, and to give himself occupation congenial to an American, he held elections thrice a year, and he celebrated the 4th of July and Washington's birthday, when they came around, by reading the Declaration of Independence, and singing the "Star Spangled Banner."

But his wife! Did he ever think of her? Ah, yes! The bitterness of that separation no tongue can tell. Often he would lie upon his back and take from his pocket the thirty-three miniatures and look at them with longing and tearful eyes. And he would get to wondering which was Emma, which was Rebecca, which Columbia, and which Sapphira. The lineaments of Ballygag were the only ones he felt certain about, but, somehow he never lingered very long over them.

And he would ask himself if any of her ever thought much of him. He would wonder if she was all alive, or if, perchance, some of her counted him dead, and had remarried. Perchance she had departed, sorrowful and broken-hearted, and only thirty-three little grassy mounds in the churchyard remained to mark the remains of her who once had been the joy of his life.

It might be that if he should ever return home he

"Often he would lie on his back and take from his pocket the thirty-three miniatures and look at them."—*Page* 176.

would find his cottage desolate, with no one to love, none to caress, and it would devolve upon him to begin life afresh by embezzling another boarding-school. The thought was bitterness to him. Only those who have learned from a sad experience what it is to lose three and-thirty wives at a blow, can realize the depth and intensity of the sufferings of this unhappy young man.

CHAPTER III.

THE VICTORY OF JONES.

MEANTIME, how did Mrs. Dunbar bear the bereavement that had come to her? For the first three or four years she was hopeful ; but gradually, as the time passed swiftly by, and no word came to her from the wanderer, she began to feel the growing agony of despair.

Often she would go up as the evening shadows fell, and stand at each of the thirty-three windows, and gaze out toward the glowing west, straining all sixty-five of her eyes (Ethelberta had a cataract), to catch a glimpse of her Thompson. But, alas ! Thompson did not come ; and as a feeling of deep sadness stole in over her souls, Mrs. Dunbar would bow her heads over the infants in her arms and weep. Perhaps she would wail out her woes in a plaintive lullaby, which was so distorted by her sobs that Ballygag's former partner would stop long enough to scold her for singing flat, and not marking the dotted notes with sufficient distinctness.

The misery of a suffering woman's heart ! Who shall

sound it? And what multiplication table can compass it where it is thirty-three times increased? There are some conundrums that have to be given up at the outset.

At last, however, she was forced to the conclusion that Thompson was dead. It was inevitable. The ship had never been heard from. No message had ever come up from the roaring sea, to tell the story of her destruction. She was gone ; and, without doubt, Thompson had gone down fathoms deep into the cruel waters with her. Mrs. Dunbar abandoned hope, and decided to mourn for him as one that had been called away to another life.

As soon as her determination became known, and she began to talk about putting on mourning, the city merchants noted an advance of two per cent. in crape and black bombazine, and the bachelor Saints began to have revelations concerning their duty to persuade her from prolonging the period of her widowhood.

Arbutus Jones was enabled to perceive with perfect clearness, what were his obligations in the premises. He made up his mind that the anguish of Mrs. Dunbar could be assuaged only by sweet words of consolation from his lips. He called early to offer his sympathies, and afterwards he would go around often in the evenings and talk with her about the virtues of the departed Thompson, for whom, however, it was impossible for him to feel any but a fictitious enthusiasm.

After a while, he became more assiduous in his attentions, and he felt, reviving in his bosom, with all its vehement force, the love he had for her when she was maidens. Often he would lead her forth in the twilight, and, while as many of her little hands as he could conveniently

" While as many of her little hands as he could conveniently hold, lay
confidingly in his."—*Page* 179.

hold, lay confidingly in his, they would stroll to some quiet, grassy dell, and she would arrange herself in a circle by the side of a babbling brook, while he sat in the centre, and whispered soft words of love to her, and walked around, and pressed each of her hands, and let the love light of his eyes shine on her faces, and warm to life the flickering flame in her hearts.

One evening he proposed to her in a lump. He asked her to be his. The Ballygag was the first to speak. She said :—

"Have you examined your heart, Arbutus? Do you love us truly?"

"Certainly! Of course! Most of you, anyway. However, sooner than lacerate your feelings, I am willing to count *you* out, and permit you to cling to the memory of Thompson."

"But I'm the one that can't be counted out. If you love me, I am yours!"

"I am willing to sacrifice my love for your sake, to save your feelings."

"You are too noble," said the late Mrs. B. "I cannot consent to such an act of heroic devotion upon your part."

"I think you would be happier, maybe, without me. I'll start you in another boarding-school."

"Loving heart! And do you think I would be willing to accept such unselfish kindness, when I could not repay you by watching over you? Never!"

"And then you know," said Jones, "Dunbar might eventually turn up and it would be so comforting for him to have at least one of his wives remaining to him. So upon the whole, perhaps, I had better let you float along as you are."

"Ah ! Arbutus ! I love you more than ever when you show yourself so ready to surrender your own joy for the good of others. Take me, oh take me to your fond bosom !"

And the former Mrs. Ballygag fell towards him with a purpose to be folded to his heart ; but Jones, with remarkable presence of mind, pretended not to see her, and addressed himself assiduously to the task of assisting Sapphira to rise from the ground. Then the whole of Mrs. Dunbar rose, and retiring a little space, went into committee to consider the question. After an animated debate, during which the Ballygag gave her views the fullest and most generous expression, Mrs. Dunbar decided by a vote of twenty-nine to three (the woman with the cataract not voting) to become the wife of Arbutus Jones !

Jones learned the decision with transports. One by one his sweetheart was held in his fond embrace, as he kissed her and promised to be true to her ; and one by one, as she looked into his manly face and found there the radiant joy of pure affection, she was filled with trustfulness and peace, and with him went back to her home full of blissful anticipations of a future which should compensate for all the suffering of the sorrowful past.

Mr. Jones was very anxious to be married speedily ; but the widow, of course, pressed for such delay as would be necessary to enable her to prepare new outfits of clothing. There are always stirring times in the business of a community when a Mormon wife or widow begins to make a movement in the matter of clothes. In this case, the appearance of Mrs. Dunbar unexpectedly in the market, caused such a revival in trade, that the merchants began to buy houses and lots, and to set up carriages under the impression that a new era of prosperity had begun. But eventually Mrs. Dunbar was ready, and the day was fixed. She expressed a preference for Bishop Potts, of Ogden, as the officiating clergyman, because she was used to him, and, of course, Jones asked the worthy Bishop to come over and tie the knots.

The wedding attracted a good deal of attention in Salt Lake City. Jones sailed up the aisle of the temple with Sapphira and Ethelberta upon each arm, while fifteen of his best friends each convoyed two others of Mrs. Dunbar. The sexton brought up the rear with the ex-widow Ballygag, who honoured the occasion by turning out in a green bonnet with yellow ostrich feathers, a crimson poplin dress embroidered with blue, with a new false front upon her head, and with a look of beaming happiness bursting through her gold spectacles.

The ceremony occupied but a few moments, and when the Bishop having made these thirty-four one flesh, the procession turned, passed down the aisle again, entered the carriages, and went to the home that was once Dunbar's, but now had come into the possession of Jones.

Dunbar! how he would have been torn with agony if he, far away upon that lonely island of the sea, could have witnessed that scene in the temple! But this torture was mercifully spared him. At the moment when his loving wife was given to another by the Bishop,

Thompson was splitting oysters open with his jack-knife, and thinking how uncommonly good they would be with horse-radish. No voice whispered the truth to him. No pangs of the heart interfered with the vigour of his gastric juice !

Of the domestic life which came to Arbutus Jones, with the golden days which followed the wedding, we need not speak. It passed away sweetly and brought him perfect contentment. But one day, a month or two after the marriage, Arbutus, upon his return home, found an elderly lady whom he did not know occupying a seat at his dinner-table. He thought at first it might be one of his wife, so he counted the row of her, and found that there were thirty-four women instead of thirty-three. A moment later Sapphira introduced the stranger as her mother.

" She has come to stay with us, Arbutus, dear, upon my invitation. I longed to have her with me; and I knew you would welcome her for my sake. Won't you, darling ?"

" Oh, certainly ! Glad to see her ! Very glad ! Of course. She is always welcome here !"

But Jones did not look as if he were really glad. A dark foreboding entered his mind. The precedent was bad ; it was dangerous. If this kind of thing began, where was it going to stop ? That was the question that he asked himself, with gloom in his soul and a scowl upon his brow.

Two days later Mary Jane's mother arrived. Mary Jane said that she had invited her mother down to spend the summer, and to give her a chance to learn to love her son-in-law. Arbutus forced a smile as he welcomed her, but it was not difficult to see that his mother-in-law would have to labour hard to induce him to return her love.

The following week Ethelberta's mother came, ostensibly for the purpose of superintending an operation upon Ethelberta's cataract. But Arbutus saw plainly through the pretence. He was far too acute a man not to know that a woman who comes for the purpose of witnessing an operation upon a cataract is not necessarily accompanied by six trunks, eleven boxes, a bedstead, two bureaus, a sewing-machine, a cooking-stove, a poll parrot, and a cat. She had come to stay. He knew it, and he grated his teeth as he strove to bear it patiently.

A month passed, and at intervals mothers-in-law continued to arrive, until there was a sum total of twenty-one in Jones's house. He began to grow desperate. One day he called the Ballygag aside. He asked her if she had a mother. She said she had not.

Arbutus clasped her in his arms and kissed her tenderly. She was amazed. He had not been lavish of caresses with her. She asked for an explanation. He said—

" I adore a woman who has lost her parents. Ah, Lucille!" (her name was Lucille), "my only regret now is that you didn't keep an orphan asylum instead of a boarding-school, when Dunbar eloped with your establishment."

As he spoke thus the door-bell rang. Lucille went out to see who was there. When she returned, she said the mothers of Columbia and Emma had just arrived with two waggon-loads of trunks and furniture.

Arbutus shuddered.

" This is terrible, Mrs. Bally—Lucille, I mean. If this thing continues I shall go mad. I did not bargain for this. Twenty-three of them already— twenty-three mothers-in-law ! My reason will totter on its throne !"

" Yes," said the former Mrs. B., " and Henrietta and Sarah and Matilda told me that they had written this morning for their mothers to come on and live here; and Sarah said she had invited one of her aunts also."

A spasm of pain flitted over the face of Arbutus Jones. He sat down upon a chair. Was the curse come upon him ? Were the fates preparing for him a scorpion whip of retribution for his destruction of Dunbar's hopes of happiness? We cannot tell. Maybe we wouldn't tell if we could.

While he sat there trying to think what he should do to avert the calamity that was overpowering him, a servant entered with a telegram. Jones tore it open and read it.

" Wh—wh—what's this ? ' My dear son-in-law : Meet me at the train on Tuesday. I am coming to board with you for a few months. I am your affectionate mother-in-law.—' REBECCA FITLER.'

" Rebecca Fitler ! Who—what—which one's she ? "

" She is Imogene's mother. I know her well. She's worse about a house than the whooping-cough. Quarrelled with her husband till she killed him," said Lucille.

" Ha ! ha !" laughed Jones, fiercely. " Twenty-six mothers-in-law and an aunt ! This is refreshing ! It is delightful ! Lucille, I am beginning to feel murderous !

If this kind of thing goes on I shall soon be in a frame
of mind which will make indulgence in assassination
seem like pastime."

" I'm afraid it *will* go on," said the late Mrs. Ballygag, looking out of the window ; " I see Geraldine's
mother coming up the front yard with a carpet-bag and a
band-box. She makes twenty-seven ! "

" Twenty-seven and an aunt ! " exclaimed Arbutus.
"Five more to hear from ! But we can rely upon them
to come, I think, can't we, Lucille ? May be I'd better
write to them for fear they forget it ; " and Arbutus
laughed a wild, hysterical laugh.

" What are you going to do about it ? " asked the late
widow B.

" Do ? What am I going to do ? I am going to do
something terrible ! Something desperate ! No man can
stand this persecution ! I don't mind having a couple of
dozen or so of mothers-in-law around, but the line must
be drawn somewhere, and I draw it at twenty-seven and
an aunt."

" You could get rid of them by obtaining a divorce,"
said Lucille.

" No ; I shan't do that. It's too expensive. Besides,
I don't want to give up the girls."

" Suppose you order the mothers to leave, and if they
refuse force them from the house ? "

" Won't do," said Arbutus, shaking his head thoughtfully. " You don't know them. An army couldn't put
them out—an army rigged out with Krupp guns and
battering rams. No, no ! We must resort to something
more desperate."

"How would it do to put poison in their tea?"

"I can't see any profit in it. They'll die. I'll have to stand the funeral expenses, and may be pay the cost of the *post-mortem* examinations."

"Well, then, blow them up with gunpowder."

"No, dear; you must suggest something more practicable. The explosion would disfigure the furniture, and it would make old Partridge, the coroner, wild with joy. Lucille, I hate that man with bitter hatred; and shall I do a thing that will give him thirty or forty inquests, and help him to pay off the mortgage on his house? Never, my dear, never!"

"I don't see how we can manage it, then," said the Ballygag.

"Let me give you an idea," said Arbutus. "I have in my mind the outlines of a malignant plot, which will rid me of these women for ever. It is an awful thing to do, this that I propose, but the case is desperate; I am driven to an extremity. Will you promise to help me in it?"

"Yes."

"Do you know any of Mrs. Brigham Young."

"Oh, yes; one of her went to school to me. She was the best girl I had at grammar. She could tell a participle as far as she could see it."

"Well," said Arbutus, "I want you to go to see her. Tell her I will give her a thousand dollars if she will persuade the Prophet to have a revelation declaring that all my mothers-in-law must be sealed at once to Partridge, the coroner! Will you?"

"You must have a very deep grudge against Partridge.'

"I have! I want him to suffer. Will you go?"

"I will; and I think I can manage the matter for you. How about Sarah's aunt?"

"Run her in with the rest! Make it as hard for Partridge as we can. Give him the whole twenty-eight."

"I'll go around at once," said Lucille, and she left the room.

A gleam of savage exultation shone from Jones's eyes, as he thought of the probable completeness of his vengeance. In an hour the Ballygag returned. It was all fixed. She had a promise that the order would be issued the next morning.

Sure enough, next morning Partridge called, looking livid with rage.

"Where," said he to Jones, "are these preposterous old hags that you are trying to shove off on me? Where are they? Trot 'em out so's I can see 'em."

"See here, Partridge, I don't want you to speak in that disrespectful manner of my wife's mothers. What do you want to see them for?"

"Oh, you needn't pretend you don't know. I'm mighty certain you fixed this thing up against me. But I s'pose I've got to take 'em. So let's see 'em."

The ladies filed in. Jones announced the news to them, as gently as he could. Six fainted on the spot. Ten simply screamed. Three said they'd die rather than marry a coroner. Three, and Sarah's aunt, smiled, and said they considered it as, upon the whole, rather a good thing.

"Well, I don't," replied Partridge. "To speak plainly you're a discouraging-looking crowd. See here, you

women who are screaming there, you needn't carry on in
that manner. You don't want me any less than I want
you !"

"Partridge," said Jones, "go about it with more
suavity. You can't possibly gain their affection if you
proceed in that manner. Woo them gently."

"I don't want any interference from you," replied
Partridge. "Here, you women! Get on your things, and
come along. I'd commit suicide to get rid of you,
if it wasn't that I don't want my successor to collect
a fee for my remains. Come on now, and be quick
about it."

Then the bride and groom filed out; Mrs. Jones,
meantime, standing in a line in the hall weeping, while
Jones kept his handkerchief to his eyes and chuckled.

When Partridge reached the front gate, he turned
around, and, shaking his fist at Jones, he shouted :—

"You never mind ! I'll pay you for this, old fellow !"

And then the party proceeded to the temple, and soon
was hopelessly bound in the chains of wedlock.

Upon the departure of his wife's mothers, Jones
rubbed his hands, and, in a gleeful mood, danced about
the room with the Ballygag. He was joyful. He had
reason for joy. But there was a dire and awful retribution preparing for him. The shadow of his doom was
slowly creeping toward him.

CHAPTER IV.

THE RETURN.

FIFTEEN years had elapsed since Thompson Dunbar tore himself away from his bride, and his happy home. Fifteen years had he dragged out a dreary existence upon his lonely rock in the midst of the sea. One day he saw a ship approaching the island, and he made frantic signals to attract the attention of those on board. Twice the ship seemed to turn away from him, but at last, to his great joy, his signals were answered, a boat was lowered, and in half-an-hour he stood upon the deck of " The Golden Horn," bound for San Francisco.

The captain gave him a suit of clothes, and loaned him some money ; and as soon as the vessel touched the wharf, a few weeks later, he leaped ashore, and took the first train for Salt Lake City.

Imagine the alternations of hope and despair that distracted his mind ! Again and again he asked himself how he should find her. Would she be all alive and well, or partially dead ? Would his children be alive ? Would he find his home as beautiful as ever ? Would he go there to obtain peace and joy, or to suffer pangs of terrible sorrow ?

As he mused, the train entered the city. It was early afternoon. He thought he would go to the hotel and learn something of the truth, before he sought his cottage. It might be less terrible if he should be prepared beforehand.

The landlord of the hotel did not recognize him.

His bronzed and furrowed face, his shaggy hair and beard, his bent form, suggested nothing of the Thompson Dunbar who had gone away a decade and a half before.

Thompson sought information from the landlord.

"Did you know a man named Thompson Dunbar?" he asked.

"Yes, indeed! Knew him well. He left here fifteen or sixteen years ago. He was a sailor, you know."

"What became of him?"

'Lost, sir, lost! It's supposed so, at any rate. No word ever came from him, or about him. His ship was wrecked, we know."

"Was he married?"

"Married! Ah! that's just it, sir! He was married to thirty-three of the loveliest girls in the city. A young and charming bride, and a swarm of the dearest children."

"Did Mrs. Dunbar take it hardly?"

"Indeed she did, sir! Cried her eyes out, nearly. Went on at a most fearful rate. Everybody sympathized with her."

"Is she all alive yet?"

"Oh yes."

"And well?"

"I believe so; perfectly. She was the last time I saw her."

"When did you see her?"

"Well, I haven't seen her myself for several weeks; but my book-keeper told me he saw three of Mrs. Jones out driving yesterday."

"I was referring to Mrs. Dunbar," said Thompson.

"I know," replied the landlord ; "I say my clerk saw three of her riding out."

"But you said he saw Mrs. Jones."

"Well, don't I say he saw Mrs. Jones! You seem to be dull of comprehension."

"Maybe I am ; maybe I am. Only you are talking about Mrs. Jones, and I am talking about Mrs. Dunbar."

"But, my goodness man ! See here ! Her name *was* Dunbar when she was Dunbar's wife, wasn't it? And when she married Jones her name was Jones. Do you understand?"

"Married ! is she married ?"

"Certainly! of course!"

"Married to Jones! What Jones?"

"Why, Arbutus Jones; been married several years.'

The head of Thompson Dunbar fell upon the table, and he did not even try to keep back the sobs which burst from his overladen heart. Then a thought occurred to him. Looking up he said to the landlord :—

"And Jones? He is dead?"

"No, sir ; alive and well, and heartier than ever."

Thompson Dunbar arose and staggered from the room. He sought the privacy of his chamber, where he could weep tears of passionate grief.

An hour or two later his mind was made up. His heart was broken, but he would have one long, last lingering look at his darlings and his children before he sought the tomb.

He seized his hat and cane, and walked rapidly toward the house where he used to live. As he came near to it he recognized it as the old place but little changed. How dear it had been to him! How much he had loved it! And now another polluted its hearth-stone. Another had whitewashed its fence! He groaned as he thought of these things.

There were children playing in the yard. One hand-some boy had run out into the highway after an errant ball. Thompson spoke to him. The boy stopped to listen. Thompson recognized the suit he had on. It had been made by a pious maternal hand from Dunbar's own wedding coat.

Thompson asked the boy to sit upon the grass with him.

"What is your name, my lad?" he asked.

"William T. Dunbar, sir," the boy replied.

"And where is your father?"

"Drowned!"

"Are you sure of that?"

"Yes, sir. I know he is. Mother says so."

"Have you no other father?"

"Yes! old Jones!"

"Do you love him?"

"No, sir; not when he licks me."

"He whips you, does he?"

"Sometimes!"

Dunbar felt his anger growing hot. He felt an impulse to go in and kill Jones on the spot; but he thought better of it.

"What would you say, my dear boy," he asked, "if I should tell you that your real father is not dead?"

"I should say you were a scandalous old story-teller."

"But I do tell you so! I am your father!"

The boy laughed, when he looked thoughtfully at Dunbar and said:—

" Did you ever read the story about George Washington and his little hatchet ? "

" Yes, my son."

" Well, you'd better go home and study up that story. George couldn't tell a lie. There'll never be an anecdote of that kind written about you."

Thompson heaved a deep sigh. He was about to reason with the lad, when a sharp female voice was heard calling—

" Billee—ee—ee—ee—ee ! Billee—ee—ee ! "

" That's me !" said the boy. " She's calling me. I must go," and he jumped from the ground.

" Who is it ? " asked Dunbar.

" Old Ballygag, we call her," said the boy. " One of pa's wives ! "

The next moment the head of Ballygag was projected over the fence top, and she saw Thompson.

" Billy," she exclaimed, " you come into the house this instant! How many times have I told you not to have anything to do with those abominable tramps that come loafing about here, sneaking little children away from their parents, and breaking their mother's heart. You'll be kidnapped the first thing you know, or lost like your poor dear father, who went down to the bottom of the Pacific Ocean and was never heard of again, leastways, by any of us who ought to have heard of him if he was alive and well, which he wasn't, Heaven bless his soul ! for how could he be when he was bitten all to pieces by the sharks ? Billy, come right in this minute :

"Bluy, come rignt in this minute."—*Page* 195.

and you, you old vagabond, move on, and don't come hanging around here looking like a long-haired lunatic, scaring people's children half to death! Move on, or I'll call the police!"

And the Ballygag grasped Billy, already upon the other side of the fence, boxed his ears a couple of times and led him in bawling.

Thompson turned sadly away and began to walk towards his hotel. A tramp! And this was a woman he had once called by the endearing name of wife! Better to have stayed upon his desert island and to have died there miserable and forlorn, than to have come home to such agony and insult as this.

He determined never to seek his home again unless he should resolve to reveal himself to his wife. But the yearning that he felt was too strong. He could not resist it. When the shadows of evening fell he sought the house again. There were brilliant lights in the windows as he softly crept through the gateway and trod with noiseless footfall upon the gravelled walk. He stepped upon the porch, and hiding behind a shutter he peered through the casement.

How beautiful that sweet domestic scene! but how horrible for him! His own dear sitting-room, and yet not his!

There she was! Emma, Sapphira, Ethelberta, Henrietta, Columbia—all of her. A few of her sat about the centre table knitting. A few of her, were ranged around the wall. Lucille (his own Ballygag) was there making over one of Thompson's shirts for Jones! Everything seemed to conspire to cut him up.

There was Arbutus Jones, his old rival, sitting in an arm-chair with smiling face, dandling three infants upon each knee. He was playing with them and with forty-two other children; and in a corner were seven cradles full of babes, among them two twins and a triplet, which were rocked by a hydraulic engine operated by pellucid water from the sparkling mountain stream. Every now and then one of Mrs. Jones would look up from her work and smile at her husband and at the pranks of the little ones. They were all so peaceful, so happy, so thoughtless of the haggard man who shivered and shuddered out there in the dusky night as with wild eyes he devoured the scene.

Thompson looked eagerly at the children. In the faces of some he traced his own lineaments, his own noble Roman nose; in others he saw distinctly the facial outlines of Jones : he saw the nose which turned upward as if perpetually it would sniff the celestial constellations.

There was a great pain in his heart. He did not know what to do. He was dazed, bewildered. His first impulse was to express his emotion by bursting in the window with a brick. But he repented him of the thought. His wife was happy. It would be most horrible for him to break in upon the even current of her lives and to bring misery to that joyous household. He could not bear to do it. What right had he to make Jones's children motherless, and their father a houseless wanderer ? He would not do so fearful an act. He would go quietly away and lay him down and die. Death would be welcome to him now. He had nothing to live for, nothing to hope for, no joy or happiness any more in this cold and cruel world.

He returned again to his lodging. That night a

raging fever attacked him. For days he was wild with delirium, but at last the fever left him, and he became conscious. His life was fast ebbing away. The physician told him that the end was near. He must finish at once his connection with the affairs of this world.

He called for his landlord.

"When I am dead," he said, "I want you to have my remains prepared for the tomb, and then I wish you to send for Mrs. Arbutus Jones to come here to look upon my face."

"Which of her?" asked the landlord, sadly.

"All of her. She loved me once. She will wish to see me."

"Who are you?"

"THOMPSON DUNBAR!"

And then his tired spirit winged its way into the illimitable ether. He was no more. Perhaps he was even less.

The last message of the unhappy Thompson was conveyed to Mrs. Jones; and she came, in melancholy array, to view all that remained of him who had won the love of her youth. It was a sad, sad scene at that reunion. Thirty-two fond women in tears, and the late Mrs. Ballygag haunted by an awful fear that she had slain him by denouncing him as a tramp, snatching his boy from his arms, and driving him from his home.

Even Jones was affected. Overcome by the spectacle of his wife's grief, he wandered off disconsolate to the barroom, and tried to find solace in a variety of mixed beverages.

Cf course Coroner Partridge came; his duty was to view the body. When the shocking story was told him,

he laughed. Partridge, a man holding a high and responsible and most solemn public position actually laughed
boisterously. Persons thought that his familiarity with
woe had robbed him of sensibility ; but that was not it.
Partridge had suddenly thought of a terrible scheme of
revenge.

The funeral was held upon the following Tuesday.
Mrs. Jones attended in full force, and each of her carried
with her a modest tombstone, bearing a tribute to the
memory of Thompson Dunbar. They buried him upon
the hillside with impressive ceremonies, and then Mrs.
Jones planted the thirty-three tombstones upon the grave
and watered them with her tears.

Mrs. Jones returned to her home sorrowful, but trying
to regard the matter with a spirit of resignation. Thenceforth she would be happy with her children.

Happy ! The next morning Mr. Partridge called.
Mr. Jones and the whole of his wife were at home. After
some preliminary and original remarks about the weather,
Partridge said—

" By the way, Jones, you know my brother Joe ?"

" The druggist, you mean ?"

" Yes, the druggist. I called, ladies, to ascertain what
you think of him."

" We don't know him," the ladies said.

" And we don't want to know him," Jones added.

" Ah, that is indeed unfortunate. I hoped the ladies
knew him and admired him," said Partridge.

" Nobody," replied Jones, sarcastically, " admires a man
who looks like a clothes-pin stuck in an apple. That isn't
our favourite style of man."

"How sad!" exclaimed Partridge, calmly. "It would be so much better for all parties if there was some basis upon which to build a genuine affection."

"Affection! What in thunder do you mean?" demanded Jones, warmly, and rising from his chair.

"Why," said Partridge, "where parties have to live together, love is necessary to happiness."

"Partridge!" exclaimed Jones, "I don't want to knock out your brains ; you have so little to spare. But I shall be obliged to do so if you keep on. I'll brain you right before Mrs. Jones."

"Mrs. Jones!" said Partridge. "What Mrs. Jones? I don't see any Mrs. Jones about here."

"No more of this nonsense," said Jones, fiercely. "Quit now, or I'll throw you out of the window."

"When I quit, these ladies go with me," said Partridge, waving his hand toward the group.

"Mr. Partridge, please explain your self," appealed Sapphira.

"Certainly, madam."

"He'd better, or I'll murder him," said Jones.

"I suppose, ladies, you consider yourself the wife of this person, Jones?"

"Certainly," was the unanimous answer.

"Of course," shouted Jones.

"Well, you ain't," said Partridge.

"Why not?" they asked.

"You were married to him while Dunbar was alive. The marriage, therefore, was illegal. It was null and void. Consequently, you are now simply Mrs. Dunbar, the widow of the late Thompson Dunbar."

"Is that all," said Jones, laughing; "we'll soon remedy that. We will perform the ceremony again this afternoon."

"Oh, no you won't, Mr. Jones," sneered Partridge. "I don't think you will."

"Why not? I'd like to know who will prevent me?"

"I will."

"How?"

"Last night, the Prophet Young had a revelation. He was commanded to seal the whole of the widow Dunbar to another man. That man was my brother Joe!"

Arbutus Jones uttered a wild exclamation, which cannot be reproduced here without injury to good manners and to the morals of the reader. The thirty-three widows fell fainting upon the floor. Partridge sent a servant to call up his carriages. They came. Jones showed some signs of a resistance, but Partridge said :—

"Come, now, old fellow, you know it's of no use. This is exactly the way you played it on me, and I took my punishment like a man. You might as well do the same. Joe'll make her a better husband than you, anyway."

Jones perceived the folly of fighting against the Prophet and fate. He kissed his darlings fondly, as they began to resuscitate, and then flying out into the garden, he sought a deep recess among the trees, and cursed Joe and all the Partridges, and the Prophet, and the Church, and Mormondom generally, from Joe Smith down to Brigham, and back again. Then he left his home for ever, envious of the rest that had come to his rival, Dunbar, in the depths of the sepulchre.

Partridge took the widow down to his brother Joe's, and Joe and he tried to persuade her to accept her fate. She did so, at last, sullenly and reluctantly ; but, nevertheless, with recognition of the fact that it was a religious duty. She was married to Joseph Partridge, and to his home she came after the ceremony. He tried to make her happy by giving her free run of the gum drops, and liquorice, and jujube paste, and fancy soap, and tooth brushes in the store. But none of these things comforted her, and life became more intolerable for her every day.

Jones did call one day, when her husband was away on business at Ogden, and proposed to her to elope with him, and join the Gentiles. But none of her were willing to commit such an awful sin, excepting the high-spirited and irrepressible Ballygag ; and Jones, after considering the matter, concluded that the enterprise, in her company, had not those fascinating characteristics which had seemed to him to distinguish it when the idea first occurred to him. He bade the whole of Mrs. Partridge farewell, for ever, and, going out into the wilderness, he foreswore civilization. He joined the Kickapoo Indians, and began practising war-whoops.

As for Mrs. Partridge, she dwindled and died, one by one, and her husband bought an acre in the cemetery, in which he placed her; and when the last was gone, he went back to his desolate home, to roll pills in agony, and to moisten his salts and senna with his tears !

Miss Hammer's Lovers.

I.

JOSHUA HAMMER sat in a rustic arm-chair, upon his porch, with his feet resting upon the railing in front of him at a greater elevation than his head.

It would be interesting if some curious scientific person should inquire why it is that a man, an American especially, never sits with perfect comfort unless his legs are extended in the direction of the planetary system. There is a bare possibility that the propensity to rest in this manner may be the lingering trace of the habit our remote simian ancestors had of hanging with arms and legs from the branches of trees. The suggestion is offered, with proper respect, to the preachers of the doctrines of Evolution.

Mr. Joshua Hammer's porch completely surrounded a large and comfortable dwelling-house which stood, one story high, in the midst of a coffee plantation, in one of the most beautiful portions of the Republic of Nicaragua, Central America. Mr. Hammer was an American, a native of New Jersey. Finding the road to wealth at home full of exceedingly formidable obstacles, he had invested his savings in a fertile tract in Nicaragua, planted hundreds of coffee-trees, built himself a fine house, and begun to accumulate riches. His wife was dead. His domestic matters were cared for by his daughter, Irene, his only child, and a singularly handsome girl. At the moment of which we write, Mr. Hammer had staying with him, as a guest, Miss Sarah Appleby, his sister-in-law, the sister of his dead wife.

Mr. Hammer sat upon the porch reading a huge volume that was bound in sheepskin. It seemed to interest him deeply, for his eyes were fixed upon the page, and occasionally, as he read, he would pass his hand, in an anxious sort of way, over some portion of his body, as if he were feeling the motion of an internal organ, and was apprehensive of a fatal interruption of the performance of its functions.

Before he had finished his perusal of the volume, a tall man, with hair and beard of a reddish hue, and manifestly not a native of the region, ascended the steps to the porch, and said—

" Good morning, Mr. Hammer ! "

Mr. Hammer removed his feet from the railing, closed his book upon his thumb, and rose to welcome his visitor.

"Halloa, Knox ! Glad to see you ! Walk up, and take a chair. By the way, Knox, it is lucky you came. Where is your thoracic duct ? "

"I have it with me; I always carry it," observed Knox, without the faintest glimmer of a smile.

"Oh, I know; but what I want to ascertain is, *where* you carry it?"

"Why, *here*," said Knox, pointing to his chest. "It extends from here to here, and—"

"That's enough! that's all that is necessary. Hang it, old fellow, do you know I believe something is the matter with my thoracic duct! I never dreamed of such a thing until this morning; in fact, I hardly think I knew I had a machine of that name inside of me; but I got to reading about it and its diseases in this medical book, here, and every time a new symptom was described I thought I could detect it."

"Your imagination is too active," said Knox.

"I don't know, may be it is. I really have an idea that it's not wholesome for me to read medical works. When I look over an article on functional derangement of the liver, it seems to describe my liver with painful exactness; when I read up on the diseases of the heart, I feel as if mine might collapse at any moment; if I study up in certain bones, they begin at once to ache; if I read about scarlet-fever, or yellow-fever, or cerebro-spinal-meningitis, I get a notion that I am a victim of each malady in turn, and that if I don't put myself under treatment at once I am a goner."

"That is not an uncommon experience," said Knox, laughing. "But why do you read such books?"

"Well, you see, Irene, she has a queer kind of fondness for them; has a taste for medical science, I really believe; and I bought a lot of authorities to please her.

She can tell you more about bones and membranes and thoracic ducts in a minute than I could learn in a week."

" I am glad she shows some partiality for the medical profession," said Knox. " The fact makes me a little more hopeful."

" Hopeful of what ? "

" Why, you see, Mr. Hammer, I called this morning to tell you that I have a notion to marry Irene, if I can get your consent."

" But, has *she* consented ? "

" Well, not exactly ; but it amounts to the same thing. She said, when I asked her, that she wouldn't tell me that she loved me better than any one else in the world, but she would admit that she was extremely partial to doctors ; and you know that I am the only physician around here."

" Humph ! " said Mr. Hammer rubbing his chin. " I'm not so sure about that. How about Sandoval ? He has been coming here to see Irene a good deal lately."

" You don't class him among respectable physicians, I hope ? " demanded Knox. " He is only a wretched little quack."

" I don't know ; I don't notice that he kills any more patients than you do."

It was a quarrel in which a prudent man like Mr. Hammer did not care to take a decided part. Tecumseh Knox, of Ohio, while studying medicine in Philadelphia, formed a close friendship with a student from Nicaragua with the unreasonable name of Diego Mendoza y Herrara De Leon Gomez Maria Sandoval ; and when the two graduated, Knox, having no prospect of finding a district unequipped with a physician which he could devastate while learning the practical part of his profession, was easily persuaded by his friend Sandoval, whom he addressed continually as "Sandy," that an attempt to interfere with the death-rate of Nicaragua might afford profitable employment to more than one enterprising man, and so he accompanied Sandoval to the home of the latter in that State.

The two remained upon the best of terms for several years, until a day came when Sandoval announced himself a convert to the principles of homœopathy, and began to attack the diseases of his patients with infinitesimal doses. Then Tecumseh Knox swore eternal hatred to him; for the human heart knows no animosity so bitter as that with which the allopath regards the homœopath. And when Sandoval subsequently entered political life, Knox at once joined the party that was in opposition to the Sandoval party, and the two organizations went at each other, tooth and claw, with a new fury born of the antagonistic medical theories infused into them.

Sandoval, just now, happened to be President of the Republic. It occurred to him one night that the neighbourhood was so healthy and the collection of bills so difficult, that there might be more profit in governing the Republic : so he had a private interview with General Flynn, Commander-in-Chief of the army, and his arguments, for some reason, were so powerful with the General, that Sandoval was able to issue a fiery pronunciamento, and to summon the army to his assistance while he went around and "cleaned out" the administration.

"He is nothing but a mean little quack," said Knox, to Mr. Hammer. "Don't call that creature a physician, I beg of you!"

"Well, anyhow, I think he has a hankering after Irene, and if she chooses to regard him as orthodox in his views, I don't see exactly what we are going to do about it. Besides, he is a President, you know. That counts for something."

"If Irene thinks so I'll run him out before morning! I can scare up a revolution in this Republic in twenty minutes at any time," said Knox. "President! Why, I'll go round and evacuate the office with the toe of my boot if Irene wants political glory."

"All right," said Mr. Hammer, "I don't care anything about it myself. Irene must settle it. I'll give my blessing to whichever one of you she chooses to take. I'd rather have you, because you're an American; but Sandy's not a bad fellow for a son-in-law. He will suit me if he will suit Irene."

'That's enough," said Knox. "That is all I can ask. You say that Irene is mine if she will take me. I'll soon settle that matter. And now I'll say good morning."

As Dr. Knox withdrew, Miss Appleby came out upon the porch and sat down in one of the chairs.

"That man, Sarah," said Mr. Hammer, "wants to marry Irene."

"He does, does he? Well, I trust she won't have him! You didn't encourage him, I hope?"

"No; I encourage nobody. Irene shall marry according to her own taste. So far as I am concerned my plan is to keep on good terms with everybody. Sandoval is

in power to-day, and he throws off my taxes because he
wants my influence. To-morrow Knox may be in his
place, and what I want is to get Knox into such a frame
of mind that he will keep my taxes off. I'm for the
government, no matter who heads it. When the government refuses to help me, I shall get up a little private revolution of my own, and help myself to the government."

"I hope Irene will never marry a doctor," said Miss
Appleby. "I hate doctors."

"They are useful sometimes, Sarah."

"Yes, useful to undertakers and tombstone people.
How does a doctor know what's the matter with a man,
when he can't see into him? If he could take a lantern,
and crawl down and explore him, he might do some good."

"Sometimes they make cures, though."

"How often? There was Mrs. Martinez; she was
taken with chills; they called in a doctor. Where is Mrs.
Martinez now? I don't know where she is, but she isn't
where she ought to be. There was Diaz's coloured man;
he was a little bilious. The doctor was sent for, and
now he is an angel—that is, of course, if there *are*
coloured angels. And Mrs. Alvarado; look how she
went! Right healthy and well, excepting a pain in her
shoulder. The doctor dosed her, and off *she* went into a
better world ; I hope she did anyhow."

"And Lerdo's Jim, too."

"Yes, Lerdo's Jim; took a few pills, and the next
thing he knew he was flitting into the hereafter. Been
alive now, if the doctors had let him alone. And Mr.
Velasquez, and Mr. Alvarado, and Miss Mendez, and the
two Escobedo girls, and old Mrs. Gadara—what's become

of all of them, I want to know? Why, they've been hustled into the tomb by doctors ! That's where they are. Don't tell me ! "

" Irene doesn't seem to dislike them as much as you do. I think she is rather fond of studying medicine herself."

" I know she is ; and, Joshua, you take my advice, and repress the propensity ! This morning she put her arms around my neck, and pretended to be affectionate ; but I was suspicious, and when I pressed her, she confessed that she was examining my jugular vein ! She said she wished she could bleed me ! Wished she could bleed her aunt ! I tell you, Joshua, it is simply murderous ! "

" She never wanted to bleed me."

" No ; but, Joshua, I strongly suspect that she has more than once mixed mild doses of medicine with your tea so as to try the effect."

" Maybe that is what is the matter with my thoracic duct."

" I have no doubt of it ! Irene means well, but she is far too enthusiastic. Last Tuesday she gave the cook some medicine for spasms·that sent the girl bounding about the kitchen floor like a rubber ball. I had to sit down on her to stop her. Irene stood calmly by, and said it was 'very interesting.' I'm afraid she'll poison us all some day—accidentally, of course ; but it will be no comfort to me, when I'm dead, to know that Irene didn't mean any harm."

The conversation was interrupted by the arrival of Irene with a person in military dress, whom she introduced to her aunt, and whom her father welcomed, as General Flynn.

" Sent the girl bounding about like a rubber ball."—*Page* 211

General Terence Flynn was Commander-in-Chief of the army of the Republic. He was small in stature, and not remarkably good looking. His hair was sandy and rather thin ; and an accident of some kind had broken the bridge of his nose, and given that feature a peculiar twitch to the left, so that if the General had made up his mind to "follow his nose" through life, he would have been turning corners perpetually.

General Flynn was the son of an Irishman who came to America twenty years before the period of this narrative, and who had engaged in the business of mixing mortar with a hoe. Terence was sent to a public school, and after finishing his education he made an ineffectual attempt to study law. Then he shipped as a sailor before the mast, and when he had knocked about the world for a few years, he sailed one day into a Central American port as first mate of a schooner. Having quarrelled with the captain, he resigned his position and went to Nicaragua, where, in a year or two, he mastered the language, and plunged into the peculiar politics of the country with hearty enthusiasm.

One of the Presidents, whom he had helped into office, gave him command of the army. As the commander of the army, usually, was the only man in the country of whom the rulers were afraid; and as General Flynn was just the kind of a person to recognize a particularly good thing when he had it, he proposed to himself to retain the position during the remainder of his life.

"I met the General a moment ago," said Irene, as the party sat down, "and he was so kind as to offer to accompany me home."

"And no soldier ever performed more agreeable escort service," said the General, gallantly.

"The General was good enough," said Irene, "to give me some information that I wanted, and I asked him to come in and finish the conversation."

"What she wanted," said the General to Mr. Hammer, "was to know if, during my experience upon the battle-field, I ever witnessed a compound fracture of the *tibia*."

"Did you?" asked Miss Appleby.

"No, ma'am. I have fought thirty-four battles in this Republic, but in the whole of them only eight men have been wounded, and one man killed."

"What killed him?"

"He was bitten by a double-nosed pointer belonging to the enemy, and the bite mortified. The Nicaraguan soldier, as a rule, has an overpowering aversion to getting hurt. He hates a war with real bullets."

"But you were wounded yourself, General," said Irene.

"So I was."

"How?" inquired Miss Appleby.

"I accidentally kicked over a loaded musket at the barracks, and shot myself in the leg. The ball is in there yet," said General Flynn, touching his calf.

"And the General says I may probe for it, some time," said Irene.

"Irene!" shrieked her aunt, "I am surprised at you! Probe for a ball in General Flynn's leg? I never heard of such a thing!"

"Indeed, ma'am; and if the young lady is fond of surgery, why shouldn't she? It'll be a work of humanity. I've given her permission to try a new kind of remedy for fever upon the army. The whole military force of the Republic is at her service, if she wants to practise for doctoring."

" Isn't it splendid." said Irene. "Oh, you are too kind, General."

" I'm afraid the mortality rate will be larger than in time of war," said Mr. Hammer, smiling.

" Oh, papa!" exclaimed Irene ; " you know you're not in earnest."

"And how *is* the army, General? " asked Mr. Hammer.

"Well, from fair to middling, sir, as well as I can make out. It's a little hard to keep the exact run of things. You see, there are fifteen thousand men on the rolls, but we can't scare up more than one hundred and thirty-five for active duty, and twenty-two of them are brigadier-generals."

" Don't they get jealous of each other?" inquired Aunt Appleby.

" Yes, in time of peace ; but when there's war I have no trouble. In the fight of last December three briga-diers stayed at home because they had notes to meet. General Curculio backed out because it looked like rain, and he had lent his umbrella ; and General De Campo wrote to say that he would be unable to come because his mother-in-law had lumbago."

" You won, though, I believe ? " said Irene.

" Yes," said the General, with a proud smile. " I put a guard around the door of the executive mansion. Then I broke in a window with a brick, and when the President appeared, I told him to get out. He said he would as soon as he could get his boots on. The rascal ! he wanted time to bag the unexpended balance of the executive appropriation ! I went in and caught him at it, and marched him down stairs by the collar."

" He must have been a hero," said Miss Appleby.

" But when we put Sandoval in, I resorted to strategy. The army, you know, had shrunk up so much, and the weather was so hot, that the men hated to go into battle; and I sent word to the President that there was a cockfight in the Plaza with a Yucatan rooster on which he had a bet. He come right out, of course, and when he got back I had Sandoval in office, with eighteen men guarding him with loaded muskets. A more disgusted man than the ex-President you never saw in the whole course of your life!"

" I have an idea Sandoval won't stay in long," said Mr. Hammer.

"Oh, I don't know. I haven't quite made up my mind. It's a mere question now of homœopathy or allopathy. Knox, you know, belongs to the Opposition, and they call Sandoval's crowd 'The Pilule Party;' while Sandoval always alludes to them as the 'Phlebotomists.' Just at this moment I'm for the Pilules, but I might be made to see that the Phlebotomists have right on their side. I think the army is rather more partial to quinine and calomel than it is to medicine that the men can't feel going right to the spot. I'd like to discuss the subject with you, Miss Irene."

" Oh, do ! I'll show you all the authorities."

" Irene! you shock me," said her aunt.

" May I, pa?" asked Irene.

" I see no harm in it," said Mr. Hammer. "I'll get

you, at the same time, to draw out a map of my thoracic duct. I'd like to see how it looks."

" And the General, pa, has promised to get me a skeleton, if you will let me have it. Will you, pa ? "

" To scare your aunt with ? "

" Irene Hammer ! if you bring a human skeleton into this house, I will leave at once ! " exclaimed Miss Apple-by. " As those bones enter one door, I go out the other."

" Oh, well ; we can discuss the skeleton after a while. Suppose now we adjourn to the library," said Mr. Hammer.

" With pleasure," said the General, as he offered Irene his arm. Then Miss Appleby joined her brother-in-law, and the whole party entered the house.

II.

THE Pilule party, a few weeks later, were still in power, General Flynn having neglected to give to the arguments of the Phlebotomists against the homœopathic theories that weight which Knox felt really belonged to them.

In the meantime, President Sandoval, when he could spare time from the duties of state, became a more atten-tive visitor at the house of Mr. Hammer. He was a man of very agreeable manners, and rather a favourite with Mr. Hammer and Irene, and appreciation of this fact by Dr. Knox filled the latter gentleman with raging jealousy. Knox, in fact, began to conceit that Irene treated him with a certain degree of coldness, and he was keenly sensible of the fact that to encounter any serious obstacle in that quarter after asking Irene's hand of her father, would be to make him appear ridiculous in the eyes of the old gentleman. Knox determined to try to bring matters to a crisis.

It was a lovely evening. Sandoval sat with Irene upon the porch, behind a mass of fragrant clinging vines, while the round moon rose slowly over the distant hills and dimmed with its misty light the radiance of the myriad fire-flies that flitted, sparkling, amid the shrubbery. The two were alone. Mr. Hammer was writing in the library, and Miss Appleby had gone to bed with rheumatism in her shoulder-blade. Sandoval was speaking softly to Irene.

" Why, look at the matter, Miss Hammer! Examine it for yourself! What do you do when your nose is frozen ? "

" It never *is* frozen in this climate."

" But suppose it should be ; would you put it in hot water ? "

" Not too hot."

" No ; you would apply snow to it ; you would bury it in ice."

" Would that cure it?"

" Yes ; for like cures like. And so if your toes were frosted. Excuse me for speaking of your toes. Say *my* toes. If my toes were frosted, would I hold them to the fire ? "

" I don't know. Would you ? "

" Of course not; I should put them in cold water ; the colder the better."

" Barefooted, do you mean ? "

" Barefooted. That is the homœopathic principle. Cold for cold, heat for heat."

" Don't you ever allow mustard plasters ? I can never approve a school of medicine that rejects mustard plasters."

" In some cases, of course. Where the malady is of a mustard character, we cure with mustard. Now, for instance, what does arnica do when taken internally ? "

" Makes you sick ? "

" No ; it produces bruises upon the skin. That is wny we use it to cure bruises."

" I will put some in Aunt Appleby's tea to-morrow morning, to see if it will," said Irene.

" And so if you are warm, and wish to become cool, do you take a cold bath ? That will make you warm. You take a hot bath, and you at once feel cool. If you have a fever, you make hot applications to the body. The principle runs all through the whole list of diseases."

" How interesting!" exclaimed Irene.

" I shall be glad to unfold the whole homœopathic scheme to you at any time. You take an odd interest in such things."

" I wish I could study medicine."

" Not for the purpose of practising, I hope."

" I don't know."

" You know how much we professional men abhor women doctors. But we will not discuss that. Why not marry a physician ? "

" That would be my preference."

" It would! You don't know how happy I am to hear you say that ! Homœopathic or allopathic ? "

" That would depend, of course, on circumstances. Your plan with frozen noses strikes me very favourably."

"Let me hope that you will be favourably impressed, also, with the author of the suggestion. In fact, Irene, I love you! Will you be my wife?"

"Really, Signor Sandoval, I—I have hardly considered the—the—"

"Remember! I do not ask you to marry a mere physician. My wife will be honoured as the first lady of the Republic, for I am the President; and—"

While he was speaking, a man came up on the porch and said—

"Is Doctor Sandoval here?"

"Yes; here I am. What's the matter?"

"Only a little trouble up here at the House."

"A disturbance?"

"Yes, a kind of one."

"I must go and see what the difficulty is."

"Oh no, you needn't," said the messenger, "it's all over."

"How do you mean?"

"Knox is President!"

"Knox? Tecumseh Knox?"

"Yes."

"Where's General Flynn? Order him to call out the troops at once This is serious, Miss Irene."

"He *has* called them out!"

"Well?"

"And they came."

"Well?"

"And General Flynn and the army have declared for Knox and the Phlebotomists!"

"The perjured villain!" shrieked Sandoval.

"Yes, sir. They sent to the executive mansion, and asked if you were home; and when the coloured girl said you weren't, they dashed in, set your trunks and bedsteads in the street, and Knox moved in. He has turned out the Cabinet, confiscated all the money in the Treasury, made General Flynn Knight of the Order of San Salvador and the Blue Elephant, and he's thinking about declaring war with Costa Rica, so as to give the brigadier-generals a chance to sack a couple of towns and go in for glory! It's the biggest thing in the way of a revolution that this Republic has struck yet!"

"Well, well," said Sandoval, sadly, turning to Irene, "I don't see how this government is ever going to make its influence felt in the affairs of Europe if things go on in this manner. It's not the right way to conduct a free republic, that's certain!"

"It has the advantage of being original," said Irene.

"Yes, but it's not sufficiently impressive! Why, those bloated old despots across there in Europe roll over and laugh when they hear about such proceedings. It seems to me that what we want here is greater respect for the dignity of the Presidential office."

"Pa will be surprised when he hears about it," observed Irene.

"Why, if they had only given me a little time! But to run a man out while he is away calling on a friend! It's not the fair thing. I'd just written to the President of Venezuela to come up and pay me a state visit, too! He'll come and find Knox in office! It is a little too mortifying! But you," said Sandoval, drawing close to Irene, "you will love me still, won't you?"

"Still! Love you still! I don't think I understand you exactly."

"I thought you intended rather to intimate that you would reciprocate my feelings."

"You misunderstood me. I did not mean to convey such an impression. To tell the truth, Signor, pa wants to keep in as much as possible with the administration, and my duty is to help him."

"This is heartrending! Misfortune seems to heap itself upon me!"

"And, at any rate, I have long had an impression that if I married at all, I should choose a man who had a trepan, or consumption, or something, so that I could study his case continually."

"I have a touch of gout, now and then, if that will be of any use to you."

"I'd rather not decide so important a matter finally just now."

"Oh, very well. I'll call again, if you will permit me. Perhaps," said Sandoval, significantly, as he rose to go, "when I come again I will be President, and have the Phlebotomists under my feet!"

When Mr. Hammer came down to breakfast in the morning, he called his servant and asked,

"Jose, who is President this morning?"

"Dr. Knox, sir; unless they had another revolution after midnight."

"Knox, eh? Well, Jose, just run into the city, and inquire how things stand. And, Jose, find out the name of the Secretary of the Treasury, and come back as quickly as you can. I want," said Mr. Hammer to

Irene, "to address a note to him before he is turned
out."

" For my part," said Miss Appleby, " I consider such
governments ridiculous. But what can you expect from
a lot of doctors?"

"So Flynn has gone over to the Phlebotomists, has
he? I expected that," said Mr. Hammer.

" They drugged him, I reckon," remarked Miss
Appleby.

" Dr. Sandoval was very indignant at his conduct,"
said Irene. " But I have no doubt General Flynn acted
in accordance with the dictates of his conscience."

" General Flynn's conscientiousness, darling," said Mr.
Hammer, " is like Sandoval's doses—microscopic!"

" He hasn't enough to stick a pin in, I'll guarantee,"
observed Miss Appleby.

" General Flynn wishes to see you, sir," said a servant,
entering the room.

"Ah! he is here, is he!" remarked Mr. Hammer.
" I'll go to him at once."

" You heard about the revolution, of course," remarked
the General, as he took a chair.

" Oh yes! Sandoval is gone, is he?"

" Yes; you see there was no help for it. The Pilule
theories are not popular in the army. Sandoval, like all
these homœopathists, would persist in trying experi-
ments; he would use the troops for medicinal purposes."

" How?"

" Why, for instance, on Tuesday he made the twenty-
two brigadier-generals take ipecac., to see if it would really
produce asthma, and it did. The result was horrible.

For an entire day there were twenty-two brigadier-generals meandering about town gasping for breath. They didn't like it; they said that they loved their country, but hanged if they were going to make themselves short-winded for her benefit."

" They got over it ? "

" Certainly; took more ipecac. But Sandoval was not satisfied with that. He compelled thirty-four colonels to take sulphur, to prove that sulphur produces eruptions as well as cures them. Why, you never saw anything so disgraceful ! The whole batch of them broke out in a kind of scarlet rash, and Colonel Grambo's wife packed up and went home to her father's, because she was afraid he'd give the children small-pox. I tell you, sir, the soldiers of this Republic are not going to stand too much of that kind of thing."

" I should think not."

" So we pronounced for Knox, and ran Sandoval out. And Knox has issued a general order to me to fly-blister the entire force and to cup and bleed every man, from the commander down, so's to get their systems straight again, after Sandoval's foolishness. The men 'll not be worth a cent for a fight if we keep on putting doctors at the head of the government."

" I'm afraid not," said Mr. Hammer.

" What I came to see you about," said the General, " was to ask you to accompany me to-day to a review. Knox is going to inspect the army. Will you come ? "

" I think I will."

" And I should like you to bring Miss Irene, also."

" I will ask her, if you wish it."

"By the way, Mr. Hammer, now we are speaking of her, do you know I have had serious thoughts of proposing myself in marriage to your daughter? Would I have your consent, if the proposition should prove agreeable to her."

" Well," said Mr. Hammer, "the fact is I'd rather you would ask her first. Knox said about the same thing to me when he was here a few weeks ago. I'd prefer to have Irene make her own choice."

" Knox! You don't mean to say Knox pretends to be in love with Miss Hammer?"

" That is what he said."

" He did, did he? If I had known that last night there would have been no revolution. That settles him! I'm for the Pilules now, ipecac., or no ipecac. Knox marry her! Well, that *is* good!"

" But the review will be held, will it?"

" Oh, certainly! Duty is duty, no matter who is President."

" We will be there, then. At what time?"

" Half-past eleven, in the Plaza," and General Flynn withdrew, the-mortal enemy of the Phlebotomists.

When Mr. Hammer drove into the Plaza, with Irene and her aunt in his carriage, the army was drawn up in a line. A brass band, in which bass drum and cymbals appeared to predominate, stood at the left playing polkas and other dance music with such energy, that the military forces of the Republic were unable to keep their legs still. Upon the staff of the flag was perched a huge green parrot, the national bird; and it was expressing its opinion of the music in the wickedest objurgations that

15

the colour-sergeant, who had taught it, could discover in the Spanish language.

The army mustered one hundred and ninety-three men, the attendance being larger than usual because of the existence of a distinct understanding that there was to be no fighting. The arms were of various patterns, from the best modern rifles to old smooth-bore muskets, which kicked with such vehemence that the marksman always retained the impression that he was fired in one direction further than the bullet was in the other. There was one piece of artillery ; but it had been loaded with wet powder during a revolutionary movement several years before, and as the powder had caked and hardened in drying, it could not be dug out, and the chief of artillery was afraid to try to touch it off with a match. So the gun was used to give dignity to the appearance of things rather than for offensive purposes.

All the brigadier-generals and colonels were present, except General De Campo, whose mother-in-law had cut the buttons from his uniform and locked up the pins, to punish him for losing money upon a horse-race ; and Colonel Grambo, who had gone to bring his wife home, and to take medical advice about the eruption upon his face.

General Flynn pranced about upon a superb charger, which was the envy of the whole army. He wore a uniform which the Duke of Wellington would have been ashamed to assume after the battle of Waterloo. He was fairly covered with spangles and gold lace, and the orders on his breast were as thick as the scales upon a herring.

The General took his place by the side of the President, but it was observed that he treated Knox with marked coolness.

Sandoval sat in a neighbouring window, watching the proceedings and gritting his teeth.

The General first exercised the troops in the manual of arms. The result of each order was a wobbling uncertainty in the movements of the muskets, and the manifestation in each man of a disposition to wait until he saw what his neighbour intended to do. But the General seemed satisfied ; he was acquainted with his army ; and when the manual exercises were finished, the evolutions began. They were so surprising that Mr. Hammer laughed. Nobody in the army seemed to have the most distant idea what he was about, and the densest ignorance was displayed by the twenty-one brigadier-generals, whose manœuvres were chiefly directed by a desire to keep themselves well to the front, where the grandeur of their clothing and the ferocity of their demeanour would produce the strongest impression upon the spectators.

While the movements were proceeding, General Flynn whispered to an orderly, and a few moments later Sandoval disappeared suddenly from his window.

Finally, General Flynn saluted Knox, and asked him if he should end the review. Knox said he should like, first, to make a speech to the troops. He rode to the front, and said :—

" Soldiers ! You have the thanks of your government for the splendour and matchless precision of your manœuvres to-day. With such an army the liberties of the people are safe from the machinations of despots,

"Knox said he would like to make a speech."—*Page* 227.

and the soil of your country from the intrusion of a foreign foe. It was to save you from the traitors who were trying to destroy you with insidious poisons that I assumed the Executive Chair. I grasped the reins of power that fell from hands which were driving us to destruction. Your valour in the past is the best surety of your fidelity in the future. Let us all renew our vows to our common country, and resolve that the last drop of our blood shall be shed to save her from foreign or domestic treason! Soldiers! I salute you! Farewell!"

The President wheeled about, and as General Flynn dismissed the forces, he rode swiftly to the Executive mansion, the General behind him.

As Knox entered, he was startled to see Sandoval sitting in the President's chair, surrounded by his former cabinet officers.

"What are you doing here, sir? What do you mean?" he demanded fiercely. "Leave this place at once, or I will put you under arrest!"

Sandoval smiled grimly, and said,

" I don't think you grasp the situation exactly. Why, my gracious, man, you don't imagine that you're the President! Don't you know that there has been another revolution?"

"General Flynn," said Knox, sternly, "have that man arrested, and locked up, upon a charge of high treason! I will make out the necessary papers at once."

" It can't be done!" responded the General.

" It can't be done? Why not?" asked Knox, turning white and edging toward the door.

" Why, because I have just pronounced for him."

"And the army? I will appeal to the troops."

"Oh, you needn't mind. That order about fly-blisters fixed them. The brigadier-generals said they'd prefer asthma to blisters."

Knox reflected in silence upon the situation.

"It's of no use, Knox," said the General. "The Pilules are in possession. You might as well pack up your traps and quit! You know well enough that Sandoval's theories are sound. You vaccinate for small-pox, don't you? And you thaw out a frost-bite with ice, don't you? I've seen you do it myself. So move on now! Go; or I'll be obliged to call in the guard."

As Knox sullenly withdrew, Sandoval said to his Secretary of the Treasury—

"Collect a tax of two per cent., at once, on all the real and personal property in the Republic. General Flynn will assist you. And try to negotiate another loan of 50,000 dollars up at the banker's. We can't run this government without money; and, besides, I'm entirely out of cigars. General, give the army leave to forage in all the Phlebotomists' hen-roosts and banana-patches; and give the men new outfits from any occupied clothes'-line that you come across! Our brave defenders must not suffer if there's not a shirt left to the civilians of the Republic!"

III.

Ex-President Knox thought perhaps he might find at the Hammer mansion consolation for some of his woes. When he called he discovered that the family had not yet heard of his misfortunes. Mr. Hammer said—

"Knox, I congratulate you upon your accession to the Presidency! It is a little rough for Sandy; but, perhaps, his turn will come again, some time or other."

"It has already come, sir," remarked Knox.

"What! another revolution? To-day?"

"Yes, that red-headed little rascal, Flynn, betrayed me! Mr. Hammer, hanged if I believe General Flynn has that high-minded kind of patriotic devotion that a soldier ought to have. Epaminondas didn't tear out the government two or three times a month; and if Lord Napier ever dispersed the British Cabinet because they wouldn't let him fly-blister the army, the information has been suppressed. I am not very particular, but Flynn seems to me to lack some of the greatest characteristics of a hero."

"That thought occurred to me also," said Miss Appleby, with a slightly scornful smile.

"Why don't you and Sandy take day and day about?" asked Mr. Hammer. "You be President on Monday, and let him act on Tuesday."

"That would be against the constitution," replied Knox. "I have too much respect for that sacred instrument to violate it."

"I am glad to hear you say that. I don't think anybody would have noticed the fact if you hadn't mentioned it," said Miss Appleby.

"Ah! here is Miss Irene," exclaimed Knox, as that lady entered. "Good morning! Miss Irene, may I have a few moments' conversation with you?"

"With pleasure."

" Shall we stroll upon the porch, if your father and aunt will permit us ? "

Irene acquiesced, and she left the room with Knox. When Knox had explained to her the political situation, he said—

" But, Miss Hammer, I should not regret the loss of power and office if I could obtain something else that I want."

" What is that ? "

" Your—your—may I say it ? your love ! "

" Oh, doctor ! I can hardly promise you that. I need not attempt to go into an explanation ; but I may mention that, among other things, I cannot be perfectly sympathetic with you in medical matters. What is your remedy for a frozen nose, for instance ? "

" Why—in fact—indeed, Miss Hammer, I cannot see what relation exists between my affection for you and my theory about frozen noses."

" Dr. Sandoval says he would put it in ice. Where would you put it ? in the fire ? "

" Ah ! Sandoval has been attempting to delude you with his vile heresies, has he ? "

" Not so bad as that, I hope ; but like cures like, doesn't it ? "

" If you burned your arm, would you hold a lighted candle to the wound to cure it ? "

" I don't know."

" If you should be half-drowned would you anchor yourself in the river to recover from the shock ? If you stuck yourself with a pin would you swallow another to make yourself well?"

"I don't think I would."

" Certainly you wouldn't! But that's homœopathy! Suppose your pa should punch out one of his eyes, would you punch out the other as a remedy? I tell you, Miss Hammer, that kind of foolishness is going to carry this country to destruction, if we are not mighty careful."

"Why, here's General Flynn!" exclaimed Irene, as that valiant warrior galloped up, and dismounted. As she rose to welcome him, Knox did not seem overpowered with joy. In fact, he sat still, and looked glum.

" Good morning, Miss Hammer! Halloa, Knox, you here?" said the General, in a cheery way. "Don't be so downhearted, old man, maybe your turn'll come next."

" The doctor," said Irene, with an intent to relieve the embarrassment of the situation, " has just been pointing out the fallacies of the homœopathic theories."

" I'm beginning to see them myself," said the General.

"You are?" exclaimed Knox, with surprise.

" Doctor Sandoval almost convinced me last night that they were true," said Irene.

" Yes, I heard that he was here last night," said the General, significantly. " He told me what occurred. If I had known that he had certain aspirations, that I needn't mention, I should never have pronounced against Knox here. Told me that he loved her," said the General, in a whisper to Knox.

" I had no idea he would be made President so soon," said Irene.

"Well, he won't hold office long, I think," said the

General, winking at Knox. "I say, Knox, do you know what he did, almost the first thing after he was sworn in?"

"No; what?"

"Actually ordered me to issue rations of cinchona bark, to see if it would give the army chills! General Tejada says that Nero, in his worst days, never gave his brigadier-generals chills; and, for his part, he don't think that's the right way to go about saving the country."

"Might as well close out the whole sacred heritage of the fathers to some efficient despot at once," remarked Knox.

"Of course, and so I've pretty much made up my mind to pronounce again for you. S'pose you run up and see General Tejada, and arrange the details with him? Promise that you'll make him a duke or something, and that you'll guarantee him from fatty degeneration of the heart for a term of years, and he'll lay down his life for you."

Dr. Knox seemed to like the idea, for he arose, and bidding good-bye to Irene and the General, he mounted his horse, and disappeared down the road.

"I'm glad he's out of the way," said the General; "I merely wanted to get rid of him."

"Are you really going to pronounce for him?" asked Irene.

"I think I shall; temporarily, at any rate, until I can look around for a better man. The army is getting disgusted with these medical Presidents."

"But you don't object to medical people, General, I am sure?"

"Not when they are as lovely as you are."

"Oh, General!"

"Yes, I am in earnest, Miss Irene. I fairly worship the ground you tread upon. Won't you give me a little love in return?"

"Ah, General, you are asking too much. I have almost vowed not to marry any man who was not sufficiently infirm to be an interesting subject for scientific study."

"Then I'm the happy man. Look at my nose! How charming it would be, if we were married, for you to exercise your skill in making it straight again! You shall try, Irene. Give me your love, and you may put that feature in splints for a month at a time."

"It *would* be interesting," said Irene, thoughtfully. "The lateral cartilages are only slightly twisted. Possibly I could pull them around with a string tied to your nostril and your right ear."

"Splendid!"

"But you would present a peculiar appearance upon parade."

"Who cares?"

"I do not suppose that the osseous walls of your nose are affected in any way."

"I know they're not," said the General, with emphasis.

"It is a very fascinating study—the nose," said Irene.

"Mine?"

"Any one. Thousands of people are actually in ignorance that they smell with their olfactory peduncle."

"Hundreds of thousands of them," exclaimed the General. "I didn't even know it myself."

"And Aunt Appleby said she wouldn't believe me, because I told her that she couldn't wink without a sphincter muscle. She said she considered me insane."

" How unreasonable ! Nothing would induce me to wink without one."

"Why, a person can't even kiss without a sphincter."

" Indeed ? "

" I know it is so."

"May I try if I can ? " asked the General.

" Oh, General, it is too bad for you to make light of such a subject ! "

The General seized her hand and kissed that. She permitted it to remain in his grasp. " I didn't notice whether a—a—what do you call it ?—a sphincter helped me then or not. Let me try again ! "

Irene smiled sweetly as the General repeated the operation. When he tried it a third time she moved her hand suddenly away, and the General's nose struck the back of the chair with some violence. When he lifted his head there were tears in his eyes.

" Pardon me," cried Irene. " Did you hurt yourself ? "

" Oh, not much."

" I see that the blow affected your lachrymal glands. They are close to the nose."

" May I take your hand again ?" asked the General, clasping it without waiting for permission.

" The hand ! " exclaimed Irene. " How wonderful it is ! I have beautiful plaster Paris models of the carpus and metacarpus up-stairs. I will show them to you some day."

" It is remarkable how much you know about such things—really wonderful," said the General. " What is the bone at the back of the head called ? "

" Why, the occipital bone, of course."

"And what are the names of the muscles of the arm?"

"The spiralis and infra-spiralis, among others."

"Well, now, let me show you what I mean. I want to take a lesson in science. When I put my infra-spiralis around your waist, so, is it your occipital bone that rests upon my shoulder-blade in this way?"

"My back hair, primarily, but the occipital, of course, afterwards. But, oh, General, suppose pa should come in and see us?"

"Let him come! Who cares?" exclaimed the General, boldly. "I think I'll exercise a sphincter again, and take a kiss."

"General! how can you?" said Irene, blushing, as he withdrew his face, after executing the feat.

"Don't call me General; call me Terence," he said, drawing her closer. "You accept me, don't you? *I* know you do, Irene, darling!"

"Terence!" whispered Irene, faintly.

"What, darling?"

"I can hear your heart beat!"

"It beats only for you, my angel!"

"And it sounds to me out of order; the ventricular contraction is not uniform."

"Small matter of wonder tor that when it's bursting for joy."

"You must put yourself under treatment for it. I will give you some medicine."

"It's your own property, my darling. Do what you please with it."

"And that wound in your limb? Is the bullet in the tibia or the fibula?"

" I have not the least idea in the world what those
terms refer to, but you may analyze me until you find it.
You may cut me all up in bits, if you want to."

" Oh, Terence ! "

" The sphincter operation is the one that strikes me
most favourably," said the General.   " Let me see how
it works again."

" And Gen—Terence, I mean ! "

" Well, sweet ? "

" Have you any objection to my studying medicine,
and becoming a real physician ? "

" Not the least bit in the world !   I'll buy you a case
of surgical instruments to-morrow."

" Oh, will you ? "

" With a saw, a carving-knife a foot long, and
lancets, and a gimlet, and everything."

" Splendid !   But, Terence ? "

" What, dearest ? "

" Not a gimlet.   Doctors don't use it."

" I thought they did.   Anyhow, I'll get you gallons
on gallons of squills, and paregoric by the barrel, and
arsenic and stuff by the ton—enough to physic the
whole of Central America."

" How can I thank you ! "

" And I'll appoint you Surgeon-General of the Forces,
and make old Knox mad enough to commit suicide."

" Poor Dr. Knox !   What will he say when he hears
that we are engaged ? "

" I don't care what he says.   If he mentions the
matter to me, I'll recommend him to marry your aunt.
He and Sandoval might toss up for her."

" Aunt is going away."

" She is ? "

" To Cuba. Her brother lives there. She is going to stay with him for several months."

" Knox can wait until she comes back."

" She is not partial to doctors."

" I remember your saying so before. Her incredulity about sphincters is simply astonishing. Let me see, how was it the sphincter acted ? "

Just as the General was kissing Irene, Miss Appleby came out upon the porch, followed, a moment later, by Mr. Hammer.

"Well, upon my word, these are curious kinds of carryings on ! Irene, do you permit gentlemen to salute you in that manner ? "

" It is all right, madame," said the General, gaily. " We are engaged. I feel as if I should like to salute the entire family."

" You may kiss Mr. Hammer, if you want to ; and the cook."

" Mr. Hammer," said the General, " Irene, here, has accepted my offer of marriage. I shall be glad to discuss the matter with you at your convenience."

" I will give you an early opportunity, sir," replied Mr. Hammer. " But I am afraid this is another revolutionary movement. Knox and Sandoval will be mad enough to do anything."

" They are not dangerous, sir ; not a bit dangerous. I will take care of them ! I am sorry, Miss Appleby, to hear that you are going away. You'll miss the wedding. I hoped to dance with you."

"I don't dance."

"We shall have the army band."

"In that case, I doubt if I should be able to dance if I knew how."

"And now," said Mr. Hammer, "suppose we adjourn to dinner. General, you will join us, of course?"

"Oh, certainly. I feel as if I were mustered in as one of the family already."

And the party disappeared through the hall door.

Two important events happened on the morrow. Miss Appleby sailed early in the morning for Cuba. She had a great dread of sea-sickness. Irene gave her two infallible preventives, Dr. Knox sent her a third, and Dr. Sandoval called to leave a fourth. Miss Appleby had still others that she had seen described in newspapers, and General Flynn gave her a patent swinging berth, which oscillated with the vessel, and was warranted to make sea-sickness impossible.

As the steamer sailed away, the friends of the family waved a last adieu with their handkerchiefs, and Irene cried so hard that the General was compelled to exert himself strenuously to console her.

Later in the day, the General called the army out, and in a short speech informed the troops that the liberties of the country were in peril, and that upon them devolved the duty of snatching the government from the hands of Sandoval and the traitorous Pilules, who were threatening it with destruction.

There were one hundred and fifteen men in the ranks, and fourteen brigadier-generals. Forming the force in battle array, the General gave the order to move upon the Executive mansion. President Sandoval seemed to have heard of the proposed attack. All the doors were shut and locked, and a dozen men stood at the second-floor windows with muskets.

As the assailants approached, one of the muskets went off by accident, and instantly thirty-eight private soldiers, nine colonels, and six brigadier-generals left the ranks to go home after something that they had forgotten.

General Flynn rode bravely up to the besieged building, with drawn sword in his hand, and demanded that Sandoval should surrender.

" I'll see you hanged first ! " replied Sandoval.

" I want to avoid bloodshed," said the General ; and at the suggestion of bloodshed ten more men and a colonel remembered that they had other engagements ; " but I'm going to take this building."

" I don't think you are," replied Sandoval. " I am the lawful President of this Republic, and I'll die in defence of my rights."

"What's the use of talking in that way, Sandy?" remonstrated the General. " You know well enough you've got to succumb, so you might as well come down at once."

" Somehow, I can't see it in exactly that light."

" If we have a fight it will only break the doors and splinter up the furniture ; and if we have a siege, why, some of the men'll be sunstruck sitting around out here in the heat. You ought to surrender out of consideration for them."

" Knox's medicine will kill 'em quicker than sunstroke," replied Sandoval.

" If I get up there, I'll pull your nose, you infinitesimal doser!" shouted Knox, in a rage.

"You'd better attend to the men who are sore from head to foot with your poisonous fly-blisters before you come around lecturing me, you salivating old rascal!" replied Sandoval.

"Will you surrender or not?" asked General Flynn.

"Certainly I won't," replied the President.

"Well, then, I'll put you and your traitorous Pilule Cabinet out in the street in less than half-an-hour! See if I don't!"

The General dismounted, and calling the remaining brigadier-generals around him, he held a council of war. A few moments later a detachment of troops commanded by General Tejada marched off down the street. Sandoval and his brave defenders watched them with mingled curiosity and alarm. After a brief interval the detachment returned, dragging a fire-engine by a rope. It was stationed beneath Sandoval's window, and the army, equipped with buckets, formed a double line to the river.

The meaning of the manœuvre dawned upon Sandoval and his adherents, and they closed the windows quickly. The engine was manned. The army began to fill the tanks with water. General Tejada seized the nozzle of the hose and mounted a ladder which Knox had placed against the wall.

When the heroic General reached the top-round, he smashed the window with his fist and turned a two-inch stream of water upon the Executive department of the Pilule government. The department, followed by Sandoval, dashed into another room. The General leaped through the window, dragging the hose with him, and pursued the fugitives. He drove them from point to point

"He turned a two-inch stream upon the Executive Department."—*Page* 242.

until they flew, pell-mell, down the main staircase. The General turned the stream upon them with full force, and they were compelled to choose between seeking refuge in the street and being drowned. They unlocked the door, and in an instant they were in the hands of a guard. Knox entered the doorway to speak to General Tejada, and that gallant soldier, being full of enthusiasm, did not recognize him and turned the hose on him with such vehemence that he was swept off his feet and carried clear out into the street.

The revolution was achieved! The Phlebotomists had won the day. Knox was sworn in at once by the chief justice, who laid down his bucket while he performed the solemn ceremony, and the Pilule Cabinet, drenched, draggled, discouraged, and miserable, was sent home in search of dry clothing.

"It was a big thing, Knox, wasn't it?" said General Flynn.

"It was genius, General, that idea about the fire-engine!"

"I am going to write a book about it. Wars are too sanguinary under existing systems. I shall recommend the adoption of squirt-guns in place of rifles, and fire-engines instead of artillery. Give me enough fire-engines and I'll whip the biggest army in Europe without killing a man!"

IV.

THE Knox Cabinet had been in office about a fortnight when Mr. Hammer received the following letter from his brother-in-law, an American merchant doing business in Havana.

" DEAR JOSHUA :

"I have sad news to communicate. Sarah reached this port upon the steamer on the 15th instant. She was greatly prostrated. She took, before starting upon the voyage, several preventives of sea-sickness, and these, combined with the movements of an oscillating berth in which she slept, made her so ill that her life was despaired of by the captain. The surgeon told me that he had not seen so violent a case of sea-sickness during the whole of his professional career. The result was that when she reached my house she took to her bed, and expired on the morning of the 17th instant. In accordance with her last wishes her remains will be forwarded to you upon the next steamer * * * * "

It happened just at this time that Major General Bussera, the Minister of War of Venezuela, who had been visiting Cuba upon public business, was stricken by yellow fever. He died within a few hours, and arrangements were made for conveying him home with much pomp and circumstance in the Venezuelan frigate, *El Cuspador*, which lay in the harbour of Havana.

By some most unlucky mischance the boxes containing the remains of Major General Bussera and Miss Appleby were precisely alike, and as they lay upon the wharf, near to each other, the Venezuelan sailors of course carried Miss Appleby away to their ship, while the dead Major-General was stowed away in the hold of the packet ship and sent upon a voyage to Nicaragua.

The manifestations of grief upon the frigate *El Cuspador*, as she turned her prow homeward, were elaborate and affecting. Minute guns were ordered to be fired during the entire voyage. A guard surrounded the bier, which was draped with black velvet and silver, and alternating brass bands played melancholy dirges night and day. It was estimated that at least two tons of powder were fired away during the trip, and that several hundred thousands cubic feet of wind were expended by the bands, to say nothing of muscular exertion.

Upon the arrival of the remains at Caracas, a state funeral was prepared, the entire city was draped in mourning, the streets were filled with people, the army was put into line, and the coffin was placed, amid imposing ceremonials, in a magnificent tomb built at the public cost. Foreign undertakers who were present said that it surpassed anything of a funereal nature that they had ever witnessed. The whole nation was in tears ; the heart of a great people was wrung with anguish, and the bills amounted to ten or fifteen thousand dollars.

The mortal part of Major-General Bussera arrived in good time in Nicaragua, and it was taken to Mr. Hammer's house.

General Flynn was present when the box came. He felt that he had a sacred duty to perform in consoling Irene in the hour of her affliction. When the covering of the box was removed Irene exclaimed—

" How much she has changed ! " and then Irene began to cry.

" I wouldn't have known her," said the General.

" It doesn't look a particle like Sarah, that is certain," remarked Mr. Hammer.

" There cannot be any mistake about it, I should think," observed the General.

" Oh, no ; of course not," remarked Mr. Hammer.

" But aunt was not bald," said Irene.

" And her nose turned down, instead of up," said Mr, Hammer.

" It is very curious," remarked the General. " But death produces wonderful changes."

" We cannot comprehend these mysteries," said Mr. Hammer, " but I should like to know how her hair happened to turn black. It used to be grey."

" And she had no double-chin," said Irene.

" Well, well!" remarked Mr. Hammer, " we must accept facts as they are. I have no doubt that it is all right."

The General led Irene away, weeping, and Mr. Hammer went to the city to arrange for the funeral. The body was interred in the cemetery on the morrow. Only the family, General Flynn, and the clergyman were present.

About a month later, a Venezuelan frigate sailed into the harbour, and sent eight boat-loads of soldiers ashore. Nobody could imagine what the object of the invasion was. President Knox, however, suspected that the President of Venezuela had come to pay that state visit promised to Sandoval.

The soldiers said nothing. They marched quickly through the streets and out to the cemetery. Proceeding to the Hammer family vault, they forced open the door, and seized the casket containing the body of Major-General Bussera. Then they placed a keg of powder in the tomb, fixed a slow-match in it, and retreated to a safe distance to watch Mr. Joshua Hammer's sepulchre fly whizzing in fragments through the air.

Then they returned to the ship with the General's remains, hoisted anchor, and sailed away.

But where was the late Miss Appleby during this outrageous proceeding? It was with difficulty that any accurate information could be obtained ; but report said that when the Bussera family discovered that they had buried another person than their noble relative, they were so indignant that they took the casket down to the beach and tossed it into the sea. Other rumours, not authenticated, however, declared that it floated away, and for a month or two it sailed around the Gulf of Mexico, bumping up against Guatemala and Belize, being shot at for a shark, and affording a roosting-place for sea-gulls. Finally the captain of a Jamaica schooner, report said, tied an old anchor to it, and sank it in sixty fathoms of water.

When these facts became known in Nicaragua, and the real purpose of the Venezuelan invasion of the cemetery was disclosed, the most intense excitement prevailed. There was a feeling that the sacred soil of the Republic had been outraged by foemen, and that the dearest rights of one of the citizens of the nation had been trampled under foot with manifestations of scorn and insult. General Tejada declared that if he could transport two fire-engines to Caracas he would bring Venezuela to her knees. General De Campo swore that blood alone could wash out the stain, and he would be one to volunteer to invade Venezuela with fire and sword—if his mother-in-law would let him. General Curculio sharpened his sword upon a grindstone, and loaded both pistols to the muzzle, apparently with an intent to destroy Venezuela single-handed ; but he was suddenly laid up in bed with a bilious attack, caused by a fa.se report that President Knox had declared war.

Knox said that war must come; but he felt as if the country needed time to prepare for a long and bloody struggle. Dr. Sandoval vowed that if he were in office he should fit out a hostile expedition at once; and he asserted, further, that the trouble might have been avoided if the deceased persons who caused it had not been put to death by the murderous treatment of the allopaths. General Flynn seemed disposed to hold his peace. He merely said that if he was wanted to uphold the government of his country, his superior officer knew where to find him.

Knox dilly-dallied so long with the matter, that Sandoval resolved to appeal to the country upon the question of Irene's aunt. He issued a proclamation, in which, pointing to the President's manifest indisposition to resent a wanton and fearful indignity to the Republic, he dwelt upon the fact that the crisis might have been avoided if General Bussera had had homœopathic treatment instead of the blistering and drenching with which Knox had for years striven to exterminate the human race; and, finally, he promised that if the people would elevate him again to the Presidency, he would obtain prompt and certain satisfaction from Venezuela.

Knox replied next day with a proclamation, in which he said that he had already made the following demand upon the Venezuelan Government, and that he should enforce it at the point of the bayonet if it should be refused :—

1. A complete and satisfactory apology.

2. An indemnity of fifty thousand dollars.

3. The fishing up of Irene's aunt from the bottom of the Gulf of Mexico.

4. Restoration, in blue marble, with Gothic finish, of the Hammer sepulchre.

5. Payment of Mr. Hammer's undertaker's bill.

While the matter was pending between the two Governments, and while some of the statesmen of Nicaragua were considering if it would not be a good idea to call a Central American Congress to discuss and dispose of the subject of Irene's aunt, President Knox, one evening, rode out to Mr. Hammer's house. On his way thither he was overtaken by General Flynn. He was surprised to learn that the General had the same destination.

" Flynn ! " said Knox, " if I tell you something, will you keep it a dead secret ? "

" Of course ! "

" I tell you because I want you to help me with old Hammer. Why, the fact is, Flynn, I have about made up my mind to marry Irene ! "

" No ! " exclaimed the General.

" Yes, sir. She has kind of half consented, and I'm going to press her this evening for a final answer. Promise me that you will trot the old man off somewhere, so as to give me a clear field ! "

" I'll see about it."

" And if you have a chance, say a good word for me. I want his blessing. He has lots of money."

" Lots of it."

" And, Flynn ! "

" What ? "

"I wish you'd just mention, accidentally, as it were, in the presence of Irene, that Sandy is a phenomenal ass, and that his medical system is a sure road to sudden death!"

"Anything else that I can do for you?"

"N—no! I believe not! Well, you might perhaps just say that I have written a note to the President of Venezuela, to say that if he don't sail out and personally dive for Irene's aunt, I'll kick him, if I have to chase him from the Gulf of Mexico to Terra del Fuego. Something of that kind."

Irene was at home, and she gave both visitors a hearty welcome. After a few moments' conversation, President Knox began to wink furiously at the General, as a hint for him to drop out and search for Mr. Hammer; but the General seemed not to notice it. The President, therefore, was obliged to confine his remarks to unsentimental topics, and he began to tell Irene about the discovery of hot springs on General Curculio's plantation, and of an effort the General was making to plant his coffee-trees around the springs, in the hope that when he bored them, as the New Englanders do their maples, the sap would run in the shape of hot coffee. During his observations, the servant announced Dr. Sandoval.

When Sandoval entered, he was rather startled to see the two leaders of the Phlebotomist party; but, after greeting Irene politely, he bowed stiffly to them, and concluded to remain.

"Have you heard anything further about your aunt, Miss Hammer?" asked Sandoval, maliciously.

Nothing," replied Irene, with some emotion.

"The Government is conducting negotiations," said Knox, with dignity. "We shall soon be able to take definite action."

"It is high time something was done, I think," said Sandoval, to Irene.

"Miss Hammer is well aware that nothing more could be done than has been done," replied Knox, winking again at the General, to persuade him to back him with the story of his note to the Venzuelan President. But the General held his peace.

"It is so unfortunate, too," said Sandoval to Irene, "that Miss Appleby did not have proper medical attendance in Cuba."

"Your method, I suppose, when a person is sea-sick, is to give them squills, or something to make them sicker," said Knox.

"My method is not to let a person die from sea-sickness in two days."

"You'd kill 'em in one day, I reckon," said Knox.

"Miss Hammer, you appreciate the absurdity of this kind of talk? Miss Hammer, General, prefers the homœopathic system," said Sandoval.

"Does she indeed?" replied the General.

"On the contrary, she inclines to the regular school. Do you not, Miss Irene?" asked Knox.

"I think," said Irene, "that my preference is for the eclectic method."

"The eclectic?" shouted Knox.

"It is impossible!" exclaimed Sandoval.

"That is the system I intend to study," said Irene.

"Are you going to study?" asked Knox.

"Yes."

" Not with a view to practise, of course ? " said San-doval.

" I intend to practise when I receive my diploma."

" To set up as a physician ? " exclaimed Knox.

" Yes."

" A woman doctor ! Well, who would have believed it ? " said Sandoval.

" Are you in earnest ? " asked Knox.

" She is," said the General.

" Well, then, of course," said Knox, with a hysterical laugh, " I need go no further."

" No further in what ? " asked the General, rather fiercely.

" Well, as I regard a woman practitioner as—as—well, I will not say what—of course, Miss Hammer, all is over between us. I retract my recent offer."

General Flynn laughed.

"What are you laughing at ? " asked Knox.

" I don't see anything amusing about it," said San-doval. " My medical society would expel me if I should confess acquaintance with a female physician."

" Gentlemen," said the General, rising and assuming a martial air, " perhaps this had better stop. Knox, you say you withdraw your offer to marry this lady ? "

"Yes, sir ! "

" Well, as she is already engaged to marry me, that performance appears to be, in a certain sense, superfluous. She wouldn't have you if you were the only man left. She hates you worse than your patients hate your doses of assafœtida "

"Engaged to you!" shrieked Knox. "Impossible!"

"And, Sandy," said the General, "your medical society won't permit you to know her? Well, sir, for fear that remarkable association should fail to act promptly, I give you notice that the acquaintance is discontinued from this date. Good morning! By the way, Knox, as you go out, just tell to Mr. Hammer your story about the President of Venezuela, and mention your views about the dimensions of Mr. Hammer's fortune."

The two physicians gritted their teeth, smiled grimly, bowed politely, and withdrew.

"Knox," said Sandoval, "this is a queer business."

"Very!"

"It means war on the administration, I think."

"On you, too."

"Wouldn't it be a good idea to tie together?"

"I think so."

"Here's my hand!"

"And here's mine; and we'll stand shoulder to shoulder in the fight against Flynn, women doctors, and the eclectic system!"

General Flynn nudged up close to Irene when the visitors had gone, and as he took her hand, he said,

"Well, that's a good riddance, anyhow. I knew they wouldn't like your studying medicine. There is not enough work for them, as it is, and there'd be less if there was a doctor that cured instead of committing murder!"

"I'm afraid they are very angry, Terence; perhaps they will do us some harm?"

"Not unless they can persuade us to take some of their medicines, and we are far too intelligent for that."

Mr. Hammer came in, and the General explained the situation to him. He laughed, but presently, becoming grave, he said,

" But, Flynn, how about my taxes ? Knox will be sure to try to collect them for all the back years, as soon as he returns to his office."

" We can settle that easily enough."

" How ? "

" Why, let's have another revolution ! I'll pronounce for you, and promise the country that as soon as you are President you will bring Venezuela to terms ; then you can knock off your own taxes. I will be your son-in-law, and we can keep this Government running as a kind of a nice little family affair."

Mr. Hammer liked the project, and he agreed to it. In the morning, General Flynn issued a proclamation in which he declared Knox deposed from the Presidency as a traitor, in consequence of his neglect to avenge the wounded honour of his country. Mr. Hammer was announced as his successor, and in a general order to the army, Irene Hammer was promoted to the position of Surgeon-General of the Forces.

Under ordinary circumstances, General Flynn would have carried the army with him, but as soon as the news spread among the men that Hammer's success meant actual war with Venezuela, quite one-half of the entire force mutinied and went over to Knox and Sandoval. Among the seceders were all the brigadier-generals but Tejada. General De Campo said that he liked Flynn well enough, but he would never accompany an army upon a campaign in summer time unless there was ice-cream in the commissary department. General Curculio said that if Venezuela had some other name he would fight her to the last gasp, but he had sworn, when he was a boy, never to conquer a country that spelled its name with a V. Colonel Grambo was actually hungry for a fight, but he was reading a serial story in a magazine, and he couldn t bear the idea of going to Venezuela, lest he should miss one of the numbers.

The half of the army that remained faithful to General Flynn did so because the men knew that the General had a habit of making his revolutions successful, and they preferred being upon the side that controlled the pay-rolls and the supplies.

On the following day General Flynn sent a note to Knox, commanding him to surrender his office. Knox kicked the messenger down the Executive stairs. Then Flynn wrote another note, saying that he should move on the enemy at once.

General Flynn's half of the army was put under arms promptly, and in a few moments it moved in from the barracks towards the town. The Knox and Sandoval army were discovered drawn up in line of battle behind a post-and-rail fence just outside the town.

When General Flynn saw it, he halted his force, and threw out four skirmishers toward the foe. The skirmishers advanced twenty feet, but as the Government force actually aimed at them with muskets, they fell back suddenly in disorder upon the main line.

General Flynn then rode bravely to the front, and commanded the enemy to surrender. In reply, Colonel Carboy, one of Knox's aids, threw an old boot at him.

The General resolved to give battle at once. Riding back to his line, he showed the enemy to his men, and ordered them to charge bayonets and take the position. Not a man stirred. " Then fire at them !" shrieked the General.

Instantly every musket was discharged, and instantly the Government army arose from behind the fence and fled. Then Flynn's army dashed forward and secured itself at the fence. A moment later Knox's army fired a volley, and at once Flynn's heroes fell back to their own line.

These brilliant manœuvres were continued for several hours; and the fence was held by each army eleven successive times. The war began to be somewhat monotonous, and General Flynn resolved to execute a flank movement. He had just issued the necessary orders, when the booming of cannon fell upon his ear. There was heavy firing for several minutes, and both armies received such a scare as they had never before experienced. Scouts sent to the top of an adjacent hill returned with the startling report that a Venezuelan frigate was in the harbour bombarding the town. No sooner was the announcement made, than the two armies arose simultaneously, and fled towards the interior, making the best speed ever known in military operations in that region.

General Flynn was left alone upon the field of battle. He felt discouraged, and naturally so. Sitting down upon a log, he picked up a piece of brick and began to sharpen his sword, when he heard sounds that indicated a woman in distress. Proceeding to a neighbouring thicket, he found Surgeon-General Irene Hammer, kneeling beside an open case of surgical instruments, sobbing.

17

" ' I think it's real mean,' said Irene."—*Page* 259.

"Why, my darling, what is the matter?"

"I think it's real mean!" said Irene, crying harder.

"Mean, my angel? What is mean?"

"Why, that nobody is wounded! You've been fighting nearly all day, and there is not even a man with a scratch to put court-plaster over! I didn't expect such treatment as this."

"I am very sorry, pet, but I couldn't help it."

"What's the use of having a Surgeon-General," said Irene, looking up with tearful eyes, "if nobody gets hurt? I don't believe this can be the real kind of war. Napoleon and the Duke of Marlborough always had wounded."

"Yes, but, Irene, dear—"

"If you really loved me, you would at least have had one sabre cut for me to sew up, or a bullet to probe for. It's a scandalous shame, that's what it is."

"If you'll forgive me, you shall have the very first case of accident that happens in the town, whether it is a man kicked by a mule or shot with a bullet."

"Will you promise?"

"Yes, on my word of honour! And, Irene?"

"Well?"

"If that frigate out there really did shell the town, perhaps there may be something for you to do, as it is— somebody blown in half, or splintered up, somehow?"

"Suppose we go right in to see if there is?"

"Very well. The armies have fled, and I am going to meet the invader alone. The Commander-in-Chief is bound to do his duty, at all hazards! The cowardly rascals!"

The General helped Irene to mount her horse, and
when he had leaped into his own saddle, the two galloped
toward the town. As they entered the main street, they
were surprised to see the flags flying, and the city in gala
attire. The General could not imagine what was the
matter. With his companion he pressed on toward the
Executive mansion; but when he approached it he was
startled to see a guard of foreign soldiers drawn up in
line before the door. His first impulse was to retreat,
but just then he perceived Mr. Hammer, now President
Hammer, leaning from a window, and with smiling face
beckoning the General and Irene to come to him.

"Well," said the General, "it is the queerest thing I
ever encountered; but as your father wants us to go, I
reckon we had better do so!"

"Of course," said Irene.

As they rode up, the guard presented arms, and the
General, helping Irene to alight, escorted her up the
stairs. As they entered the President's room, Mr. Hammer greeted them, and said—

"Ah! glad to see you! You have just come in time.
Let me introduce you to President Maracaybo, of Venezuela? Mr. President, my daughter! General Flynn,
the Commander-in-Chief of our army!"

"Delighted to meet you," said President Maracaybo,
as he shook hands with the General and Irene.

"You are very kind," said Irene.

"Gives me much pleasure, I assure you!" said the
General. "Only I don't quite understand the—the—"

"Of course you don't," said President Hammer,
laughing. "His Excellency has come to pay us a long-

promised visit, and we propose to give him a hearty welcome."

"But the cannonading that we heard?" said Irene.

"He came in the frigate *El Cuspador*—splendid vessel!" said Mr. Hammer, "and she was firing a salute."

"Our international complication, then," said the General, "is in a fair way of being arranged?"

"Bless your soul, man, there is no complication," said Mr. Hammer.

"How then—what is—how about the—the—that is, how about Irene's aunt?" demanded the General.

"Your Excellency must answer that question," said Mr. Hammer, turning to the visitor.

"Certainly," said the latter gentleman.

Then he arose, opened the door of the adjoining room, and remarked—

"My love?"

A lady appeared, took his hand, entered the room with him, and lifted her veil.

It was Sarah Appleby, Irene's aunt.

Irene uttered a little scream, and fainted. The General turned as white as the wall.

"You here!" he said. "We thought you were dead!"

"Is it really you, aunt?" asked Irene, faintly, as she opened her eyes.

"Certainly it is! Who else should it be? How are you, my child? I am glad to see you again, I assure you. And, General, you seem to be well, as usual?"

"Yes; but—but—how do you explain the—"

"It was all a mistake, sir," said Irene's aunt. "I was not really dead, only in a condition of suspended ani-

mation—a mere case of catalepsy. I revived the very
next morning after they put me in that abominably damp
tomb. If I find out who circulated those wicked stories
about me floating in the Gulf, I'll pull his nose."

" Well, Miss Appleby—" began the General.

" No," interposed President Maracaybo, "not Miss
Appleby! She is now Madame Maracaybo! She is my
wife. Her case interested me so much that I became
interested in her. She accepted me, we were married,
and here we are !"

Irene flew into her aunt's arms, and kissed her tenderly Then President Maracaybo approached, and said—

" Permit your uncle to salute you, also !" and he kissed
her affectionately. He was about to repeat the operation,
when the General said—

" Once is enough, I think, your Excellency," and led
her away.

" So you will be at our wedding, after all ?" observed
the General to Irene's aunt.

" Oh, yes."

" And I shall dance with you ?"

" You may, if you can persuade the army band to
remain quiet long enough."

" And I will dance with my niece," said President
Maracaybo.

" I'll make the band play, and stop you, if you do,"
replied the General, with a look between a smile and a
frown.

The wedding followed within a week, and it was the
most brilliant festival ever witnessed in the Republic. All
the brigadier-generals were present in full uniform. They

swore allegiance to the Hammer Government as soon as they were perfectly sure that the war was over. President Hammer put an end to the revolutionary business, and he conducted affairs with a strong hand. His first act, after the wedding, was to send Knox and Sandoval into perpetual exile. They went to Yucatan, and began to practice medicine with the result that the death-rate of the country, in a single year, increased a little over fifteen per cent.

Mr. Skinner's Night in the Under-World.

I.

I N the reading-room of an hotel at Eisenach,
Central Germany, Mr. Bartholomew G.
Skinner, of Squan, New Jersey, United
States of America, sat with his feet upon
the edge of a table.

Mr. Skinner had acquired a fortune at
Squan. He began as the keeper of a summer
hotel, and with money earned in this avocation
he had engaged in speculations in land upon a large
scale. Having bought up vast tracts of "pine barrens"
in West Jersey—great stretches of sandy loam, on which
grew nothing but stunted pines, scrub oaks, and huckle-
berry bushes; he cleared them, laid out farms and
villages, invited immigration, and advertised far and wide
over the civilized earth the cheapness of his lands, the
fertility of the soil, and the healthfulness of the climate.
People came, saw, bought, and took up their residences
there; and so it came to pass that while Mr. Skinner

amassed a fortune, thirty or forty thousand persons acquired cheap homes, beautiful towns dotted the former desert, and vines, and peach-trees, and waving grain stood in luxuriant growth where nature had for centuries supplied nothing but vegetation that was useless to man.

Mr. Skinner was, in a high and noble sense, a bene-factor of his race. The man who turns a great wilderness into a lovely garden as he did, deserves even a richer reward than he counted when he summed up his profits.

Mr. Skinner was travelling through Europe for enjoy-ment. He was a man who had had little education in his boyhood; but he had read much, and thought much; and concerning the practical affairs of life he was fairly well informed. He was a practical man, and he prided himself upon the fact. There was no nonsense about him, and not a great deal of sentiment, excepting that which has a basis of solid common sense. The natural movement of his mind was always toward the bottom facts; and where a matter was clearly within human ken he never accepted theory, or tradition, or guess work, but proceeded to examine it for himself, in his own way, and to form his own conclusions.

The contempt entertained by Mr. Skinner for some of the methods, ideas, and superstitions which he encoun-tered during his journeying, could hardly be expressed, and he did not often try. He fully realized that every-body's way could not be his way; that large allowance must be made for differences of condition in which men are brought up, and that only a fool goes through the world condemning aloud everything that does not conform to his standard. But Mr. Skinner was not a silent man. He liked to talk, and he talked with directness and confidence. He was utterly simple, and without affectation—so much so, that those who had been accustomed to stand in awe of persons, whom Mr. Skinner never hesitated to regard with easy familiarity, mistook for rudeness what was really nothing but absolute unconsciousness that there was any occasion for a manifestation of reverence. A man of intense simplicity is apt to give great offence to those who are keenly sensitive to the requirements of a very artificial etiquette ; and Mr. Skinner often did so. But he never willingly offended, for a kinder heart than his never beat in a human bosom.

Mr. Skinner was reading a book as he sat with his feet nearly as high as his head. It was a Traveller's Guide, and the passage that interested him at that moment described the Horselberg, just beyond Eisenach, and told in a very prosy way the wonderful story of Tanhaüser.

Mr. Skinner had never encountered that legend before. He read it through twice, first hurriedly, and then more carefully. Then he turned the book over upon the table, rose from his chair, and went to the window.

He looked out, and there, in full view, was the very mountain alluded to in the story. Mr. Skinner stood for several minutes gazing at it, with his hands behind his back. He appeared to be considering something. Presently he turned about and rang the bell. When the waiter appeared, Mr. Skinner said to him in English :

" What mountain is that, over there ? "

" The Horselberg, sir."

"Is that the hill Tanhaüser went into?"

"Yes, sir; so they say."

"You've read about it, have you?"

"Yes, sir."

"Do you believe that story?"

"Oh, I don't know, sir. I think I do. Everybody here believes it."

"Ever been over there?"

"Many a time, sir."

"To the place where Tanhaüser got in?"

"That's what they say, sir."

"I want you to take me to that spot."

"All right, sir; when?"

"Late this afternoon. I want to get there by the shortest known route."

"Very well, sir."

"You come into this room at seven o'clock precisely, and I'll be ready."

"Yes, sir," said the man, as he withdrew.

As Mr. Skinner walked back to the window to take another look at the mountain, he said to himself:

"If there's anything in that story I'm going to find it out. If Tanhaüser could get in, why can't I get in? And if I do get in, I'll bet a dollar I'll play a better hand than he played, see if I don't!"

Then Mr. Skinner sat down by the table and began his eleventh letter to the *Barnegat Advertiser*, the newspaper through which he conveyed to the people at home his impressions of Europe.

At seven o'clock Mr. Skinner was in the room equipped for his undertaking. He had a traveller's satchel containing a few articles swung over his shoulder; he had placed a loaded revolver in his pocket; upon his arm was a light overcoat, and in his hand he carried an umbrella.

Presently the servant entered, and ordering him to lead the way, Mr. Skinner started, stopping for a moment as he went out to address a note to the proprietor of the hotel, who was temporarily absent.

After a long walk, and some rather stiff climbing, the goal was reached.

" This is the place, is it ?" asked Mr. Skinner.

" Yes, sir ! "

" Humph ! Well, you can go home now," said Mr. Skinner, putting a bit of money into the man's hand.

" Not going back with me, sir ? "

" No ; I intend to stay here all night. I'll return in the morning, most likely. You needn't wait ! "

The man looked at him with mingled amazement and curiosity, but as it was plainly apparent from Mr. Skinner's manner that he was not convulsed by extraordinary emotion of any kind, and was neither contemplating suicide, nor likely to be much affected by supernatural manifestations if any should appear, the man turned slowly about and began to retrace his steps.

It was early twilight, and Mr. Skinner's first act was to take a look at the place. It was upon the mountain's side, a sort of a small plateau, covered with grass and a sparse underbrush. The mountain rose high and black above him, bare and rugged to the top. Trees were thickly clustered upon each side of the plateau, and beneath him in front the ground sloped away somewhat precipitously, its sides clothed with verdure, excepting here and there where the rain had washed the earth into gullies, or the stones had slid downward and marked their narrow paths by stripping away the grass.

Out beyond the base of the mountain he could perceive through the gathering dusk the indistinct outlines of the town, with now and then a light shining from a window.

Mr. Skinner admitted to himself that the loneliness of the place was somewhat oppressive ; but he was in search of truth, and he had not expected to be quite so comfortable as he would have been at the hotel.

It grew darker, and the air became chilly. Mr. Skinner put on his overcoat ; then he threw his umbrella upon the ground, seated himself upon it, and lighted a cigar. Upon the whole it was not disagreeable ; there was a flavour of adventure about it which pleased him.

As the darkness deepened the lights in the town increased in number, and he even thought he could distinguish his hotel by the glow about the front windows.

It was a magnificent night. The stars twinkled brightly as he looked up at them, and he felt a good deal of satisfaction in recognizing most of the constellations. Those were the very planets that he used to study from his own front porch at Squan. They had an air of old acquaintanceship which was delightful. He had not seen anything since he left the States that reminded him so strongly of home. It was a little odd to think of those heavenly bodies sweeping over Squan, missing him, and after crossing the continent and the Pacific Ocean finding him sitting on his umbrella out here on a wild mountain in Germany.

The damp earth and the heavy odours of the vegetation about him brought up peculiar recollections also.
We remember smells longer than anything else in our
experience. The Horselberg, on that calm and peaceful
night, had the odours that greeted his nostrils on the
second night at Gettysburg, when he lay upon the hillside, in the dusk, with his regiment, too weary of blood
and carnage even to think of to-morrow's battle, which
would bring death to thousands about him, and woe to
other thousands far away from the battle-field.

And so he mused and smoked, and smoked and
mused, as the hours went slowly by. Once or twice he
caught himself nodding ; and then he would rise and
walk about for a little space to rouse himself.

At last, however, his thoughts became confused, and
he knew no more until suddenly he was conscious of
the faint reverberations of a distant town clock. He
counted the strokes mechanically, and there were
TWELVE.

He had been asleep quite an hour. He was about to
get up and walk again, when he heard a noise close to
him, very faint, but distinct and musical. In a moment
he saw that the turf about about him was lighted by a
glow softer and less clear than moonlight ; and he perceived that a host of tiny figures capered about amid the
grass.

All of his senses instantly were upon the alert. He
pressed his finger-nails strongly against his palm, to be
sure that he was not dreaming. No ; he was wide
awake—he thought himself sure of that ; and although
he felt a most intense curiosity, and he realized that his

heart was beating with accelerated motion, he was per fectly cool and fearless.

Looking steadfastly, he could perceive that the moving creatures were miniature men and women, dressed in fantastic garb. They danced about to and fro, here and there, uttering few sounds and seeming wholly unconscious of the presence of an observer. Mr. Skinner knew that they were elves ; they belonged to the story of Tanhaüser.

An hour ago he did not believe in the existence of such beings. Would anybody believe him when he should relate his experiences? What would the solid, practical common-sense of Squan respond to a story of an actual experience with elves? He had an instinctive feeling that it would never do to include anything of that kind in his next letter to the *Barnegat Advertiser.*

Mr. Skinner sat perfectly still, and watched the pretty creatures making their evolutions. He had half a notion at one time to put out his hand suddenly, and seize a couple of them. There was a fortune waiting for the showman who should offer such an attraction to the people. Tom Thumb and his kind would be nowhere compared with such atoms as these. But he thought better of it. They seemed so innocent and happy that he could not bear to injure one of them. And for money too ! He had enough of that without doing a cowardly action for the sake of it.

They came nearer and nearer to him, and he could see that they were numbered by tens of thousands. Every blade of grass and every barley-corn of earth swarmed with them, They danced, and rolled, and kicked, and leaped, and tumbled; and as they came to his side and turned somersaults upon the ferule of his umbrella, some of them began to throw their caps into the air. One cap finally fell upon his hand. He did not mean to do it, but, somehow, involuntarily, his fingers

"Involuntarily, his fingers closed upon it."

closed upon it. In the twinkling of an eye the whole army of elves vanished, the glow faded from the grass, and there was silence and deep darkness.

"Queer!" muttered Mr. Skinner to himself; "all gone, every imp of them. Let's see what it is I've got, anyhow."

He struck a match and looked. It was a tiny cap, too small to go upon the end of his finger.

"Well, there's something like proof if I ever want to tell what I saw! I'll keep it."

He never knew precisely whence came the impulse that moved him to do so absurd a thing as to remove his hat and to place that little thimble of a cap upon his head ; but he did so, and no sooner had it touched his crown than there was heard a sound of rushing wind and a confused murmur of voices. He felt himself whirled about by some unseen force, and before he could make a movement of resistance, he found himself lying in what appeared to be a dimly-lighted cavern, flat upon his back, with his umbrella in one hand and his hat in the other.

II.

"Not very pleasant," said Mr. Skinner, as he sat up and looked around ; "but it's original and mighty interesting ! I'd pay a reasonable price to know what it was that picked me up and flung me in here. I didn't see a thing. I'm in for it now, though, sure as you're born."

Mr. Skinner got upon his feet, and after feeling his revolver, to ascertain if it was handy for use, he examined the cavern. It had rocky walls, absolutely bare, unless where stalactites here and there hung from the roof. Straight before him it opened through a narrow way into a space beyond of which he could see little, excepting

that far, far in the distance he discerned what appeared
to be a mere point of very brilliant light.

Hardly had he gotten upright than the walls of the
tavern rang suddenly with a chorus of wild, shrieking
laughter.

Slightly startled by this fiendish noise, he looked and
saw coming toward him swiftly what looked something
like a squall of snow. Before he could think about it,
he was enveloped by a crowd of figures of misty
whiteness, which swept round and about him with
amazing velocity.

It was a moment or two before he could realize
precisely what was the matter; but he soon began
to mark the outlines of hideous forms, which grinned
at him in a horrible fashion and seemed to menace
him.

" Ghosts ! or my name is not Skinner ! Well, I never
thought I'd strike anything like this ! "

The whirlwind of shadows encircled him with accelerated speed, and as they came closer and closer to him,
the demoniacal yells became more fierce and terrible.
Mr. Skinner was surprised at his own calmness. Leaning
upon his umbrella, he observed the performance with
rather a critical air, and after a brief interval of silence
he remarked, without being certain that he was addressing anyone in particular :

" It's of no use. You can't scare me with any of your
whooping and howling. I can stand this sort of thing
as long as you can. I'm not one of the hysterical
kind."

Still the spectral storm raged wildly about him, and

still the cavern echoed the voices that came out of the tempest.

"Oh well!" said Mr. Skinner, at last, sitting quietly down and crossing one leg over the other, "if it makes you feel better to waltz around that way, just go on! I can wait! Only I'm going to explore this den, if I have to stay here a week to do it!"

Suddenly, as he spoke, the ghostly crowd left him and flew shrieking down the passage whence it came. One figure alone stood before Mr. Skinner. It looked somewhat like an old man, with long hair and beard, and with a face of majestic sternness.

Mr. Skinner saw the form so vividly, that he at first thought it to be a real human being ; but when it stood between him and the passage-way, and he perceived that he could see the distant light right through the old man's mantle, he comprehended that he had a genuine ghost to deal with.

"Unhappy man," said the spectre, "why did you dare to penetrate to this secret chamber?"

"Well, in the first place, I'm a free and independent American citizen, travelling upon a passport signed by the Secretary of State, and I've got a right to go where anybody else goes ; and, in the second place, I was pitched in here, head over heels, without my consent, by some of your people."

"Are you not afraid to stand in the presence of the awful spirits of the dead?"

"No, I'm not! Certainly not! You can't frighten me? What are you, anyhow? You're nothing but a little bit of vapour, or carbonic acid gas, or something

" I am not afraid of anything I can poke my umbrella through,
like that."—*Page 277.*

If there was a chimney here and a strong draught, you'd be sucked up the flue. You couldn't help yourself. Afraid! I'm not afraid of anything I can poke my umbrella through, like that, and that!" and Mr. Skinner stirred about with his umbrella in the middle of the spectre.

"You are very audacious; but you will never escape from here," said the ghost, solemnly; "never, never!"

"I won't? We'll see about that. I've left my direction with the United States' consul, down at the town below here, and if I'm not back again within a specified time, he'll be up here and blow your old mountain to flinders! You don't seem to be acquainted with the party you have to deal with."

"It is strange," said the spectre, with the faintest suggestion of embarrassment in its hollow tones, "we are not used to being regarded with such calmness by mere mortals."

"I know it!" answered Mr. Skinner; "I know it. People generally are frightened into fits when they think they see a ghost; but I made up my mind long ago that if I ever met one I was going to investigate him. S'pose we sit down here and have a little talk?"

The spectre did not move; but it struck Mr. Skinner that he detected upon the misty countenance some evidence that the ghost felt that it was hardly holding its own. Mr. Skinner had the advantage, and he knew it.

"I want to ask you now, for example," said Mr. Skinner, sitting and locking his fingers over his knee, "how it feels to be a disembodied spirit? Never hungry, are you?"

The ghost slowly shook its head.

" Costs you nothing for food ; don't have to buy any clothes ; no aches or pains, or anything of that kind ? "

The spectre still nodded negatively.

" I thought not," said Mr. Skinner, "and nothing spent for travelling expenses either. I reckon, now, if you wanted to take a fly over to America you could get there in a jiffy : crawl through a keyhole when you felt like it too, I've no doubt ? "

" Yes," said the ghost.

" It's mighty singular," said Mr. Skinner, reflectively. " I've felt that way myself at times, in dreams. It must be rather agreeable, upon the whole. No taxes and no work to do. But, say, what's the fact about your fellows haunting houses and graveyards ? Ever do anything of that kind ? "

" Sometimes."

" I wouldn't have believed it two hours ago. But what's the sense of it ? What's the use of scaring people with that kind of foolishness ? Why don't you keep off and behave ? "

" You could not understand it if I were to tell you."

" I'd like to have a chance to try, any way. But, no matter, let that pass. I wish you'd tell me, though, what's going on in here. Whose place is it ? "

" These are the realms of Venus. You shall see them ; I will lead you."

" Will you ! That's clever ! I'm glad I met you ! " and Mr. Skinner attempted to pat his companion on the back, but his hand went through the figure.

"How soon will you be ready to start?" asked Mr Skinner.

"Now!"

"All right! But wait a minute! No objection to my smoking, I suppose?" said Mr. Skinner, lighting a match. "Maybe you'll have a cigar? Oh! excuse me ; I forgot. Of course you don't care for such things? Now," said he, shouldering his umbrella, "if you'll push ahead I'll follow."

"I will go!" said the spectre.

"One moment! As we are going to travel together I think I ought to—that is, I,—beg pardon, but have you a name?"

"I am the Erl-King! One of the poets, Goethe, wrote of me. You have read it, perhaps."

"What! you don't say! Yes, sir, that poem is in every 'Speaker' in our school district. You ran off with a child. I tell you what, old man, it wouldn't do to try any of those kidnapping pranks in our country ; the people wouldn't put up with them. Where is the little one?"

"In the court chamber. You shall see."

The journey began. The pair entered the narrow passage way, and Mr. Skinner, whose powers of observation were in full play, noted that the walls were cut so smoothly that not a crevice or scratch could be seen upon them.

"That's a mighty nice piece of work," he said, rubbing nis hand upon the wall. "How did you cut that? With hand tools or atmospheric drills?"

"It was not done by mortal hands!" said the shade.

"No?" exclaimed Mr. Skinner, as the pair proceeded upon their journey. "And this too !" he said, as they emerged into a long gallery higher and wider than the passage way leading to it. "This beats any rock-cutting I have seen yet. I say, if anybody ever wanted to run a railroad tunnel through this mountain would your folks consider a proposition for a right of way ? "

The ghost slowly shook its head.

"It's a pity, too," said Skinner, sadly, "for it don't seem right to have work like that wasted."

"It's not wasted," said the goblin.

"Well, of course, each of us looks at it differently That's only natural. Now, it strikes me that to bore a magnificent hole through a mountain for nothing else than for a parcel of goblins to prowl about in, is a sinful waste of effort. However, it's none of my business."

As he spoke there was heard a faint sound of the crowing of a cock.

"Halloa! What's that? Sounds like a rooster? "

"It is a cock crowing outside of us, upon the hill-top."

"Outside, eh? I thought, at first, maybe you kept chickens, and it struck me as kind of singular. I couldn't imagine what a ghost wanted with poultry."

A few steps further on the pair came to the edge of a precipice, and Mr. Skinner could see, beneath, a black, rolling stream, from which clouds of light vapour ascended; while upon the other side, perhaps a hundred feet distant, the rocks rose sheer and ragged to the level of the height upon which he stood.

Across the chasm was a sort of bridge, not wider than

a hand's breadth, and having nothing but the naked footway to support the traveller who should try to cross it.

"What is this?" asked Mr. Skinner.

"This," said the spectre, "is a river of boiling pitch, which must be passed by every mortal who penetrates to these realms."

"How do visitors get across?"

"Upon this bridge. Some do not succeed. Dare you venture it?"

"I think I shall. Is it the custom to walk over?"

"It is," said the goblin, with what seemed to be a look of fiendish exultation upon its misty countenance.

"Humph!" remarked Mr. Skinner. "Nobody can account for the foolishness that there is in the world. Now, my way of getting over is different. Hold my umbrella a moment; won't you?"

As the goblin could not comply with this request, Mr. Skinner put the umbrella under the top of his satchel. Then he got down and sat astride of the bridge, and aided by his hands he made a series of small jumps which brought him safely to the other side in a few moments.

The goblin was there to meet him, and Mr. Skinner noticed that it had an air of severe disappointment. When he got upon his feet he said :

"That is the poorest contrivance for crossing a stream that I ever saw. Why don't you rig up something better?"

"We are contented with it!" said the ghost, gloomily.

"I'll tell you," remarked Mr. Skinner, producing a

"He made a series of small jumps." — *Page* 281.

pencil, and making a calculation upon the back of an old letter which he fished from his pocket. "I know a man in my country who'll run you an iron truss bridge over that chasm for twenty-four hundred dollars, and keep it painted for ten years. Something substantial and safe. If you say so I'll write to him?"

The goblin, with a mournful look, shook its head.

"All right," said Mr. Skinner, "it's your concern and not mine. But, I'll tell you, if money was any object with you there are people who'd give a handsome bonus for the privilege of boring for oil right around here. I know, old man, from what I've seen in Pennsylvania, that there is petroleum where that pitch comes from. Do you care to speculate in the matter? No? Oh, very well, I thought it might be friendly to mention it."

As the shade of the Erl-king moved forward, with Mr. Skinner following, the character of the gallery underwent a change. The walls were separated by larger distances, and the vault above them rose to a greater height. The rocks, instead of showing their nakedness, began to display lavish adornment. Sometimes they were covered with masses of trailing vines which hung from them in graceful festoons ; sometimes great bunches of beautiful ferns were clustered upon the walls, their long and feathery branches sweeping downward to the floor. At brief intervals the verdure gave place to a mosaic work of splendid jewels. Mr. Skinner was amazed to find hundreds of square feet of the walls glistening with diamonds, emeralds, rubies, amethysts, and other precious stones, of enormous size, and cut with the most exquisite skill.

The sun did not shine upon them, and there was no
artificial light that he could discover; and yet the mass
of jewels flooded the vast chamber with a radiance that
dazzled his eyes. It was the most glorious vision that
he had ever encountered. It surpassed in the richness
of its colouring and the splendour of its wealth everything
that he had ever read of in the Arabian Nights, or
dreamed of as he pored over the wildest fairy tales. He
trod upon a pavement encrusted with stones, each one of
which would have enriched an empire, and he saw about
and above him walls inlaid with such superb art as no
jeweller of mortal clay could hope to rival.

His guide would have hurried on, but Mr. Skinner
wanted to tarry a while and enjoy the spectacle. It is
not every day, he thought, that a plain man has a chance
to study such a scene. This alone, he said to himself,
was worth all the trouble he had taken, and all the danger
he had encountered. A description of the chamber, in a
letter to the *Barnegat Advertiser*, would fill New Jersey
with excitement; and, before the year was out, the Erl-
king's goblin would have half a thousand Jerseymen
knocking at his door and wanting to come in.

"Ah!" said Mr. Skinner to his guide, "I know now
why you do not want visitors. I understand why you
would like them to tumble off of that bridge. You've got
millions and millions of dollars invested there."

" This is nothing; they are baubles," said the ghost.

"What! Oh, well, of course they're not of much use
to you. But I think I could get some practical good out
of half a bushel, or so. That diamond there, for example,
would supply half the women in my State with breast-

pins, and make them perfectly happy. Are you handing any of these around—among your friends, I mean ? "

The ghost made no sign of affirmation, and Mr. Skinner added, as he gave a final look at the display,

No matter. I don't covet them. Only, I thought it would be nice to take one or two along, to remember you by."

" You will not find it easy to forget me, in the place to which you are going," answered the Erl-king, with what might have passed for a sneer. " See ! " and the spectre waved its shadowy hand.

Mr. Skinner turned and looked. Before him, at the foot of a gentle slope, lay a scene of weird and wonderful beauty. He saw a vast garden stretching away in front of him, and to the right and the left, towards boundaries which, somehow, were so indistinctly defined that he could not surely say what were the dimensions of the place, or its proportions. It had not the wildness of undisturbed Nature, but still less did it appear with the symmetry of human art. The beautiful confusion into which the untrained earth flings the forms that spring from her bosom, was not there. Some hand had prepared the outlines of the garden, but upon a scheme such as no mortal man could have devised. There were grace and beauty, but these were evolved from an order which was elfish in its eccentricity, and which appeared even wilder than chance itself.

There were myriads of walks twisting and writhing into strangest shapes, beginning nowhere and leading no whither ; and these ran in and out among fantastic groupings of shrubbery, which expressed no definite notions of forms, but conveyed suggestions of a purpose to fill the mind of the observer with a sense of the un-canny.

The trees were covered with foliage which had a greenness not precisely that of the outer world, but so differing from it that one could not tell precisely wherein the difference lay. The sward, of the same strange hue, was covered with flowers of novel and peculiar shapes, and glowing with colours that had no counterpart in nature. Here and there cataracts fell from eminences upon the plain, but the water, as it tumbled, was governed by some force which turned it into queer figures, so that one might imagine it to possess life and volition of its own.

After its descent, it ran away through tortuous chan-nels among the grasses, bubbling, and leaping, and play-ing fantastic tricks, as no earthly water could have done. The fountains, that burst upward from the plain at various points, also dashed and flashed in obedience to some law which was excepted from the code of nature.

A flood of strong and penetrating light poured over the whole garden ; but there was no sunshine, no distinct radiance of any kind. The shadows merged into the light imperceptibly, and the waters gave back but a faint reflection to the source of their illumination. The leaves danced and fluttered, and the surface of the streams were lightly ruffled, but there was no breeze; the birds flew about upon odd courses from bush to tree ; and they seemed to sing ; but no note of their music fell upon the ear. The cataracts tumbled in silence ; no sound of falling waters came from the fountains.

There was splendour and beauty, but over it all was the hush of death. It was a place that might have been made a home for joy, but it was joyless and horrible. There was life, movement, activity ; but only such animation as that which stirs within the realms of dreamland —mysterious, noiseless, and unreal.

As Mr. Skinner looked down upon the scene he realized these things, and, perhaps, for a moment, he had a sense of oppression, as though he were in a nightmare. But he readily freed himself from this feeling, and his curiosity was strongly excited as he noted several figures, apparently of human beings, passing slowly to and fro, in attitudes of dejection, along the avenues of the garden.

" Who are those people ? " he asked of his guide.

" Those are mortal men who have come here as you have come, and whose fate it is to linger here for ever."

" Why don't they quit, and go home ? "

" Only two of all who nave entered this realm have gone away, and they returned when they were summoned. That is the doom of all ; to tarry or to return."

" Who were the two ? "

" Tanhaüser and Thomas of Erceldoune."

" Are they down there now ? "

" Yes."

" Well, if you don't mind, I'll get you to introduce me. I would like to know one of them."

They walked down the declivity and into the garden. Mr. Skinner examined everything carefully.

" Land like that," he said, pointing to a grassy tract which stretched away to the left, " would bring forty dollars an acre in West Jersey. I know a man who gave that price for some not quite so good."

The ghost made no reply.

"I don't see," continued Mr. Skinner, "that you do much with the property. Now, there's a field I know would be first-rate for watermelons or sweet potatoes ; a light, sandy soil, but rich and easily ploughed. If I were you I'd put at least an acre in melons and another in tomatoes and lima beans ; but then, of course," said Mr. Skinner, suddenly remembering the unsubstantial nature of his companion, " you don't care as much for such things as I do. It's a pity, though, so much territory going unimproved. It would be far better for those people there if they had a regular job of spading and hoeing to do every day."

They walked on as he spoke, and as they passed a tree that was filled with fruit Mr. Skinner plucked from the branches something that looked like an apple. When he bit it, he found that it was but a mass of dust.

"A decent cider apple-tree would be a blessing in such a place as this," he said.

"This," said the goblin, pausing near to one of the wanderers in the garden, " is Thomas of Erceldoune."

The man turned as his name was uttered, and Mr. Skinner went up, with some vivacity of manner, seized his hand and shook it.

"Glad to know you! I've met nobody since I came in here but my ghostly friend and some others like him, and it's a satisfaction to meet a genuine man."

"Alas!" said Thomas, sadly, "is still another victim

added to those who have come here to find endless
misery ! "

" You don't take exactly the right view of it," said Mr
Skinner, cheerily, " I am not a victim. Not a bit of it."

Mr. Skinner felt a deep pity in his heart for this
wretched man. He could not determine clearly whether
Thomas of Erceldoune was young or old. He looked as
if he might not have lived more than three decades, and
yet there was something about him that suggested
vigorous manhood which had been suddenly stopped in
its development and kept for untold years precisely at the
point at which it was when its forces were petrified. The
air of sadness that he wore was the visible sign of
despair. From this man's soul hope had flown for ever
and for ever.

" How long have you been here ? " asked Mr.
Skinner.

" I do not know. Sometimes I think but a day ; at
others I seem to have dwelt here for a thousand years.
It was in the fifteenth century that I left my earthly home
for the last time."

" You don't say ? Why, that's nearly four hundred
years ! "

" Yes ; it must be so long."

" How did you get here ? "

" I came first to gratify my curiosity. Then I was
permitted to go back to my home. But I knew that they
would summon me ; I knew it ! And one day while I
made merry at a feast with my friends, one came to tell
me that a hart and a hind were coming up the highway to
my door. No one but myself perceived that my time had

come. But I was conscious of the meaning of the visit of those strange messengers, so I arose and followed them away, away, blinded by my tears and my misery, until they lead me here."

"Do you know what I would have done if I had been you?" asked Mr. Skinner.

"See here, old fellow, cheer up."

"No."

"Why, well, instead of quitting home I would have had venison for supper."

"That is a strange thing to hear in this place!"

"I know, but I mean it! See here, old fellow, cheer

up! You're mistaken if you think I am going to stay in
here. Indeed I'm not. And if you will come along with
me, and stick to me, I'll run you out when I go. I don't
know exactly how, but I'll do it if I say so!"

"It cannot be!"

"Oh, come now, that is nonsense! If I get you off you
can go over the ocean with me. I'll settle you on a little
place somewhere in Atlantic County, make you snug and
comfortable, and you can start fresh in life. Is it a
bargain?"

"Impossible!"

"I don't know that you care much for politics; but if
you come with me to Jersey, and you're in want of money,
I could arrange, maybe, to have you run for something—
the Legislature, or some other paying office, enough to
make you easy. Let me see; are you an Irishman?"

"I am from Scotland."

"Scotch, hey? Well, that is unfortunate! You'd
have a much better chance in my country if you were
Irish. We Americans think we rule ourselves; but we
don't. The Irish govern us! But I'll do the best I can
for you, so get together your things and come along."

But Thomas of Erceldoune did not answer. He hung
his head, and turning about slowly walked away.

"Won't come, eh?" said Skinner.

The retreating figure shook its head slowly and
mournfully.

"Young man," called Mr. Skinner, "you may never
have another chance like this. It's the wildest nonsense
to reject it. You come along with me and we'll stir up
this den of goblins so that they'll be glad to get rid of us

at any price. I'll take you under the protection of the
American flag, and we'll see whether anybody will dare to
hold us! Won't go? Well, it's too bad! too bad!"
and Mr. Skinner looked after the unhappy man, and
watched him until he disappeared behind the shrubbery.

"No, he will not go," said the goblin. " He knows
better than you do the awful power that holds you both
in thrall."

"Not both, old gentleman. I see you are still delud-
ing your cloudy noddle with the idea that I am going to
stay."

"You will stay," answered the goblin, "and, as it did
to Thomas of Erceldoune, so a hundred years will seem
to you but a swiftly passing day."

" Ah, my venerable friend," replied Mr. Skinner, "you
can't play that upon me. I have an American lever
watch and a pocket calendar for the current year.
There'll be no time rolling by without my knowing it."

"We shall see," answered the ghost, with an air of
not feeling quite so certain about it as he had done
before.

"And, meanwhile," said Mr. Skinner, " s'pose we
push on and complete this exploration. I want to see
the end of the journey."

III.

The spirit of the Erl-king made no reply, but drifting
slowly across the garden it entered the portal of what
seemed to be a vast building of some kind, though so

puzzling and uncertain were its outlines, and so indistinct the light that shone about the place, that Mr. Skinner could not by most careful scrutiny determine if it was really a structure, or a wall of the solid rock hewn into symmetrical shape.

He followed his guide through the doorway, along a wide hall which rang beneath his footsteps, and thence through another wide portal into a long chamber of such height as he could not clearly discern. A table stretched from one end of the room to the other, and gathered about it was a great host of figures, whose greyish whiteness could be perceived without difficulty through the dusky atmosphere.

"This," said the goblin, "is the Hall of Heroes. Here are gathered the immortal parts of men whose deeds upon earth have made their fame eternal."

"Soldiers, I reckon," said Mr. Skinner. "Who are they?"

"There," replied the ghost, "sits Arthur, and about him are gathered the glorious Knights of the Round Table. All are there, the true and the false together. There is Charlemagne with his warriors, his crown upon his head, his good sword by his side. Near to him Red Bearded Frederick sits with his six knights. Thrice his beard enwraps the stony table in front of him, and thrice more still must it enfold it."

"Why don't he shave?" asked Mr. Skinner, calmly.

"Here," said the spectre, not deigning to reply, "the three great Tells join with the throng. The legend is that they sleep a mortal sleep within the mountain.

.But their eyes of sense will never more unclose. And with them are the shades of valiant men of all degrees, a company of the mighty and the heroic."

" What are they at ?" asked Mr. Skinner.

" It is a festival. They sit here, shadows of their ancient selves, but with souls that feel the impulse of the former fires, to hold revel and to recount the deeds of the wondrous past."

" A kind of a dinner party," suggested Mr. Skinner. " I'd like to join them. I don't see anything to eat ; but I s'pose I am safe to get a spectral steak or a goblin chop, and that's good enough when a man is not hungry."

" Beware how you thrust yourself upon these awful shades !" said the Erl-king. " They will not brook levity or familiarity."

" I guess I will sit at the table and look on, anyhow." And Mr. Skinner, advancing, took a seat tolerably close to one of the ghosts, and, assuming an easy attitude, observed them.

There was a murmur of voices among them, but of voices such as no tongue ever shaped into words. And ever and anon the warriors, who seemed clad cap-à-pie in ghostly armour, moved as if to raise beakers to their lips, and to drain them to the dregs. Nobody appeared to notice Mr. Skinner's presence ; but after a while that gentleman began to display signs of uneasiness, and, presently rising, clearing his throat, and looking calmly around, he said, as if he were addressing an ordinary meeting of mortals :—

" Gentlemen, your chairman has not called upon

me to respond to any sentiment, possibly because he's
not familiar with the modern custom upon festive occa-
sions, or perhaps because, not knowing me, he may have
persuaded himself that I would feel some diffidence in
addressing such a company. I do not wish to obtrude
my opinions upon you ; but since my entrance to these
regions, I have acquired the conviction that it would be
an act of philanthropy for an intelligent outsider like
myself to make an effort to freshen up your views a little.
I intend, therefore, to offer a few remarks, which I trust
will be received in the spirit of friendliness which moves
me to present them.

"Of course, gentlemen, my notions of things must
inevitably differ widely from yours. You were dead and
buried hundreds of years ago, and your sympathies are
largely with a past that was wholly ignorant of matters
of high importance with which I am perfectly familiar ;
and I have the additional advantage of still possessing a
physical body, and not being compelled to stay underground all day, and to go out only at night, and even
then presenting the appearance of having been sliced out
of a fog-bank."

Here the Erl-king cautioned Mr. Skinner not to go on.
But he continued :

"Without going deeply into the work of contrasting
the methods of your time with the methods of mine, I
may be permitted to remark upon the oddity of the circumstance that while individual soldiers of your age
encased themselves with iron stove-plates and helmets,
the vaporous semblance of which you now wear, we have
adapted such means of protection only to ships, with the

result that the chief purpose of the existence of a portion of mankind just now is to make ships that no existing gun can penetrate, and when that is done, to invent a gun that can sink that ship.

"The point of interest is that men are still as busy killing each other as they were when you were around; and that while we are proud to pity the ignorance and folly which characterized you when you spent your lives in fighting, we have not become so wise as to perceive that to settle a quarrel by shooting men with a revolving cannon is not any more sensible than to chop them up with axes and to brain them with clubs, as you folks used to do."

The Erl-king hinted to Mr. Skinner that he was touching a delicate subject; but the speaker proceeded :—

"However, the matter to which I wished principally to allude interests you more directly. I say, frankly, that until I dropped in here, I never had any solid faith in the reality of ghosts. I regarded the whole thing as a mass of superstition. I see now that I was wrong. But having confessed this much, I think I ought to say to you, who probably have some influence over the affairs of your kind, that the sooner some one of you starts an energetic reform movement in the ghost business, the better will be the result. Gentlemen, I am a practical man—a utilitarian, if you will ; and I must say that it grieves me, when I look around upon this grave and dignified company, to think of the ridiculous character of the methods in which you manifest yourselves to mankind. If I were a goblin, and I retained a particle of my self-respect, I would keep away from graveyards at night ; I would refrain from haunting houses, and prowling about, making noises to scare timid women and children ; I would refuse to come out at so-called spiritual *seances* and thrum diabolical music upon cracked guitars, and tilt tables at the bidding of long-haired and wild-eyed mediums. If a ghost who has been respectable in life cannot put in his spare time in the outer world in better ways than these, my advice to him is to stay in the bowels of the earth right along, and to let honest people alone."

The Erl-king mentioned to Mr. Skinner that they must move on at once. But Mr. Skinner said that he would close in a moment.

" Apart from the silliness of such proceedings, gentlemen, they are disgustingly useless. Now, if I were a ghost I would use my powers to reveal to living men truths that would be of service to them—such as knowledge of the spiritual state, and information, perhaps, as to the location of veins of coal, of the metals, and so forth ; or, if these things were forbidden, I would rent myself out for exhibition for the benefit of good objects of various kinds. A genuine ghost, for example, could always find employment when Hamlet or Macbeth is performed at the theatres ; and if you can flit about with the rapidity commonly attributed to you, some of you might earn good wages carrying messages for persons to places which the telegraph does not reach."

The Erl-king said that there would be danger in speaking further ; but Mr. Skinner added :

" One word more. You hold in wicked bondage down here in the garden a lot of people who have a right to their liberty. Now, what good it does you, or the head person who governs this place, to practise cruelty of that kind, I can't imagine. My opinion is that you ought to let them go, and to give them each a pocketful of the

"While Mr. Skinner was speaking, the assembly sat in profound silence."—*Page* 299.

jewellery I saw back here, a piece, for damages done to them. If you don't agree to this I intend as soon as I return to my hotel to get out a writ of habeas corpus, if such a thing is to be had in the German Empire ; and most likely, if there is any fuss made about it, I will organize a railroad to run along here, and I will have a locomotive whizzing through this mountain in a way that will make you wish you could die again ! That is all I have to say. I am obliged to you for your attention ; and if any of you ever want to communicate with me don't hunt up a medium, but come direct to me at Squan, New Jersey, in the day-time, and if the light annoys you we'll have a comfortable talk in the cellar or the smoke-house."

While Mr. Skinner was speaking the assembly sat in profound silence, and upon some of the faces could be detected a look of bewildered amazement. When he finished, he said politely :

"Good morning," and turned to go.

"How do you think it struck them?" asked Mr. Skinner of his companion.

"You are a marvellous man, and a bold one," replied the spectre, almost timidly. "I thought they would rend you in pieces. Strange ! Strange ! that such things should happen within these realms !"

"I told you I'd give you some new ideas," said Mr. Skinner ; "and now, which way are we going?"

"Straight forward."

"And what then?"

"Soon you will be ushered into the splendid court of Aphrodite, the mistress of these realms, and the power whom you and I and all must obey."

"A ghost, is she?"

"A being of transcendent and wondrous loveliness."

"Well, let me know before I get there, for I should 'ike to fix myself up a little."

They pressed onward through a succession of apartments, each of which was more magnificent than that which preceded it, until they entered a chamber that was adorned with strange, but beautiful objects.

"That," said the guide, "is a plant which gives to him who possesses it the power to ward off evil spirits. He who looks in this mirror sees all his future life in full detail depicted before him. The water of yonder bubbling fountain compels complete forgetfulness of the past. He who eats of the fruit that lies upon this table gains such vision that he can see the riches that are hidden in the bosom of the earth. Here are gathered all the resources of magic, and all the marvels that men have dreamed of when they have thought to pierce the veil that shuts out the supernatural from the natural."

"When you get tired of making an inventory of the effects," said Mr. Skinner, "perhaps you will come along."

"We are now," said the goblin, reverently, "upon the threshold of the throne-room of the glorious Aphrodite. Through that doorway we shall be ushered into her majestic presence."

"Wait a minute, then." And Mr. Skinner, unslinging his satchel, placed it upon the table, among the fruit that improved the eyesight, and began rummaging in its depths. A moment later he took out a clean collar and a hair-brush. Placing himself before the mirror of life to come, he untied his cravat, removed his shirt-collar, put it carefully in his satchel, buttoned on the fresh one, tied his cravat, gave it two or three pats with his fingers, and then surveyed it with a look of satisfaction. Then taking off his hat, he smoothed his hair with the brush.

When the operation was completed he returned the brush to the satchel, snapped the catch, resumed his hat, and, turning to the goblin, who observed him with what seemed feelings of horror, he said, "Now I am ready. Shall we go right in?"

The shade of the Erl-king approached the door, which swung slowly and silently upon its hinges. Mr. Skinner followed the goblin through the portal.

The scene upon which he was ushered transcended in dazzling splendour anything that he had ever witnessed. He saw a vast temple, whose walls were massive slabs of gold and pearl, covered by some cunning hand with grotesque but beautiful designs of elaborate workmanship. Huge pillars of sapphire and emerald rose from the floor and swept upwards to a roof of snowy crystal, through which a clear, soft radiance poured in a flood which made every nook and corner of the apartment as bright as though the noonday sun looked in upon it.

The floor was of onyx, laid in a wondrous pattern, such as no human mind has ever devised. The doors were made of ebony, inlaid with silver ; and, at intervals, there stood tables of carved ivory, of amethyst, of frosted gold, and chairs of porphyry, and chrysolite, and sardius. Great mirrors of burnished silver hung from the walls, and before them tiny fountains leaped into the air, and fell into jewelled basins. Upon all sides there were riches, beauty, magnificence, and exquisite art, such as no treasure-house upon earth ever presented to the eye of man.

At the end of the room, beneath a canopy bespangled with gems, two golden thrones were placed, and, sitting upon one of these, the visitor saw a woman, so fair, so noble, so crowned with a matchless and wonderful beauty, that he thought all the loveliness of woman that he had ever looked upon was but as deformity in comparison with it. She was clad in a snowy robe of gossamer fineness, and of most delicate grace ; and upon her forehead glistened a diadem of jewels of surpassing splendour. About her, as she sat, were gathered a court of other women, scarcely less beautiful, and, as the visitor approached them, he heard strains of music of piercing sweetness, which swelled and throbbed through the crystal arches with vibrations which the ear might have heard for ever and for ever without satiety.

As the visitor came nearer, it seemed to him that that glorious company had been expecting him, for, when the Erl-king said to him, "This is Aphrodite, the Queen," she upon the throne smiled graciously upon him, and gave him hearty welcome to her court, while those who surrounded her echoed her words, and appeared eager to do him honour.

"All very well," said Mr. Skinner, to himself; "but how about Tanhaüser, and Thomas of Erceldoune, and the other poor wretches in the garden? I have no doubt that they were received in the same manner."

"We have waited for you," said the Queen, most graciously, "and we rejoice that you have come to dwell with us. Happy is the mortal who is permitted to linger in the company of the immortals!" And she extended to him her white hand, that he might kiss it.

Mr. Skinner grasped it, shook it warmly, and said,

"Thank you, madame; you are very kind. I was travelling through the neighbourhood, outside here, and I thought I'd just drop in. But I can't stay. Sorry; but I have an engagement in Berlin on the twenty-second."

"When you have tasted the delights of this realm you will not wish to go. The world from which you come has nothing to offer that can rival the fascinations of this."

"Well, madame, tastes differ, you know. This is gorgeous, and elegant, and all that; but, as a steady thing, I really think I should prefer Squan."

"Sit here," said the Queen, pointing to the throne by her side. "It is the place of honour—it is yours. The greatest men of your race have longed to occupy it; some have done so, and counted it the highest pleasure."

"It's handsome, that's certain," replied Mr. Skinner, running his hand over the golden carvings. "Handsome, but I must say that I've seen furniture that would beat it for comfort. Now I wonder that, instead of sitting about on a hard yellow affair like this, you don't order a few stuffed chairs. for common use? There's a cabinet-maker, near where I live, that would get you up a dozen with springs for almost nothing, and be glad of the chance."

"You," said the Queen, laughingly, "are the only guest who ever thought our temple less than faultless."

"Well, madame, I'm a prosy sort of a man, who always looks at the practical side of things. Now, do you know what I would do if I owned this place?"

"I cannot tell."

"Why, I would rig up some kind of a stove, and keep a coal fire going, to take off the chill. It must be dreadfully damp, underground here."

The Queen and her maids of honour laughed merrily at this, and Mr. Skinner thereupon added,

"The best thing that I find here is a little good-humour. My friend, the Erl-king, here is much too solemn to be an agreeable companion. A week with him would make me melancholy for life."

"You shall always be merry here," replied the Queen, with a sweet smile. "These are the realms of joy, and I will give you a better companion than your guide. Which of these will you choose to be your partner through all the years to come?" And she waved her hand toward the throng which stood around her.

"None of them, madame!"

"What! None?"

"Excuse me, madame, but I don't think you comprehend the existing state of things. I am a married man already. In my home, far across the sea, I have a wife whom I love. She is not so handsome as these, maybe, but her homeliness is not actually alarming ; and when it comes to housekeeping and plain cooking, she has no equal from the Hudson River to the Capes, if I do say it myself. While she lives I intend to stick to her."

Mr. Skinner was gratified to perceive that his remarks, uttered with some warmth, did not give offence. A ripple of laughter swept over the crowd.

" You have not much love for the beautiful, I think," said the Queen.

" Oh yes, madame. When it comes to good looks, this place takes the palm, without a doubt. I was aware of that. I have often seen statues of you, out in the world. A little scarce of clothes, if you will pardon me for saying so, but uncommonly handsome ; everybody admits that."

" Men praise me, do they ? " asked Aphrodite.

" Oh, yes ! Of course. In the matter of personal appearance, I mean. My guide-book, which I was reading over at the hotel throws out an insinuation that there is a little too much paganism down here for Europe in the nineteenth century ; but in the country that I come from we don't meddle with people's religious opinions."

The Queen made no response.

" I do think, though," continued Mr. Skinner, passing one leg thoughtlessly over the arm of the throne and speaking reflectively, " that it might not be a bad idea to organize a missionary movement in these parts. There's Elder Cooper of the Barnegat Meeting ; he has a powerful gift as a persuader, and if you'd allow him to get up a revival-meeting in here somewhere, there is no telling what might happen."

"We will not speak of that!" replied the Queen in a tone of light displeasure.

"Beg pardon if I was rude? The thought occurred to me, and I expressed it frankly without meaning to hurt anybody's feelings."

As he spoke he was surprised to see a great throng of children come running into the apartment. They gathered close about him and gazed at him with childish wonder. Mr. Skinner looked into their faces, and while it was clear that they really were children, it seemed to him that there was something about them which told of more years than their stature counted. They had all the signs of youth, and yet he could not rid himself of an impression that their youth had left them long centuries ago.

As they ranged themselves before him, he said to the Queen,—

"Your's madame?"

"Oh no! these are the little ones who left their homes in Hameln to follow the music of the Pied Piper."

"Seems to me I have heard something about it," observed Mr. Skinner; "how long ago was it?"

"Six centuries have passed since they came trooping into the mountain behind the Piper. One hundred and thirty of them came, and they are all here!"

"Well, well!" replied Mr. Skinner, "it's mighty queer, and sad too. How do you treat them?"

"We love them."

"Do you educate them? No academies down here, I

'spose? Never let them go to Sunday school? Would
you mind then if I asked a few questions?"

"You shall do so."

Mr. Skinner stood up

"Put your hands behind your backs, children; that's
it ; now hold up your heads and look straight at me.
What is the capital of Indiana? Speak right out!
Nobody knows? How is Ireland bounded? Come,
answer! Don't know? Well, I declare! How many
are four and eight?"

The children stood silent, and eyed Mr. Skinner almost
mournfully.

"Well, now," he proceeded to say, "let me try you in
spelling. Can you spell 'Baker' for me? Begin!
'B—!' Go on! B-a- b-a-. Somebody try it! Can't
do it? I was afraid not. Can you spell 'Boy'? Begins
with a B, like the other! Don't know that either!"

The Queen said that they knew nothing of earthly
things.

"Well, madame, permit me to say that it's a blamed
shame the way the education of these children has been
neglected. You want a schoolmistress down here worse
than you want a parson. That's my opinion, and I don't
care who knows it!"

Mr. Skinner found himself getting angry and warm.
Opening his satchel, he took out a package and said :

"Children, here's some candy for you. Hardly
enough to go around, but it's all I have, and there is no
confectionery store handy. I'd give you some money to
buy fire-crackers, too, only I know you'd never have a
chance to spend it!"

" You love little children, I perceive," said Aphrodite.

" I do.   I love them too well to like to see them poked underground alive, and kept there six or seven hundred years.   It is a great wrong."

" They are very happy here."

" Well, maybe they are ; but it's not the fair thing. I'll tell you what I'll do.   You turn the whole batch over to me, and I'll take them along, and either bind them out or stow them away in an orphan asylum, where they will be decently brought up.   Is it a bargain ? "

" We cannot part with them."

" Who takes care of them ?   Who washes and dresses them, and fixes them up ?   You have no servants ?   No ? I hardly thought you could persuade nursery maids to live underground here.   That is the only advantage you have that I can see."

" What ? "

" No bother with the servant-girl question.   It pesters the life out of women up above.   The hired girl we had just before I left home," said Mr. Skinner, with an absent look upon his face, as if his mind was contemplating some curious experience of the past, " parted with us because we complained of her frying the oysters in Mrs. Skinner's pomatum."

Aphrodite did not seem especially interested in this fragment of domestic history, and she motioned for the children to go.   As Mr. Skinner watched them moving away, he said, putting his hand in the satchel :

" I just happened to think that I had a bottle of cough medicine along with me, that might be useful to the little ones.   You are welcome to it if you want it."

Her Majesty apparently did not hear him, for she gave a signal, and again the hall was filled with the rapturous music that he had heard a brief while before. Instantly the floor was filled with beautiful dancers, who whirled about in riotous fury through a dance, which became wilder and wilder as it proceeded. Mr. Skinner observed the performance in silence.

"Is it not beautiful?" asked the Queen.

"Beautiful," replied Mr. Skinner; "but a little too violent for my taste."

"Shall you not join them?"

"I am obliged to you; but it is with the utmost difficulty that I manage to hobble through a plain cotillion. Round dances I'm opposed to. If I should step in there I should be so giddy in a minute that I could not stand. Your music is fine though. Who attends to that for you?"

"The Pied Piper; his real name is Orpheus."

"Ah! I'm not a very good judge, although I know the best from the worst. I am a subscriber to the Barnegat Brass Band, down where I live; and that organization took the first prize at a brass band tournament at Newark last summer. Some think it is superior; but I dont know. I have always had my doubts about it."

"Music is ever beautiful," said the Queen.

"Well, possibly, your experiences have been more favourable than mine. Sometimes when the band comes out serenading at night I incline to think that the art is overrated. Do you sing?"

"No; I listen to others."

"I'm not much of a singer myself," said Mr. Skinner,

prodding an emerald tile in the pavement, absently, with the ferule of his umbrella; "but when I am at home I do sometimes turn a tune in the privacy of my family."

"Will you sing for me? Oh, I know you will!" exclaimed the Queen.

Mr. Skinner had a feeling of diffidence for the first time since he entered the mountain.

"Well, madame, I would like to oblige you, but to tell the truth, I—my voice is so poor that—"

"You will not refuse me?"

"But I am such a poor singer, that I know you will not be pleased," and Mr. Skinner laughed a nervous little laugh.

"I am sure you will try, will you not?" said Aphrodite.

"Well, if you insist on it, I s'pose I must," replied Mr. Skinner. "Let me see," said he, rubbing his chin and looking thoughtfully up at the ceiling; "I only know one piece, and not much of that. How does it begin?" and Mr. Skinner cleared his throat vehemently, twice. Meanwhile the entire company of dancers, and all the lovely maids of honour had gathered in front of him awaiting with interest the performance. Mr. Skinner felt himself getting uncomfortably warm. He cleared his throat again, and said:

"I'll do the best I can; it begins in this way: 'On Jor—dan's stor—my—y ba—a—anks I stand, And cast ——' Wait a minute. I have not got the right pitch. That's too high. Let me try again: 'On Jor—dan's stor—my—y ba—a—nks I stand, And cast a ——' That won't do; it's too low. Once more: On Jor—dan's

stor—my—y ba—a—anks I—I stand, And cast a—a
wistful eye, To Ca—a—nyan's fair and ha—a—appy land,
Where my—y possessions li—i—ie.'"

As Mr. Skinner stopped he observed that everybody
looked very solemn, and he thought the room somehow
had lost some of the brilliant light that had filled it. He
was conscious that he had not made a very favourable
impression as a vocalist, and in a kind of desperation he
yielded to an impulse to try again.

" I think probably I can do that a little better if you
will bear with me : ' On Jor—dan's stor—my—y
ba—a—nks I——' "

Before he could complete the line, a sudden pall of
darkness fell upon the splendid scene before him ; he felt
a mighty rush of wind upon his face, and then he was
whirled around and around with the greatest violence.
He seemed for an instant to lose consciousness, and when
he opened his eyes they looked straight upward at the
serene beauty of the blue sky.

He found that he was lying flat upon his back upon
the plateau to which he had come yesterday evening.
Beside him lay his umbrella and his satchel. Above him
the sun was shining brightly, about him the cool breeze
rustled the leaves upon the trees, while the music of the
birds was wafted to him from the neighbouring forest.
He thought that the fair earth and the sunshine and all
the things that Nature presented to the eye had never
seemed so beautiful.

How did he get here? That was almost the first
question that thrust itself upon his bewildered mind.
Was it the sacred nature of the words that he had tried

to sing that had offended his audience, or was it the atrocious character of his vocalization. He could not tell. He felt that he would give a moderate sum of money to ascertain.

He looked out over the edge of the plateau, and there, beneath him was the town. He could see the people moving about in the streets, and there was a crowd in front of his hotel. Perhaps they were discussing his adventure and wondering what his fate could be. What should he tell them? The more he thought about it, the less certain did he feel of the reality of the strange and weird scenes through which he had passed. The impression of their actuality was strong upon his mind, but could he say absolutely and positively that he had not dreamed it all? He had a decided impulse to scoff at the idea. The Erl-king, the ghosts, and the children, the man to whom he talked in the garden, surely he had encountered them and talked with them! But did not his common sense revolt at the theory that he had been tumbled into the cavern and tumbled out again without knowing how or by whose hands!

His perplexity increased as he reflected upon the matter. Then, suddenly, he thought of the talk he had heard about one hundred years in the mountain passing as swiftly as a single night ; was it possible that this had happened to him? He looked at his watch. It marked six o'clock. That proved nothing. The scenery about him, and particularly the town looked the same as they had done when he last saw them. He determined to go down to the hotel and satisfy his mind.

When he reached the hotel he assured himself that

only one night had passed. Upon reflection Mr. Skinner resolved not to speak of the matter to any of the other people about the view, but to keep his own counsel ; and to this day he cannot positively say whether he followed Tanhaüser into the mountain or merely had a tremendous nightmare upon the outside of that eminence.

Miss Wilmer's Adventure.

MR. RICHARD SMITH and Mr. Arthur Gibbs were guests at a large party given at the house of Judge Campbell in the town of Wington. When the evening was half gone, they were standing at the upper end of the drawing-room, talking and watching the moving throng beyond them, when Smith suddenly exclaimed :

"Who is that insignificant-looking little woman over there? She has a throng of men about her ; but they certainly can't be attracted by her beauty. She is the plainest woman in the room!"

"Don't you know her?" said Gibbs. "Why, she is the famous Wington heroine!"

"Indeed! A heroine, eh? Well, I confess my ignorance. Really, I was not aware that this prosy place boasted a heroine."

"Well, then, you have to hear a story of endurance

and fortitude which, when you look upon that slight figure, seems really incredible."

" I am ready to have the tale unfolded, my lad, whenever you are disposed to oblige me."

So the two young men sauntered out to the library, and, throwing themselves into easy-chairs, Gibbs began :

" You must know, in the first place, that my heroine has held that position just about six years. She came here half-a-dozen years ago from New England in response to a call from the gentlemen who manage the common schools of this county. She was a teacher by profession, and her name was Susan Wilmer."

" 'Susan' is very mild for a genuine heroine ! "

" She was placed in charge of a certain little red school-house, away out yonder among the hills, near to that small collection of buildings called Maysville."

" I've been there," said Smith. " Two houses—a store and a blacksmith's shop."

" Well, she took the school, and she laboured there for many months trying to teach the young ideas how to shoot, from very poor soil, I imagine, judging from the specimens I have seen of her pupils. But nobody in town cared whether she was successful or not. She did not live in the village, because of the distance, but had taken board at the only respectable farm-house in the neighbourhood, about a mile and-a-half over the mountain So her arrival did not excite any very great remark, in the usually excitable village of Wington, excepting, perhaps, when she came into church the first Sunday after her arrival, when, of course, all the girls in the building looked her over as she walked up the aisle, and went through the customary mental arithmetic to determine the cost of her clothing."

" That had to be done, of course," remarked Smith.

" But she was plainly dressed, and the young ladies not having had their envy excited, as usual, indulged their contempt for the new comer. Nobody welcomed her, spoke to her, or showed by any sign that they recognized her presence; and I may say, that during the whole of the first six months of her stay here, she was never invited to a house in the town, or asked to indulge in any of the amusements for which Wington is famous, all the year round. She never made a friend or even an acquaintance, among the people. It was a dull and dreary life enough, I think, and I doubt not some of the kinder-hearted among the elder ladies of the town would gladly have shown her some attention ; but although polite when addressed, she was reserved and diffident in her manner, and not easily approached."

" But you don't seem to be getting on toward the heroics," said Smith.

" The farmer with whom she boarded," continued Gibbs, " had a son, who ——"

" O, I see !" exclaimed Smith. " The farmer's son is sick ; she nurses him ; a tender passion developes ; he marries her out of gratitude; the regular thing, you know ! "

" Not by any means. This young man was employed as an amanuensis by a gentleman named Wylie, who lived on the adjoining estate and was very wealthy. Wylie was a man of thirty-five years, a widower, with one little girl of six or seven summers. He was a first-rate fellow, liked and respected by everybody throughout this whole region. Wylie wanted to have his little girl instructed in the rudiments of education; and, living alone, he could not very well have a governess in the house. So, upon the recommendation of his secretary, he concluded to have the child attend the red school-house, where Miss Wilmer taught. It was his custom to send the child in his carriage, and at the time of dismissing the scholars to have his man in waiting to convey Miss Wilmer and her pupil to their respective homes. Well, this arrangement was satisfactory to all parties, and during the summer months everything went on smoothly, and without any cause for complaint on either side. The child learned rapidly, and conducted herself with about the average propriety. On the 1st or 2nd day of November of that year, the school was dismissed at about four o'clock in the afternoon, but Wylie's man not having arrived with the carriage, Miss Wilmer sat with her solitary scholar in the school-room, to wait for him.

"An hour passed, and it began to grow dark, and yet the carriage did not come. The man had gone to town, and was detained by a broken axle. Miss Wilmer concluded not to wait any longer, but to attempt to walk home, thinking she could reach the farm-house before it was dark, and then have the child sent over to her father's place by one of the men of the family.

"You know how suddenly night comes on among these mountains? When the sun has set, the darkness hurries in upon us with a speed of which people who live in a level country have scarcely any conception. Well, Miss Wilmer and the child, had scarcely gone a third of the distance, before it was as black as pitch, and the heavens were so obscured by huge banks of clouds, that not even the faint twinkle of a star served to light up their path, darkened as it was, too, by the network of overhanging branches of trees, which moaned, and rustled, and creaked in the wind. But the road was an easy one, and Miss Wilmer was so thoroughly familiar with it, that she strode along with confidence, rather regretting that she had undertaken the task, but determined to persevere, despite the fearful cries of the child, whom she strove to reassure with words of comfort and encouragement.

"The road wound directly around the mountain, at a considerable inclination. On one side rose the rocks covered with stones, grey moss, and ferns, intermingled with tangled bushes and vines, and strewn with decaying leaves, while a few oaks and evergreens grew from the side, and leaned over the road as if they were trying to peer into the valley below them. On the other side the mountain descended at a considerable declivity, and was covered with trees, huge boulders, and a heavy under-growth, excepting where, here and there, the bald rock reached down perpendicularly into some chasm, formed centuries ago, when the tired earth, weary with the throes of her pristine convulsions, yawned with her granite lips, and left them unclosed for ever."

"'Yawned with her granite lips,' is good," observed Mr. Smith.

"Along this path, then, Miss Wilmer went, trying to

keep close in to the mountain's side, and to avoid all possibility of making a misstep over the opposite edge of the road. Once she came to a tree which was prostrated upon the hill above her, and which hung with its branches over the way. She ran against these in the darkness, and, drawing back, attempted to go around the obstacle. She had hold of the child's hand, and her grasp instinctively tightened as she felt the little one slip away from her, and bring her whole weight suddenly to bear on that one arm. The child gave a piercing scream as she fell, and by the flutter of her white clothing below in the darkness, Miss Wilmer saw that she was on the edge of one of the most frightful precipices upon the mountain.

" To grasp the child's arm with her other hand was the first movement, and with all her strength she endeavoured to lift her up and place her on the road. But the woman's fright had partially unnerved her, and robbed her of much of her little strength, and to her dismay, she found herself wholly unable to accomplish her purpose. She perceived with the intuition of desperation, that her only hope of supporting the child, existed in her lying flat upon the ground. This she did, and holding on by one of the arms, she gradually worked her other hand up to the body, and caught hold of the dress. But would this bear the weight ? it certainly did not lessen the danger that her strained fingers would gradually lose their power, and relax, so that their precious burden would be dashed to pieces in those black and shuddering depths below. Those were the days, you remember, when women and girls wore hoop-skirts. With a desperate effort Miss Wilmer clutched the steel springs of the child's skirt, and taking the four lower springs in her hand, she twisted her arm into them so that they formed a loop around her wrist, and then, feeling that her hold was secure, she dropped the arm of the insensible child, and, tearing off her hood, with her spare hand she bound the strings as well as she could round the wrists of both hands, and between the steel springs of the skirt, so that it could not possibly slip off, the larger part of the weight bearing upon the right arm.

"The pain was terrible beyond expression. The sharp steel edges of the springs, dragged down by the weight of their burden, cut into her flesh like knife-blades. The arm was almost torn from its socket, and the tense muscles seemed to be slowly tearing to pieces with the fierce strain upon them. But the brave girl did not flinch. She lay there with both arms hanging over the edge of the rock, in patient agony waiting for that help which she knew might not come for hours. Indeed, she felt that anyone might drive over her prostrate body in the darkness, without her being able to scream or to utter a cry for help.

"All kinds of thoughts whirled through her brain— fearful, ludicrous, and sorrowful. She thought of her school, and of the children gathering there to-morrow, and missing her, and wondering why she did not come; and she herself wondered if they would be sorry to learn that she was dead ; and if they would forget her, when another teacher came. And then came a flood of recollections of the scenes which had occurred there ; of the little peculiarities of each of the scholars, their queer sayings, and laughable answers to her questions, and of the times when she had punished them. What would they do with her body when she was found? Suppose she should be buried while not yet dead! Horrible thought! Would any of the town people go to the funeral? Would anybody be sorry she was gone, and shed tears over her? Bitterly and sadly, she could not think of one who would.

"You know, the old story of the manner in which a drowning man, in the few seconds of time which elapse between the consciousness of the approach of death and insensibility, reviews his whole life in the intense and awful energy of his mind, compelled by despair. I believe this to be the case in every instance where a person is placed unexpectedly in imminent peril of his life. The mind never forgets anything. The individual may lose all command over the memory, and be incapable by any effort, of summoning up recollection of circumstances or facts, but they are there, and may be called up at any time accidentally. And so, before Miss Wilmer's mental vision, in that supreme hour, passed in review the events of her life with almost microscopic exactness. Her childhood, and its happiness, her early womanhood, and its trials, and the disappointments, the joys, the hopes of her later years—all came up before her, and with them was a certain assurance that this was to be the end of all ; that she was to die in this place. These, and a million other thoughts, flashed across the seemingly infinite space of her mind, as she lay there, and then her fancies grew wilder and became confused, and brilliant colours danced before her and she fell into a swoon.

"As the evening wore on, and Miss Wilmer failed to

return, the farmer with whom she lived, became somewhat uneasy, and walked over to Wylie's place to ascertain if she had gone there with her charge. Wylie was
surprised and alarmed when the farmer announced his
errand, but, as the carriage had not returned, he concluded
to wait for a while, thinking perhaps they had gone to
town in the vehicle and were detained. After walking
about uneasily for half an hour, he determined to go down
the road to the schoolhouse to satisfy himself that no evil
had befallen them. Each taking a lantern, he, the farmer
and his son, proceeded out toward the mountain. Each
of them had an indefinable fear that some accident had
happened, and as they walked silently along the winding
road they scrutinized every part of it closely with the
flickering light of their lanterns.

"In a short time, Wylie's secretary caught a glimpse of
something white lying in the road; hurrying toward it,
he perceived it to be a woman's dress, and a moment
more disclosed Miss Wilmer lying at full length upon the
edge of the declivity. The first thought that flashed
through the minds of all was, that she had been mur-
dered; but Wylie almost instantly discovered his child,
and, with a cry of horror, sprang forward to rescue her
from her peril. His blood ran cold within his veins, as,
eagerly seizing her, he looked down into the unfathomable
darkness of that abyss, rendered more appalling by the
obscurity in which its terrors were involved. To tear
away the iron from the brave arms which it had bruised
and torn, was the work of an instant, and Wylie, forgett-
ing the insensibility of the noble woman at his feet,
lifted his child in his arms, and caressed it with inex-

pressible tenderness, while the farmer and his son leaned over Miss Wilmer's prostrate form, and, after binding up the wounds upon the bleeding arm, endeavoured to restore her to consciousness.

" It now became apparent that a vehicle must be procured to convey the sufferers to their homes, and Wylie's secretary went back to obtain one. In the meantime, Wylie succeeded in restoring the sensibility of his child, and she began to cry with fright and bewilderment, but, overcome by fatigue, she soon fell asleep upon her father's shoulder, and he then began to realize the heroism of the brave woman who lay before him. He had not thought that delicate, shy little creature capable of such presence of mind and such fortitude, and he began to wonder why he had never before perceived in her the elements of greatness. He had scarcely done more than notice her heretofore, but now he saw that he had been, as other men often are, worshipping heroism afar off, while here it was, in its purest and best form, at his very door.

" When the carriage came, Miss Wilmer was lifted tenderly and placed in it, and the whole party returned to their homes. All that night Miss Wilmer remained insensible, and when at last she woke to partial consciousness, she became wildly delirious, and raved about the child, the precipice, and the frightful death which ever seemed impending before her. For three days the fever raged within her, with not a gleam of returning reason, and it seemed doubtful, indeed, if the dimmed spark of life would not go out entirely. At length, however, the crisis passed, and she came out of the delirium, prostrated in body and mind, scarcely comprehending her situation, or remembering the accident in which she had borne so valiant a part.

"You may be sure Wylie did not forget her, and it was not only a sentiment of sincere gratitude that drew him to the house, two and three times every day. He had been thinking about her heroic deed, and he began to comprehend that a woman can possess higher, and better, and more enduring qualities than personal beauty, desirable as that may be. And so he called at the farmer's frequently, and the room of the sufferer was filled with the fragrance of the flowers that he brought, and her table was covered with innumerable dainties and delicacies purchased by him.

"Miss Wilmer knew from whom all these came, but she was too feeble to do more than simply feel grateful to the giver. But after a while, when she became strong enough to be carried downstairs, with that wrenched and hurt arm bound to her side, Wylie found it convenient to drop in very often and sit by her, and to converse in his pleasant, affable way. She was shy of him at first, overawed by a sense of his importance and social superiority. But nothing could long withstand his kind sociability, and Miss Wilmer soon found herself looking forward to his visits with positive pleasure, and before she entirely recovered she was, I think, in love with him.

"But you know the rest. You know how it always turns out, under such circumstances. Very soon it was announced that Miss Wilmer was engaged to be married to Mr. Wylie. The town people had all heard of her adventure, and of her brave conduct, and she was praised warmly for what she had done. But the shrewdest village gossip was hardly prepared for this result. Nobody had dreamed that Wylie would marry the poor little school teacher, even if she had saved his daughter's life. There were plenty of girls who had been making a dead set at the rich widower for years, and these, with their managing mammas, gave vent to their bitter disappointment in the customary way, by pretending to sneer at his bad taste, and by saying all the hard things they dared of Miss Wilmer.

"But this was behind her back. That fine old patriarch Job, when he recovered his lost property, you remember, was loaded down with presents by friends who had forgotten him in his adversity, and so now everybody was obsequious to Miss Wilmer, and those who had neglected her and cut her when she had no expectations, suddenly discovered that she was a remarkable young woman, and would prove a valuable acquisition to the select circle. Miss Wilmer understood the precise value of this adulation, and declining all invitations from the 'best' as well as the second best people, busied herself preparing for the wedding.

"On the appointed day the ceremony was performed in the church, in the presence of an admiring, jealous, excited crowd of ladies from the whole country round. That evening Wylie gave a tremendous reception at his house, at which everybody was present, and he clearly demonstrated that he was the happiest man in the country. This is the anniversary of that wedding, and the entertainment is given in their honour. Mrs. Wylie bears upon her arm the indelible marks of the suffering she endured upon the night of that terrible adventure, and if you will come downstairs, I will introduce you to her, and you will observe that she will offer you her left hand ; and that's the whole story of the adventure of Miss Wilmer, the Wington heroine."